Moriz Rosenthal in Word and Music

Edited and with an
Introduction by
Mark Mitchell and *Allan Evans*

Moriz Rosenthal in Word and Music

A Legacy of the Nineteenth Century

Preface by Charles Rosen

INDIANA UNIVERSITY PRESS
Bloomington and Indianapolis

This book is a publication of

Indiana University Press
601 North Morton Street
Bloomington, IN 47404-3797 USA

http://iupress.indiana.edu

Telephone orders   800-842-6796
Fax orders   812-855-7931
Orders by e-mail   iuporder@indiana.edu

Library of Congress Cataloging-in-Publication Data

Moriz Rosenthal in word and music: a legacy of the nineteenth century / edited and with an introduction by Mark Mitchell and Allan Evans ; preface by Charles Rosen.
    p. cm.
 Includes bibliographical references and index.
 ISBN 0-253-34660-6 (cloth : alk. paper)
 1. Rosenthal, Moriz, 1862-1946. 2. Pianists—Biography. I. Mitchell, Mark (Mark Lindsey). II. Evans, Allan, date
 ML417.R74M67 2006
 786.2'092—dc22

2005008640

1 2 3 4 5   11 10 09 08 07 06

To Beatrice Muzi

Concert artists, like dogs, always grow to resemble their patrons. Most of today's (examples: Gieseking, Casadesus, Heifetz, Serkin) resemble bank presidents or New Deal intellectuals. Most of yesterday's (examples: Paderewski, de Pachmann) resembled haughty princes of the blood. One lordly, athletic survivor of the time when artists wore the royal purple is orange-whiskered Polish Pianist Moriz Rosenthal . . .

—*Time* (January 4, 1943)

Contents

Preface

When Moriz Rosenthal made most of his recordings in the 1920s and 1930s, the recording industry largely restricted its productions of piano music to short works lasting less than four and a half minutes,[1] and consequently he was never to leave a permanent witness of his interpretations of the long Romantic masterpieces for which he was most famous like the Schumann *Fantasie*, the Weber Sonata in A-flat, and the Brahms Paganini Variations. In fact, I never heard him play these works, as I first met him when he left Vienna like so many distinguished artists to escape Hitler in 1938 (we had the same dentist, who introduced us—or, more precisely persuaded him to listen to me play), and by then he had almost ceased to perform in public. In the eight years that followed until his death in 1946, I remember only one concert in New York, which took place in Town Hall (I recollect that he played the *Allegro de Concert* by Chopin, the only time I have ever heard that work performed). During those years I studied with him and with his wife, Hedwig Kanner, a famous pedagogue and a pupil of Leschetizky. In spite of the fact that he then rarely performed in public, he certainly retained much of his famous technique, as I heard him play the "Minute" Waltz in thirds and sixths much faster than most pianists could play the simpler original.

I saw him fairly often. When I left the Juilliard Preparatory Center, to study with him and with his wife, I was eleven years old. A contract that my parents signed, which I came upon after their death, specified that I was to have one lesson a week from her and one a month from him. However, I actually had two lessons a week with Hedwig Kanner-Rosenthal, and she almost invariably said after each one, "Now go and amuse the old man." So I generally saw him once or twice a week for those years. Since he now performed so little, I think he was often bored and enjoyed company. In spite of his immense reputation for caustic remarks about other pianists ("Now you have the tempo, you can put in the thirds," was his comment on one of de Pachmann's less successful salon renditions of Chopin's Etude in thirds),[2] he was a very kind and generous man. In fact, during all that time, he rarely told me that I was wrong about something in the music: "I have a different idea of this piece," he would say gently and go slowly to the piano to demonstrate (he always sat two yards or so away from the piano to listen, not close by).

He almost never discussed technique with me, in spite—or perhaps because —of his formidable reputation as a technician: Josef Hofmann (whose technique was second to none) once said that he did not know what piano technique could be until he heard Rosenthal. His emphasis was almost always on phrasing. The only exception was that he taught me to play octave glissandi, showing me

how to do them at a controlled tempo, not too fast and not as a kind of char-
acterless smear. The trick was to place the weight on the fifth finger, not the
thumb, and to make sure that the fifth finger was absolutely rigid and power-
fully held in position. "Practice it every day for ten seconds," he told me, "and
after a week, you will have mastered it. More than ten seconds, and you will get
a blister on your finger." This kind of controlled octave glissando is necessary
only in a few places, above all Beethoven's "Waldstein" Sonata and Concerto in
C, and Brahms's Paganini Variations. I did learn something more about technique from him, however, by watching his hands, as his method of teaching
proceeded largely by demonstration. What was most astonishing to me from the
first time I heard him play a few phrases was the economical and visually almost
undetectable way of bringing out inner voices and varying the touch within a
chord, and to see him play, as well as to hear him, was an inspiring experience.
He had an incredible accuracy in playing very wide skips.

While on the subject of technique, it should be mentioned that the account
in *The New Grove Dictionary of Music and Musicians* about his acquaintance
and friendship with Brahms is inaccurate: it did not begin "when the composer
heard Rosenthal perform his Paganini Variations." The true story is more amusing, although after a lapse of fifty years I am not sure if I was told it by Rosenthal
himself or by his wife. Rosenthal was playing a concert in Vienna in a hall where
there were round tables on which one could place one's drinks—probably beer,
I imagine. Brahms was in the audience, but seated with his back to the concert
platform, and the young Rosenthal could only think of how to make the famous
composer turn around. He was performing Liszt's *Reminiscences de Don Juan*,
reputed to be the most difficult of all concert pieces, as Busoni claimed. About
two minutes into the piece there is a long scale for the right hand in chromatic
thirds that goes up and down the keyboard: when he reached this place, Rosenthal played parallel chromatic thirds in both hands, and Brahms of course
turned around to watch. After the performance, indeed, he asked Rosenthal if
he would play the Paganini Variations.

The incident has two significant aspects. The ability to play rapid chromatic
thirds in the left hand for more than a short distance is almost gratuitous as they
are practically nonexistent in the piano repertoire, certainly not to be found
on the level of the great display in this passage from Liszt's transcription of
Mozart, so that Rosenthal's improvised feat was extraordinary. More interesting
is Brahms's reaction for the musical politics of the time. The antipathy between
the schools of Brahms and Liszt was basic to the Viennese musical life, but
Brahms saw no difficulty and even a certain attraction in winning over the
greatest performers of the Liszt camp to perform his works. Earlier, the finest
of Liszt's protégés, Carl Tausig, became a friend and even presented Brahms
with the autograph manuscript of the "Venusberg" music from Wagner's *Tannhäuser*, which he owned, and Wagner made furious attempts to get it back
(Brahms only returned it when he was given the printed score of *Die Meistersin-
ger* in return).

Rosenthal went for long walks with Brahms, and often spoke about him.

(About his studies with Liszt he was more reticent: when I asked him what the lessons were like, he said only that it was difficult to get Liszt out of the café and back to the studio.)[3] He told me that it was Brahms who arranged for the post-humous publication of Wagner's mildly scandalous letters to a seamstress about his silk underwear, giving precise indications of what kind of stitching to use on each part of the garments. Discovering the man who owned these letters, Brahms persuaded him to release them to the press.

On one occasion, when I played the Handel Variations of Brahms for him, Rosenthal stopped me in the middle of the 17th variation, and asked "Why do you get faster here?" "It's written 'più mosso,'" I replied. Rosenthal got up, walked to the piano and looked at the music, and then said, "Brahms let me play his music any way I liked, and I am afraid that I abused the privilege. You are quite right." I still find that kind of courtesy of a distinguished 80-year-old man to a 14-year-old student incredible, and even more revealing is the respect for the integrity of the text from one who had been so free with it.

Rosenthal was also capable of considerable humor, even about the music most personal to him. When I was young, I had rather austere tastes, and I once said to Rosenthal that I did not care for the somewhat sentimental section in A flat from Brahms's fine Rhapsody in E-flat, op. 119, no. 4. Rosenthal remarked, "That passage always seemed to me like the gesture of a man who has been having a great time on the town for the whole evening, and later sitting on his bed before retiring, tosses his slippers away," and he illustrated this with the first bar of Brahms's melody. Now that I have grown to like this page of Brahms, I unfortunately have Rosenthal's image come to my mind at this place every time I perform the piece.

His wife was a brilliant and selfless piano teacher, representative of the great Viennese tradition, willing to work enthusiastically for hours with students and amazingly respectful of the individuality of each one. The Rosenthals were a devoted couple. When he applied for American citizenship, my mother went down with him to the bureau. Among the questions asked, since his wife had been married before, was whether her previous husband was alive or dead. He replied anxiously, "Dead, but he died naturally," evidently fearful that he would be accused of having taken steps to get rid of him. On one rare occasion I had a lesson with both of them: the piece was the Liszt *Hungarian Fantasie* for piano and orchestra (while Rosenthal beat time with a meatball on his fork). At the final section in F, she stopped me and said that it was too fast. He immediately interrupted: "I always performed it at that tempo," and she replied firmly, "You played too fast."

He kept himself in form technically by exercising, mostly by lifting weights, and he was proud of the muscular power of both fingers and arms. Like Claudio Arrau, he played a Baldwin since the company provided a free instrument.[4] The action of his piano was fairly stiff. As is clear from his autobiography, in his early youth he worked very hard, practicing scales four hours a day, but he once oddly said to me, "If you have to practice for more than two hours a day, you will never be a pianist." (Unfortunately, I need three to four hours.) I think he was warning me that intense work for exhausting short periods is worth more than long hours of diffuse playing. One can play for eight to ten hours a day, but more than three to four hours of deeply concentrated attention brings no extra dividends for me.

His own playing was extraordinary in its variety of tone color, rivaled perhaps only by Hofmann's. On the occasion of one of Hofmann's last Carnegie Hall recitals, I went with Rosenthal as his wife was ill. I found myself in a box with Rosenthal on my left, and Josef Lhévinne on my right. I remember that Hofmann brought the program out on stage with him and placed it on the piano, referring to it after each piece to see what came next. One of the works was Beethoven's Sonata in E-flat, op. 31, no. 3. After the scherzo Rosenthal turned toward Lhévinne and said, "Too fast"—which it was. After the minuet Lhévinne turned to Rosenthal and said, "Too slow." Afterwards, they went backstage to congratulate Hofmann, speaking not in English but, I think, in German (Hofmann and Rosenthal were Polish.)

Rosenthal's emphasis on musical structure is clear in his playing as well as in his fragment of autobiography. He condemns von Bülow for playing the final appearance of the main theme of the finale of Chopin's Sonata no. 3 in b at a tempo slower than the opening, although in fact many pianists do this, paying little attention to the "non tanto" in the tempo mark of "Presto non tanto," and starting at a speed that makes it difficult to negotiate the much faster accompaniment of the last pages. (Rosenthal suggested to me that one should play the last appearance of the theme in the right hand with one finger: this is a fingering also indicated by Emil von Sauer in his edition, so perhaps the idea originated with Liszt, with whom both Rosenthal and Sauer studied. In any case, it is a typical device of Chopin, who indicated this kind of playing with one finger for emphasis several times in his works.)

Rosenthal writes that he resented the fact that Mikuli never explained the structure of a fugue to him when teaching the *Well-Tempered Clavier*. When I was fourteen, he told me to start learning the Beethoven *Hammerklavier*, op. 106 (he must have known I would enjoy this), and to start by bringing the fugue to him next time with an analysis. He did not mean any analysis in depth, but wanted to be sure that I knew when the theme was inverted, augmented, in cancrizans, or in stretto. This is one of the large works that I regret never having heard him play.

Most revealing is his criticism of Mikuli for never having called attention to the descending scale in the bass of the second theme of the first movement of Mozart's Concerto in A, K. 488 (bars 98–106). "[He] let this piece pass me by without so much as commenting on the artistry of this terrific section," Rosenthal writes. The observation is interesting. Why is something so common as a descending scale so important? It is Rosenthal's ear which has seized the significance intuitively. The left-hand descent of E–D-sharp–C-sharp–B–A-sharp–A continuing with an octave leap to G-sharp–F-sharp–E is paralleled in diminution in the right hand as the basis of the melody, and the echo of soprano and bass endows the passage with extraordinary resonance, above all from the expressive move from A-sharp to A natural. The emphasis on the relation of subsidiary to principal voice was one of the greatest powers of Rosenthal's own playing.

He achieved this by his mastery of touch. He was well aware of this in his remarks on the contrast of his studies with Mikuli and Joseffy. Mikuli brought the modern *cantabile* and *legatissimo* touch, while Joseffy preserved the more old-fashioned, indeed, eighteenth-century, tradition of the detached or *perlé* technique (a touch condemned by Beethoven in a letter to Czerny but still used by Beethoven often enough with the indication *non legato*). The combination of Mikuli and Joseffy allowed a great range of effects, and to this was added Rosenthal's control of pedal effects, or what he called the "syncopated pedal." This means not pedaling with the struck note or chord but before or after (before, to increase the resonance; after, to preserve clarity).

Rosenthal never abused the pedal; he did not beat time mechanically with his right foot as so many pianists do, or apply the pedal everywhere unremittingly, changing only for the harmony. Above all, he understood the way the pedal can function for the counterpoint. He also astonishingly knew the value of a nonpedaled tone color. He insisted that I play the finale of Chopin's Sonata no. 2 in b-flat absolutely without pedal until the final bar: "No wind in the cemetery," was his sardonic comment. Even more significant was his direction that the pedal be omitted in bars 37 and 39 of the Largo of Chopin's Sonata in b. The effect is exquisite, the first time diminuendo and the second crescendo, after the rich pedaled sonority of the previous and succeeding bars, adding a different kind of resonance that isolates these moments, and is deeply expressive. It is only recently that I realized that Rosenthal's effect was based upon the original indications of the Chopin text, a remarkable example of how fidelity can stimulate the imagination.

His interpretation of Chopin's mazurkas corresponds to accounts of Chopin's own playing. He did not impose upon them a Viennese waltz rhythm as many other pianists tend to do, even Polish ones. He did sometimes systematically double the value of one of the beats throughout a phrase, making 4/4 measures, and contemporaries of Chopin claimed that the composer played his mazurkas that way. When, on at least two occasions, friends of Chopin remarked on this to him, he became angry, denying it, and was convinced only by their counting aloud while he played—and he then remarked that this was the national style. I have been shown an interview with Rosenthal from the early years of the twentieth century, in which he was asked if the correct rhythm of the mazurka could at times be 4/4, and (amusingly like Chopin) he denied this indignantly, saying that it was impossible. But he himself often did this, for example, in the A major central section of the Mazurka in a, op. 17, no. 4. The fact is, of course, that it is only 4/4 for an objective counting and does not really sound like it, but like 3/4 with a lilt. The authenticity of Rosenthal's interpretations came probably not so much from his Polish birth but from his studies with Mikuli, one of Chopin's pupils, and with Joseffy, the editor of perhaps the most influential Chopin edition before the end of the twentieth century.

Rosenthal's rubato was never wayward. He lingered instinctively on the most expressive moments of a melody, giving full weight to the harmonic values. But he did not play every note with a monotonously unvarying expressivity. The extreme grace of his playing came very often from his refusal to give the usual commonplace accents to the ends of phrases. Frequently avoiding both the banal emphasis and the slowing-up at these points, he throws the cadence away, so to speak, diminishing in strict tempo with a cavalier elegance, as if he disdained a more plebeian explicitness.

In this way, one of the greatest technical workmen of the keyboard played like a gentleman. When young, he had abandoned public concerts for some years to study at the University of Vienna, and when I knew him, he could still read the Greek classics in the original for pleasure.

Charles Rosen

Acknowledgments

We would like to thank the following people for their help with this project: Paula Best, for providing copies of the programs from Rosenthal's historical recitals at Wigmore Hall, London; Gino Francesconi, for providing a list of the repertoire Rosenthal played at Carnegie Hall, New York; Dr. Ingrid Fuchs, for providing access to Rosenthal's writings in the archives of the Gesellschaft der Musikfreunde, Vienna; Steven Heliotes, for providing copies of articles, letters, and other "Rosenthaliana" in his collection; Michael Hofmann, for his help clarifying some of the thornier passages in Rosenthal's German; Angela Hughes, for making available Rosenthal's letter to Herbert Hughes; the late Adele and Oskar Kanner, for making Rosenthal's written and recorded legacy available; Dr. Antonio Latanza of the Museum of Musical Instruments, Rome, for providing prints of photographs of Rosenthal; Donald Manildi of the International Piano Archives, for making available the manuscript of "Mahleriana"; Russell W. Miller, Jon M. Samuels, and Jonathan Summers, for providing invaluable discographic information; and John Wilton, for restoring photographs.

Thanks also to Miki Bird, Elizabeth Garman, Janet Rabinowitch, Suzanne Ryan, Robert Sloan, and Donna Wilson of Indiana University Press.

Kaikhosru Sorabji's review of a Rosenthal concert published in *The New Age* is reproduced by kind permission of The Sorabji Archive, Easton Dene, Bailbrook Lane, Bath BA1 7AA, England, from whom copies of all of Sorabji's musical scores and literary writings may be obtained. The review of a Rosenthal concert published in *The Musical Times* and Rosenthal's subsequent "Letter to the Editor" are reproduced by kind permission of that publication. Fritz Kuttner's translation of "The Night Rubinstein Played Bratislava," which originally appeared in the now defunct *Stereo Review*, is reproduced by kind permission of *Sound & Vision*.

Moriz Rosenthal: A Chronology

1862: Born on December 18, in Lemberg, a highly cultured city on the eastern edge of the Austro-Hungarian empire (now L'viv, Ukraine). Lemberg owed its vitality to the fact that it had been under so many crowns before it became part of the empire: Poland, Sweden, Austria, and Russia.

1872–1874: Studies with Karol Mikuli, a pupil of Chopin.

1875: Rosenthal's family settles in Vienna so that he can study with Rafael Joseffy, himself a pupil of both Franz Liszt and Carl Tausig.

1876: First public performance (Chopin's Concerto in f, with Joseffy at the second piano, and solo pieces by Beethoven, Mendelssohn, Chopin, and Liszt); further concerts in Belgrade and Bucharest, where he is appointed pianist to the Romanian Court (the Princess, later the Queen, who published poetry under the name Carmen Sylva, long remained a friend of the pianist's); first meeting with Liszt (October, in Vienna), with whom he studies from 1876 to 1878 and from 1884 to 1886.[1] Liszt told Ludwig Bösendorfer, who had arranged the audition, "In diesem Knaben steckt ein Künstler der nicht stecken bleiben wird" (In this boy there hides an artist who will not remain hidden for long).

1878: Gives concerts in Paris (Salle Pleyel and possibly other venues), St. Petersburg, Warsaw, etc.; with Liszt in Weimar (April to August). In an article written on the occasion of the centennial of Liszt's birth, and published in *Die Zeit* (Berlin), he would recall:

> At Tivoli, where in the autumn of 1878 it was my good fortune to be [Liszt's] sole pupil, I found him essentially different; he appeared to me then in a warmer and highly artistic light. Going to the Villa d'Este every afternoon, I would find the Master composing in his study; sometimes on the terrace, gazing pensively into the blue distance. The sparkling Roman autumn, the picturesque beauty of the place, the Master's lofty teaching—everything merged within me into a bliss which I can still feel today. (Adrian Williams, *Portrait of Liszt by Himself and His Contemporaries,* Oxford: Clarendon Press, 1990, pp. 560–561)

1880: Hears Liszt play in Vienna (Bösendorfersaal, under the auspices of the Wagner Society); the first and only time he will hear the pianist play in public.

1880–1884: Studies in Vienna at the *Gymnasium,* then the university, where he attends lectures by Brentano, Hanslick, and Zimmerman. He takes no degree.

1884: Makes mature debut in Vienna (January, in the Bösendorfersaal); meets Johannes Brahms; in May travels to Leipzig for the premiere of Adalbert von Goldschmidt's opera *Helianthus,* where he meets Liszt;[2] presently, in Weimar, is one of the pupils of Liszt photographed with the master. (When photographed with his pupils Liszt was almost always seated, in order to emphasize that he had said what he had to say, while the pupils were young and should be ready to move forward. In this photograph, reproduced here, Rosenthal, Arthur Fried-heim, and Alexander Siloti link their hands to form a symbolic chain of inheri-tance from Liszt.)

1888: Debuts in America. His first appearance (November 9) is a joint concert in Boston with a teenage fiddler named Fritz Kreisler, who is also making his debut in America. Rosenthal gives his first concert in New York (Steinway Hall, near Union Square) with Kreisler on November 13, 1888, during the Great Bliz-zard. Of the pianist's contribution (Liszt's Concerto in E-flat, the "Aria" from Schumann's Sonata op. 11, Henselt's "Si oiseau j'étais," a nocturne and the Bar-carolle of Chopin, the Chopin-Liszt "Maiden's Wish," and Liszt's *Don Juan* Fan-tasie), the *New York Tribune* (November 14) reports:

> To New Yorkers there is nothing novel in brilliant piano-forte playing, but it can
> fairly be questioned whether ever before an audience composed of experienced and
> discriminating music lovers in this city were stirred to such a pitch of excitement
> as was the case last night. This does not mean that our people have never heard
> more artistic playing, but primarily that they have never been so amazed and be-
> wildered.

All told, he will give more than a hundred concerts in America on this tour.

1895: Debuts in England.

1896: Begins second American tour. On November 28, he is scheduled to play Ludwig Schytte's Concerto in c-sharp, op. 28, in Chicago, but falls ill with ty-phoid and must return to Europe for a long period of rest. Some newspapers report Rosenthal's illness as bronchitis.

1898: American tour. On December 10, Rosenthal plays Liszt's Concerto in E-flat with Theodore Thomas and the Chicago Orchestra; his first appearance with the orchestra.

1902: First concerts in Paris since his appearances at the Salle Pleyel as an *enfant prodige;* Russian tour; concerts in Bucharest, where, according to a cable from a correspondent for the *Musical Courier,* "[his] piano recitals are setting this city topsy turvy. Public amazed; such success hitherto unknown in Southern Eu-rope." The King of Romania bestows on him the officers' cross of the Romanian Order of the Crown. Carmen Sylva presents the decoration to the pianist along with a scarf pin, pictures, and a number of books bearing dedications in her own hand.

1903: Serves on the jury for the Prix Diémer in Paris.

1904: Four recitals in Berlin (Beethovensaal), the first of which is attended by Conrad Ansorge, Ferruccio Busoni, Leopold Godowsky, and Xaver Scharwenka.

1906–1907 Season: A tour of North America (Canada, Mexico, and the United States) comprising some seventy-five concerts; received at the White House by President Theodore Roosevelt.

1908–1909: A projected tour of North America, which guarantees Rosenthal $80,000 for eighty concerts, fails to materialize.

1909: Appears in London for the first time since 1900; serves on the jury for the Prix Diémer and gives four recitals in the same city (Paris) at the Salle des

Agriculteurs, which the pianist Arthur Shattuck described in his memoirs as "the ugliest concert hall in Christendom. Its only redeeming feature was its perfect acoustics."

1912: Emperor Franz Josef bestows upon Rosenthal the title of "Imperial and Royal Court Pianist"; concert in Munich (Odeon).

1914: Berlin, Rome (two concerts at the Augusteo), etc.

1917: In Vienna, Rosenthal plays his first series of recitals tracing the history of the piano repertoire.

1918: Plays a series of seven historical recitals, also in Vienna.

1921 (or earlier): Marries Hedwig Loewy Kanner.[3]

1921: In January Rosenthal makes his first appearance in London since World War I, playing Chopin's Concerto in e with the British Symphony Orchestra at Kingsway Hall. Between October and December, again in London (Wigmore Hall), he plays his series of seven historical recitals.

1922: Plays Liszt's Concerto in E-flat in the Concerts Pasdeloup (Paris).

1923: Returns to America on the Majestic; challenges Vladimir de Pachmann, who has called himself the greatest pianist in the world, to a pianistic "duel" in Chicago.

1924–1925 season: American tour.

1926: Three recitals in Berlin. Returns to America on the Berengaria for recitals in New York and Chicago, and a fortnight of teaching at the Glenn Dillard Gunn School of Music (Chicago). Presents "Three Historical Concerts" at the Princess Theater, Chicago (April and May), in the first of which he plays all the works on his program through Mozart with the lid of the piano lowered.

1927: Makes his first disc recordings, for Parlophone/Odeon, in November.

1928: Spends the early part of the year in America, giving a faculty recital at the Curtis Institute of Music (February 8, Philadelphia), then returns to Europe. Concerts in Vienna (November 5, Grosse Musikvereinsaal), Trieste (December 1, Teatro Comunale), etc.

1929–1930 season: American tours.

1931: Concerts in Bad Gastein (in aid of the city's Artists Home), Berlin, London, Madrid, Vienna, Stockholm, Amsterdam, Copenhagen, etc.

1934: First tour of South America. From a "Conversation with Moriz Rosenthal" (*Neue Freie Presse,* October 25, 1934):

> "I traveled for three whole months," Professor Rosenthal tells us, "beginning in the middle of July and ending in the middle of October. Even though I have traveled through almost the whole world, I had never made it to South America. But I had heard a lot about the unhealthy climate, and I was a little worried. But I had to honor the invitations at some point and shipped off to the foreign continent. I utilized the stopovers in different harbors that lasted several hours to get a closer look at the southern cities. I gave four concerts in Rio de Janeiro, seven in Buenos Aires, and I also played in Rosaria, La Plata, Montevideo, Sao Paulo, and Bahia Blanca. The audiences were very knowledgeable in music and suffered from a virtual Chopin fanaticism. I only had to announce a Chopin-Abend and it was already completely sold out. I also performed works by Beethoven, Schumann, Schubert,

Debussy, and Szymanowski. I am very satisfied with my success and that of my concerts."

1936: Three concerts in Rome (Augusteo). In April and May Rosenthal plays a new series of "Seven Historical Concerts" at Wigmore Hall (the programs for which are very close to those of his 1921 series); performs at the unveiling of the Liszt monument in Eisenstadt (summer). In November arrives in America on the *Normandie*.

1936–1937, 1937–1938 seasons: American tours.

1938: Following the *Anschluss*, the annexation of Austria by Nazi Germany, settles in New York; celebrates the Golden Jubilee recital of his American debut with a recital at Carnegie Hall (November 13), which he performs on a special "Golden 'Golden Jubilee' Piano" made expressly for this occasion by Baldwin, a company founded in the year of Rosenthal's birth.

In New York lives at the Great Northern Hotel between 56th and 57th Streets ("neither great nor northern," he likes to say) and socializes with his colleagues, just as he did in Vienna. With Josef and Rosina Lhévinne, or with Simon Barere, frequents the modernist Automat (a bygone institution offering single portions of food behind windows which would open after a coin was inserted) in preference to the more *mondaine* Russian Tea Room.

1941: Plays his last public concert, a recital at Town Hall, New York (November 15).

1942: Friends and colleagues celebrate his eightieth birthday with a "Gala Testimonial Concert" at Hunter College in New York (December 18).

1944: Becomes an American citizen.

1946: Dies on the afternoon of September 3, in New York. He had suffered from Parkinson's disease for some years. His body lies in state at the Universal Chapel (Lexington Avenue and 52nd Street) before being interred the Ferncliff Cemetery in Hartsdale, New York, in a private ceremony.

Moriz Rosenthal in Word and Music

Introduction

I had many happy years and many not very happy years. [Music] was my only consolation sometimes. If there should be no art it would be impossible that we should know what the other feels. Music gives you an image of the life in a very shortened measure, so that you can see not only the beginning of a catastrophe but the effects. It makes life easier to bear, for it lets us see the consequences of evil that our life is too short to see.

—Moriz Rosenthal (1942)

1

The sound he drew out of the piano was entirely his own; yet Moriz Rosenthal's musicianship also amounted to a resume of nineteenth-century music history. His *legato* touch came from Chopin through his pupil Mikuli; his awareness of compositional elements was developed by Liszt; his Brahms (none of which, regrettably, he ever recorded) was shaped by an association with the composer himself.[1] As for his friendship with Johann Strauss II, it is memorialized in the form of ingeniously crafted piano-paraphrases. An exceptionally clever American journalist found Rosenthal's performance of waltzes from Strauss's *Die Fledermaus* so intoxicating as to violate the Volstead Amendment —the law providing for the enforcement of prohibition.

Rosenthal stands apart from all other pianists because his astonishing technical abilities were married to a rare intellectual erudition—a knowledge of literature (he knew all of Heinrich Heine's and much of Rudyard Kipling's poetry by heart), history, philology, medicine, chemistry, mathematics, philosophy, and society that few pianists have ever matched. For him, the ancient world or the eighteenth century was not "the past," but a cosmos parallel to his own. According to Theodore Bullock, Arthur Friedheim, who also had a classical education, often held philosophic conversations with Rosenthal "which both men enjoyed intensely because, in them, they could not only open their hearts to each other but also pun back and forth in six languages—German, Russian, English, French, Latin and Greek[2]—an exotic exercise in pure mental gymnastics in which they both reveled immoderately."[3] Indeed, Rosenthal's knowledge of the classics was so deep that in his commentary he could casually manipulate arcane Latin quotations, or invoke such significant but obscure figures as Herostratos.

Rosenthal's philosophical inclinations, not to mention his training, often found expression in his writings on music. In his lesson on Schumann's *Carnaval* (*Etude*, January 1933), for instance, he perceived depths where most musicians have not, writing of "Papillons":

It is very questionable if Schumann tried to depict only the fluttering of butterflies in his little piece . . . Already his *Papillons* op. 2 had another and deeper meaning. In a letter he explains that he was not trying to imitate the butterflies but meant the wings of soul which carry the Psyche to eternal heights. Schumann was surely most able to express through his music such a sublime picture. He reached these heights in his *Davidsbündlertänze,* in his *Fantasie,* his *Kreisleriana* and *Humoreske* but, frankly and in spite of my glowing worship for Schumann, we must admit that he failed to convey this transcendental mood in his *Papillons* op. 2 or in the "Papillons" of his *Carnaval.*[4]

And of "A. S. C. H.—S. C. H. A. (Lettres dansantes)":

The rhythm is not a valse rhythm, as generally is supposed, but (influence of Chopin, whom he admired at this time beyond all bounds!) the rhythm of the mazurka (accent on the *third* quarter note) whereas the *valse* is accented on the *first* quarter note. The poetic idea seems a very deep one. About:

> *When all is over, our ashes will dance*
> *around the sun.*

Many of Rosenthal's contemporaries looked upon him almost as a god, marveling at his art and fearing his wit. When Mark Hambourg, the eminent London-based Leschetizky pupil, was teaching his daughter Michal, he urged her to attend every Rosenthal concert that she could in order to "properly learn Chopin."[5] Even Ignaz Friedman, when he was preparing the editions of Chopin's piano music for Breitkopf & Härtel and Universal that Debussy would later use as a basis for his own for Durand, consulted with Rosenthal in preference to such renowned Warsaw-based Chopin scholars as the pianist Aleksander Michałowski.[6] His faith in Rosenthal's perceptiveness was well founded, as the following examples illustrate. From Rosenthal's lesson on Chopin's Waltz in e, op. posthumous (*Etude,* October 1933):

The second theme shows many characteristics of Chopin's early style. Schumann wrote once that he recognized composers by their basses. Thus the second theme opens (measures 24, 25 to 32).

In the left hand is a chromatically descending chord of the sixth. The bass notes [bars 25–32: E, D-sharp, D, C-sharp, C, B, B, E] form a motif which, strangely enough, appears in the "Crucifixus" of Bach's B Minor Mass, upon which Liszt composed his magnificent variations.

The Bach original is a half-step higher, in F Minor.

This similarity of themes may be a mere coincidence; but it should not be forgotten that Chopin often reminds us of Bach—in the second theme of his F Minor Concerto, for instance, where he attempts (and indeed not without success) to sound the heights and depths of the *Chromatic Fantasie*—with the aid of Bach— and again in his Mazurka in B-flat Minor, op. 24, [no. 4] where he uses, in the opening measures, the inversion of the theme of an organ fugue.

From his lesson on the just-mentioned Mazurka in b-flat (*Etude,* February 1940):

Measures 54–61 form a weird *intermezzo,* with the augmented fourth of the B-flat Minor scale.

Lina Ramann, the authoritative biographer of Franz Liszt, states, with all the aplomb and assurance born from utter want of knowledge, that Liszt invented the Hungarian Scale, characterized by the augmented fourth.[7] But Chopin's *Mazurka-Intermezzo* shows this scale about twenty years earlier than Liszt.[8] Bizet's *Carmen* also shows traces of this weird theme of Chopin's.

From his lesson on the Scherzo in b-flat, op. 31 (*Etude,* January 1932):

The highest F is also more difficult to play accurately than in Chopin's day. For this F was the highest note of the treble in the keyboard in use at that time. It was impossible, therefore, to play a false note *above* the F, and the player could take this last note with great security and boldness. This circumstance illustrates the fact that Chopin, even in the extremest fever of creating, was conscious of all the advantages of the keyboard, and ever employed them for full expressiveness.

Rosenthal knew his Chopin *à fond.* Robin Legge writes:

It happened that one night some years ago the conversation of a number of musicians turned to the subject of memory, when Rosenthal, who was present, made a bet that if we would show him any single bar in any work by Chopin he would play that work. One of us selected a work in which was a two-bar rest. We covered up the remainder of the page and showed the "two-bar" to Rosenthal. For a moment he seemed nonplussed. Then a seraphic smile broke over his face, and he said, "Very clever, gentlemen. Will you permit that I see, or will you tell me, the key signature of this piece, and I will play it." And he did after we had given him the required information. For, it seems (so Rosenthal explained), that Chopin's music contains only two examples of the two-bar rest.[9]

Rosenthal's mastery of Chopin had no magic source: it was, he emphasized, the fruit of long and loving work, and when a colleague took credit for being the first to bring out the "philosophy" in Chopin's music, for example, Rosenthal expressed his irritation by wittily remarking, "Ah! I see, Chopin-*Hauern.*"[10]

There were some, however, who believed that Rosenthal was an even greater interpreter of Beethoven than of Chopin. While Liszt himself had championed works such as the *Hammerklavier* Sonata—as Berlioz, Wagner, Widor, and others attested—with his retirement from public performance in 1847, he had made it one of his goals as a teacher to pass on his awareness and understanding of Beethoven's music to his pupils.

In "Last of the Pianistic Titans" (*Hi Fi/Stereo Review,* February 1965), Louis Biancolli asked Rosenthal if Liszt put Chopin above Beethoven as a composer. "In his heart he did," Rosenthal answered.

"But he never admitted it. You know, there is a secret history of Liszt which only I know. It has partly to do with Chopin, and this much I will tell you—you see, there were two Liszts, the Liszt who as a young man had conquered the whole world and was at the height of his fame, and the other Liszt, the one fighting desperately for his existence. That surprises you, eh?"

"I had always assumed Liszt was a supreme egotist who never had any doubt about his being a genius, not even as a young man," I said.

"That is a very serious mistake. If you recall, Liszt himself tells how he heard Paganini and determined to rise to the same level of virtuosity."

"That, I believe, is the accepted story."

"Well, that was not quite true," Rosenthal went on. "What really happened was that Liszt had heard Chopin play. The effect was almost tragic. He was crushed by the overwhelming grandeur of the man. What do you think he did? He retired to study six hours a day for four years."

"You mean to study the piano?"

"Not so much the piano. During those years Liszt read Homer, Dante, Shakespeare, and the Bible over and over again. Mind you, he did not do all this to reach Paganini. He was trying to develop his individuality so he could reach Chopin."

"But why did he have to make up that story about rising to the level of Paganini?"

"Because Liszt hated to admit that this incitement came from a pianist. It was more practical to give Paganini the credit for the revolution."

At the time that Rosenthal was studying with Liszt, Beethoven's music was rather new and not without enigmas; Rosenthal was among the first to clarify its structural and emotional significance. Nor did he try to make Beethoven more approachable by limiting his repertoire to the "Moonlight," *Pathétique,* and "Appassionata"; he played op. 109 more often than any other of Beethoven's sonatas. The only sonata he played more often, in fact, was Chopin's in b.

2

Early descriptions of Rosenthal's playing concur on his panache and his physical strength, which constituted the ne plus ultra of piano technique. One writer, neatly conflating two observations by the composer and critic Hugo Wolf that are not so neat on their own, described Liszt as the lion of the piano, Anton Rubinstein as the tiger, Friedheim as the panther, and Rosenthal as the devil. Hans von Bülow called him "Rosen-Thalberg" and "the Jupiter of octaves, the Pope of scales, and the President of the Republic of Staccato and Legato." Arthur Schnitzler wrote in his diary on May 1, 1909, that in the finale of Schumann's *Etudes symphoniques* Rosenthal broke a hammer—"an unheard of occurrence with a Bösendorfer."

Certainly no other pianist of his day could rival Rosenthal for his technical vehemence, at least in his youth. "In the 'storm and stress' period he certainly was possessed by his phenomenal technic," Richard Specht wrote in an essay on the pianist ("Moriz Rosenthal," *Die Zeit* [Vienna], 1906).[11] "His accomplishments of that period caused one to gasp. They were intoxicating and deluding, somewhat disquieting and fear-inspiring. He electrified, raised his audience to a frenzy of fascination; but it was not a pure feeling, and one too often felt that one's mind had been misused." Rosenthal's performances of Brahms's Paganini Variations and Liszt's *Don Juan* Fantasie, as well as his own workings up of

Strauss waltzes, were, in the highest sense, exploits.[12] In consequence of such performances of such works, he himself was the architect of his reputation as a titanic pianist notwithstanding his bantam-cock height: 5'1" or 5'2". And yet this reputation was misleading. For the pianist who swam across Lake Como to visit Anton Rubinstein, who sparred with the Welsh heavyweight Tommy Farr and lifted weights, who climbed mountains and practiced jujitsu, who wrestled and fenced, was no less capable of performing feats of the most intense delicacy. It is obvious that the effect of immensity and splendor in Rosenthal's playing obscured other of its virtues. And yet can Rosenthal be blamed if more members of his audience came away overwhelmed by his playing of Schumann's *Carnaval* than Chopin's Waltz in c-sharp? In any case, he prepared each of his performances with extreme devotion; better, for him, fewer performances which were of substance than numerous mediocre ones.

Certainly it is reductive to characterize Rosenthal, as critics have often done, as a piano hussar, a pianist of dare-devilry in his youth and middle age—more at home, as one subtle critic noted, on the Fourth of July than on All Souls Day— who became a more "poetic" interpreter late in life when he could no longer be technically spectacular. (Many young lions of the present day, however, could not hold a candle to him even at that point.) Contrary to received opinion, his poetic side was not something he increasingly had to fall back on as his technique diminished. Indeed, the habit of pigeon-holing a musician as exclusively virtuoso, poet, pedant, philosopher has everything to do with what listeners need from music and its interpreters: in Rosenthal's case, a belief in, or a need to believe in, the glory of youth, its energy and recklessness, and the consolation that in their decline a kind of wisdom, an easiness, comes. (Who doesn't want to believe that he has learned something from having lived?)

Rosenthal's technique was strong until the end of his career. His recording of the D-flat Nocturne of Chopin (op. 27, no. 2) is a case in point, if a quiet one: the *fioritura*, which most pianists, and all lesser pianists, approach as tiny etudes, is so organic, so spontaneous, that one hardly realizes at first what a supreme accomplishment it is. A more brilliant example is his performance of Liszt's *Hungarian Fantasie* with the Chicago Symphony Orchestra in 1938, of which Claudia Cassidy wrote (August 9, 1938):

> Moriz Rosenthal at the piano is a curiously potent figure. A pudgily leonine figure in dress clothes of another day, the 76-year-old pianist remains inflexibly himself and his playing opens the shadowy door into another generation where you are the anachronism, not he. . . .
>
> Few of us, nowadays, would choose Liszt's ornate Fantasia on Hungarian Melodies as the piece to take to a desert island where symphony and soloist had opportunely been shipwrecked. Yet it had its charms last night as Mr. [Hans] Lange and the orchestra skipped nimbly in and out of Mr. Rosenthal's huge and imposing performance. The pianist's own Carnival on melodies of Johann Strauss was as true to its period as Franz Josef's sideburns. The printed program had an old-world quality that made some of us feel brusque and impatient intruders cavilling at ornament.

3

As an interpreter, Rosenthal saw himself as an avatar of the "Grand Manner," which he described in a conference with R. H. Wollstein ("The 'Grand Manner' in Piano Playing," *Etude*, May 1937):

The grand manner of playing? A great many people speak of it as though it were the special manifestation of a special period of time, like crinolines or snuffboxes. . . . No, the grand manner did not "come in" at one special date, and "go out" at another. The grand manner is, very simply—a grand manner. A manner of playing which forms itself upon grand concepts, makes such concepts personal by grand enthusiasms, and paints its pianistic pictures in bold, brilliant, grand strokes. It is a matter of personal convictions, personal inspirations, personal thought. . . . The more typical representatives of this modern day seem less concerned with a free outpouring of generous enthusiasms, than with the practical means of achieving some goal. It is not considered "smart" to give unfettered expression to one's deepest emotions. One must be nonchalant and practical.

Any age could produce musicians in the grand manner, he postulated, if only "the representatives of that age will take the trouble to cultivate those habits of thought."

Part and parcel of Rosenthal's conception of the grand manner was his belief in heroism, upon which he expounded eloquently in an interview with R. H. Wollstein ("Is Culture Progressing in Musical Art?" *Etude*, November 1931). "The modern school of interpretation has left stark, cragged heroism behind," he said. "It strikes, at best, into a sweet, well-regulated field-vale-and-woodland order of feelings. I have even heard the argument put forward that a musician should not *feel* at all—he should simply perceive the emotions he wishes to arouse, cerebrally!" This is not to say Rosenthal believed that a musician should *only* feel; quite the contrary. "Don't make the common mistake of trying to separate the emotions and the intellect," he said. "The intellect is the seat of the emotions." [13] He also once said: "Music that reaches only the mind lacks its chief reason for being."

Rosenthal blamed this want of heroism on World War I:

Among the many splendid things that the war killed, it killed the ideal of personal bravery, of personal heroism. Our ancestors saw the ideals of knighthood fall into disuse with the introduction of firearms; not alone the methods of warfare changed, but, gradually, the entire system of life. And the same process is being duplicated in our own day. The throb of splendor, of heroism, attendant upon the hazards of personal encounter in war, fell into the discard with the arrival of shrapnel and tanks. And a "tank and shrapnel" philosophy extends beyond the battle-field into every human act. There is little heroism in this post-war life; people have grown cynical, dulled. They call heroism a "gesture" and wonder what is "the good of it." As well ask the "good" of truth and beauty and sacrifice. It is this spirit of post-war cynicism, of benefit seeking, of tank mechanism that has crept into today's playing. It has come unconsciously, of course, but, nonetheless, there it is.

While few critics denied Rosenthal his "grand manner," some saw his "technic" as an impediment to its fullest expression. For them, "technic [was] the tragedy of Rosenthal's career," the price of the adroitness with which the gods had favored him being a lack of soul. Vladimir Horowitz didn't credit Rosenthal with even this much, telling *New York Times* music critic Harold Schonberg that Rosenthal "had dexterity but . . . no real technique, and I don't think he really knew how to play the piano."[14] No one was more aware of the conflict than its living embodiment. "What shall I do about it?" Rosenthal asked. "I can't give my technic away, can I?" Significantly, Rosenthal distinguished between problems of touch, which he considered intellectual, and problems of technique. Yet in a letter to Joseph Bennett (March 23, 1898), he declared: "That the chief interest I take in musical reproductive matters lies in the correct phrasing I confess openly."[15]

It may not come as a surprise to learn that Rosenthal himself was nonetheless often jealous of his colleagues and on occasion could be downright cruel to them. The pianist Arthur Shattuck recalled:[16]

> Emil Sauer, in one of his inspired moods, was playing the Schumann *Fantasie* at the Grosser Musikvereinsaal in Vienna, when Rosenthal purposely walked into the loge directly over the stage. Sauer, looking up and seeing his colleague, became momentarily upset, which was exactly what Rosenthal intended. At the close of the recital, Rosenthal went down to the artist's room, which was rapidly filling with Sauer's devoted admirers. Rosenthal's greeting was the tactless jibe, "Well, Emil, things don't go quite as well as they formerly did."
>
> In all the thirty years I knew him, I never heard him say a kind or fair word of any of his fellow artists. Yet he was at all times interesting and entertaining.[17]

Much of Rosenthal's famous, and often devastating, wit (Robert Goldsand considered him the equal of George Bernard Shaw and Oscar Wilde on this front) was a mechanism for contending with this jealousy. (Ignaz Friedman is one of the few who ever bested him: An unexpected meeting at a train station led Rosenthal to observe, "My, Friedman, but you are getting gray!" and Friedman to reply, "Yes, but naturally!" Rosenthal hennaed his hair in his later years and kept his *kaiserlich* moustache his whole life.) Paderewski was Rosenthal's chief bête noire and, consequently, a favorite victim.[18] Upon hearing him in London, Rosenthal was reputed to have remarked: "He plays well, but he's no Paderewski."

In his memoirs, Conte Enrico di San Martino Valperga, a longtime president of the Accademia di Santa Cecilia in Rome, wrote that Rosenthal's preoccupation with Paderewski's successes amounted to a "chronic malady" that led him not merely to play exactly the same programs, down to the very encores, that the Polish pianist presented in Rome,[19] but to demand the same honorarium. This once led to a profound—and indeed deserved—humiliation for him:

> After the concert, which was, overall, a beautiful and well-deserved success, the great Rosenthal presented himself at the box office and asked for his fee. The cash-

ier, who naturally had been forewarned by me, replied with an expression of great surprise: "But what fee?" The Maestro then asked if I had given special orders. And when the cashier replied that I had told him that Rosenthal was coming to Rome under the same terms as Paderewski, the Maestro said: "Exactly, therefore I wish to have the same fee." The cashier coldly replied that Paderewski not only had never accepted so much as a lira when he came to Rome, he had in fact offered gifts to the Academy. Rosenthal took it quite badly.

I retain a rather lengthy letter of Rosenthal's in which he tries to explain the misunderstanding; and naturally, after having inflicted this fright upon him, I ended it by conceding to him a suitable honorarium.[20]

At times Rosenthal's anxieties seem even to color his accountings of musical history. For example, in his lesson on Chopin's Waltz op. 42, which he judged to be the most difficult, at least technically, of all Chopin's waltzes, he offers an interpretation of Chopin's decision not to study with Kalkbrenner, "that excellent pianist and very indifferent composer," that says more about him than about either Chopin or Kalkbrenner:[21]

The end of the matter was that Kalkbrenner required Chopin to promise to remain with him as pupil three years and during that time not to appear in public. But Chopin's family, as well as his teacher of composition in Warsaw, Elsner, suspected some trick, and feared that Kalkbrenner wished to restrain Chopin from playing in public for three years in order to make Chopin's style his own, and then to adorn with it the insipid virtuosity of Kalkbrenner. In other words he wished to *learn* from his pupil in order that he might put to his own use the fruits of his genius. This was hardly ethical; yet Kalkbrenner's self-satisfaction was so great (on this point read Heine's criticisms of the music in Paris) that he may well have thought that he was superior to Chopin, who was then very modest in manner.

That Rosenthal identifies himself with Chopin in this passage is indicated by the fact that he offers contradictory explanations for Kalkbrenner's demand that Chopin not perform in public during his period of study: first, that Kalkbrenner wished to remake Chopin in his own image; second, that Kalkbrenner hoped to remake himself in Chopin's image.

It is clear that Rosenthal was deeply and persistently troubled by the idea of a lesser talent usurping or diminishing the aura of a greater one. This is shown again in his responses to reviewers critical of his own performances, among others "H. C. C." of *The Times* (London) and "G. C." of the *Musical Times*. ("Wonderful! Now you see how infinitely greater 'G. C.' is than Rosenthal," the pianist wrote in a letter to the editor.) These reviews and Rosenthal's letters to the editor are included here; also H. C. C.'s magnificent rebuttal ("As Others See Us"). Rosenthal's "issues" surface yet again in his lesson on Chopin's Waltz in e, in which he characterizes Julian Fontana's editing of Chopin's posthumous works in terms of arrogation: "And now the moment was come when Fontana might execute the most subtle, artful, immortal revenge, a moment which must have given Fontana intense joy! The wren perched upon the wings of the eagle and flew with him up to the sun! No one knew the difference between Chopin and Fontana; both were acclaimed, both celebrated in equal measure."[22]

The most persistent expression of Rosenthal's insecurity emerged in his contract negotiations. In the autumn of 1921, in London, he performed seven historical recitals and planned to follow them up with two further recitals devoted exclusively to the work of modern composers. He wanted to perform the historical recitals and one "mixed" program in America the following year. Several of the letters he wrote in an attempt to bring this about reveal, among other things, that he kept close watch on how much his colleagues were being paid. On October 14, for instance, he noted in a letter that "[Richard] Strauss receives 1,000 Dollars, which is not surprising, given his position as the foremost current composer. Even Morini gets 700 Dollars and Miss Riesan as her accompanist."[23] Rosenthal then went on to demand, in addition to a sleeping car and choice over the piano he would play, a fee of $750 per concert and, if the gross profit of any concert amounted to more than $2,000, 40 percent of the surplus. In the end, he rejected the terms offered him. "Now after ample consideration I cannot say anything but 'No,'" he wrote, "for the following reasons:

> Diamond offers me 25 concerts at 400 Dollars each = 10,000. He said nothing about the time he would require, so I have to reckon with a long period of time.
>
> Of these 10,000 Dollars 1,000 Dollars must be deducted for commission since Diamond quite unnecessarily brought in the impresario [Albert] Backhaus [brother of the pianist Wilhelm Backhaus].
>
> For the sea voyage to New York and back, and for the journey from Vienna to Liverpool and back, for all the traveling in America, luggage, tips, sleeping cars, I estimate around 2,000 Dollars, so that 7,000 Dollars remain.
>
> I have to be prepared for the tour to last 120 days, maybe even longer. Since I have to represent in front of interviewers and others and *must* have a piano in a sitting room, the costs for a hotel (which *15 years* ago cost *20* Dollars per day!) and catering etc. would amount to at least 30 Dollars per day, i.e., 3,600 Dollars. So 3,400 Dollars would remain of the whole trip. Let's compare what I earn in Europe: Last season in England I earned 2,050 Pounds, that is approximately 8,000 Dollars, from January 5th 1921 to February 20th 1921, i.e., in around 45 days.
>
> In Spain I had a fixed contract from March 1st to the end of April, which ran over 24,000 Pesetas = 4,000 Dollars according to the exchange rate of that time. Furthermore, more than 20,000 Lira in Italy and decent earnings in Germany and Bohemia. You will agree that Diamond's offer is simply unreasonable. Two weeks ago I was offered 30 concerts at 600 Dollars each, and I posed my salary conditions.
>
> I hope to be able to give you good news soon because I know that you would be particularly pleased about it.
>
> On the other hand, I will admit openly that I found Diamond's offer an insult. Nevertheless, please believe me that I am most grateful to you for your efforts!
>
> I am sure that Diamond will one day regret not having made me a serious offer.
>
> ...
>
> I am writing to you in so much detail so that you don't think my requirements are exaggerated. I would have accepted 30 concerts at 600 Dollars each with a considerably higher option, particularly if D[iamond]. had paid for my travel. To accept 400 D, when young women violinists get 6 and 700, would be irresponsible toward myself.

By contrast, when Rosenthal's ego was not on the line, he was a gracious and charming correspondent. Witness this note he wrote to his friend and admirer Eileen Wood:[24]

> March 3 (night), 1938
> Dear Miss Eileen,
> The Lord is my witness that I phoned you no less than six times between 8.30 and 10 evening and heard that you were busy *all the time!* In my despair I clutch my pen and write. I am departing tomorrow the 4th March for drowned California (I wish, [. . .] would be with me) and will concertize at: Los Angeles (twice), San Diego, San Francisco, Tacoma, Kalispell Mont. [Montana] and Chicago. Will afterwards dive up again at New York and swim to Europe. . . .

Little more than a week later, Hitler announced the *Anschluss,* or annexation, of Austria by Nazi Germany. Rosenthal would not swim to Europe. Indeed, he would never again return to Vienna.

Another example of Rosenthal's generosity was his sincere interest in pedagogy. With Ludvig Schytte he developed a *Schule des höheren Klavierspiels: Technische Studien bis zur höchsten Ausbildung* (Fürstner, Berlin), or *School of Modern Pianoforte Virtuosity: Technical Studies for the Highest Degree of Development.*[25] He also edited many of Liszt's works for the "Tonmeister" edition (Ullstein Verlag, Berlin). Among his pupils from Vienna, New York, and Philadelphia, where he taught at the Curtis Institute of Music from 1926 to 1929, the most renowned were Webster Aitken, Robert Goldsand, Hedwig Kanner (whom he would later marry), Poldi Mildner, and Charles Rosen. Rosenthal was averse to dilettantes asking him for lessons, however. The Italian pianist Francesco Caramiello recalls that when one of his great aunts sought a lesson from Rosenthal, he put her off by asking her what need she, with her "Perugino-like hands," had of him.

Rosenthal's art survives today on the disc recordings that he began making in his sixty-fifth year. (He came to recording much later than other pianists of his generation.) In *The Great Pianists: From Mozart to the Present Day,* Harold Schonberg has written that Rosenthal's late playing hardly ever rose above a *mezzo forte,* yet improved restoration techniques now demonstrate this not to have been the case, as the accompanying CD demonstrates. Not only do these recordings reveal the scope of Rosenthal's dynamic range, they also showcase his vital sense of rhythm, which projected a sense of inevitable forward motion and musical integrity. In "Sport and Art: The Concept of Mastery," a 1969 essay, Hans Keller wrote that "instrumental mastery, teleologically the servant of expression, has often succeeded in making expression its servant." Rosenthal's late playing is an emphatic renunciation of this argument.

Sal Murgiyanto writes that Sardono, a noted Balinese dancer,

> looks at his development as a dancer and choreographer the way a Buddhist looks at the cosmos which can be differentiated into three regions: the region of sensuousness (the lowest), the region of form (the middle), and the region of formlessness (the highest). The actual practice is not one of discrete and separable areas but, rather, a continuum varying in emphasis and focus. In Tantric Buddhist ritual

performance, the kinetic, corporeal aspects are fundamental paths into the more subtle realms of consciousness.[26]

Rosenthal's late playing might be said to fluctuate among these three regions of the Buddhist cosmos. Keys, hammers, wires, pedals disappear. History and tradition are made immediate. An emotional and spiritual landscape is made into sound, and sound is made into an emotional and spiritual landscape.

"Whenever I hear Moriz Rosenthal play," Richard Specht wrote, "a name forces itself upon me in peculiar association: Friedrich Nietzsche.

> Nietzsche especially would have enjoyed Rosenthal's art; and this merely because his requirement—everything beautiful ought to run smoothly—has been complied with. It is true, Rosenthal's playing does not show any trace of heaviness; it shows *limpidezza* and the "calm ocean." It has been completely purged of materialism and has reached such a sparkling spirituality that to the average critic it seems to exclude the element of sentiment altogether. But this is entirely wrong; it is only that here the soul sentiment has in it nothing unconscious, dull or obscure, and that in its sublimity it is very far from that somewhat obtrusive "soulful playing" which has a fatal smack of the "commonplace" of dressing-gown and slippers,[27] and of cheap sentimentality. Therein also he touches Nietzsche. Rosenthal's art possesses something fascinatingly proud; it does not insinuate itself with flattery; it conquers by iron and yet flexible energy, and, compelled to choose, it would prefer austere reserve to the usual amiability.[28]

4

As a memoirist, Rosenthal is not content merely to recount the events of his life from the vantage point of old age; instead he recreates for us the perspective of the child, and then the young man, who experienced them. In this way Rosenthal the writer was the twin of Rosenthal the pianist, whom one critic praised for his ability to make the past present—or perhaps the present the past: "[His] last program was woven entirely of romantic stuffs. What could more surely invoke the music chamber of the [Eighteen] Eighties than the 'Spring Song' [of Mendelssohn] or Weber's very genteel Waltz? Yet these were not specimens seeming to be viewed under glass. Rosenthal has the faculty of transporting his hearers to a different time and a different place and making the music there vital to them."

In his autobiographical writings, Rosenthal recalls the excitement of his youth as a student, as well as the uncertainty of his twenties and thirties, when, as a recognized but not yet fully established pianist, he hobnobbed with the musical luminaries of Vienna and tried to make a vivid impression upon Brahms and his circle. Soma Morgenstern, a writer and close friend of Joseph Roth, recalled: "When he called the famous pianist Rosenthal, who called Brahms's wit the sharpest he had ever heard, as a witness, [Wilhelm] Furtwängler's remark: 'And that really means something coming from Moriz Rosenthal . . . ' was met with lively merriment, as was the statement that Brahms had often asked women for advice too but never listened to it."[29] The remaining vignettes are equally impressive for their precision and vitality.

Alas, the autobiography ends *in media res:* no mention is made of how Rosenthal met and befriended Albéniz, Busoni, Thomas Mann, Arthur Schnitzler, Johann Strauss II (a portrait of whom hung in Rosenthal's apartment in Vienna), and many other cultural protagonists of his age. Few episodes from his career are detailed, and one can understand why; as the excitement of youth gives way to the plateau of middle age—the frequent tours and repeated performances; the trains, hotels, trans-Atlantic crossings, and dinner parties that define the life of the traveling virtuoso—the impulse to record necessarily wanes. One gets a keen sense of what Rosenthal's life turned into from a letter he wrote on December 14, 1927, to Sigmund Herzog, apologizing for not being able to attend a party Herzog was organizing for the soprano Marcella Sembrich.[30] "Not only do I appreciate this great singer very highly," Rosenthal wrote,

> I was also born in the same town (Lemberg) and we took lessons in the theory of harmony together from the same teacher (Prof. Slomkowski). We are also both working at the Curtis Institute now. Unfortunately I am playing in <u>Minneapolis</u> on December 16th and in <u>Portland Oregon</u> on December <u>22nd</u>. I will therefore have to spend December 18th, which happens to be my birthday, on the train in my solitary "drawing room."

Occasional visits with friends, or holidays either at his villa in Abbazia (now Opatija, in Croatia) or at Bad Gastein and Bad Ischl in the Tyrol, provided a necessary respite from this hectic life. Notably, Rosenthal speaks very little, in these pieces, about his private life, including his late marriage to Hedwig Kanner.

While we may regret that this written account is incomplete, what is missing is more than compensated for by Rosenthal's other writings—his layered descriptions of actions and reactions, his accounts of meetings with influential people, his analyses of musical works—and by his recordings.

Note on the Texts

The works collected here do not, of course, represent every word that Rosenthal wrote, but they succeed in showing something of how he lived his professional life and of what he thought while he was doing so. The works by writers other than Rosenthal are offered to contextualize Rosenthal's own.

Between 1932 and 1940 Rosenthal contributed "lessons" on the interpretation of six compositions to the *Etude:* Chopin's Scherzo in b-flat (January 1932), Waltz in e, op. posthumous (October 1933), Waltz in A-flat, op. 42 (April 1934), Funeral March (March 1935), and Mazurka in b-flat, op. 24, no. 4 (February 1940); and Schumann's *Carnaval* (November 1932, December 1932, and January 1933). These were, by the *Etude*'s own testimony, "of monumental value" to the "self-help student" and the music teacher alike. At the same time, the *Etude*'s presentation of these lessons frequently bordered on the crass. For instance, an announcement of one of Rosenthal's lessons read, in part, "This most brilliant of living pianists got as high as $100.00 a lesson in America. In a future ETUDE he gives to all readers an incomparable lesson on the great Chopin Valse in A-flat, opus 42." Mark Hambourg was not the only pianist who groaned when the *Etude*'s request for a "lesson" or article arrived in the morning post.

As the intent of this volume is literary rather than pedagogical, we have included only excerpts from these lessons. A road map through the Scherzo in b-flat—"This dramatic introduction modulates to the relative (sometimes called parallel) major, D-flat; then through F Major back to B Minor; is repeated in part; modulates to F Minor; and then remains for sixteen measures in D-flat Major"—would be as coals to Newcastle to the professional pianist, and a distraction to a reader who seeks primarily to know Rosenthal the writer. Likewise the "historical" background that usually precedes Rosenthal's analyses owes a considerable (and unacknowledged) debt to his reading of Hugo Riemann's still valuable *Musiklexikon*. Finally, Rosenthal often recycled anecdotes and information from other essays, published and unpublished alike, for use in the lessons.

The numerous "conferences" to which Rosenthal submitted for the *Etude* are not included here in their entirety either. As used by the *Etude*, "conference" appears to mean the reworking of Rosenthal's answers to an interviewer's questions into a first-person narrative putatively written by Rosenthal himself. The best example of the extent to which Rosenthal was ill-used by the magazine is a piece titled "If Franz Liszt Should Come Back Again" (*Etude*, April 1924), in which the pianist is prompted to ventriloquize for the dead composer, offering a paean to American musical life on his behalf: "If Liszt should return now and come to America, he would stand amazed at the great demand for music in the new world. He would be amazed at the numerous fine halls, the music schools springing up everywhere, and it would delight the soul of this most progressive of all true and great pianists." The obvious purpose of this speculation is to burnish America's ideal of its own musical culture with the benediction of old Europe. On such occasions, Rosenthal seems like a great actor being obliged to perform in a student play.

Since many of the *Etude*'s readers were music teachers and students, Rosenthal often had to simplify his prose to suit the editorial necessities of the magazine's audience in a way that he did not in his autobiography or in those articles he wrote out of a sense of personal conviction. In these pieces Rosenthal often resorted to inventing or describing "programs" for the works in question even though he pointed out more than once that Chopin had no commerce with them. In his highly pictorial lesson on the Funeral March, for example, Rosenthal wrote: "Chopin himself, who disliked every program, confiding in the musical power of his ideas, answered jestingly a pupil, who asked him about the meaning of this *Unisono-Finale:* 'There is gossip between the right and left hand.'"

More significantly, the *Etude* placed what would have to be called moral constraints on Rosenthal's articles. This is demonstrated by comparing two of Rosenthal's versions of Chopin's last meeting with George Sand, the first from his letter to Herbert Hughes, published here, and the second from the *Etude* ("The Genius of Chopin," February 1926). In his letter to Hughes, he gives the grown-up story, writing, "[Sand's] lovers were quite numerous"; describing her relationship with Chopin as what it was, a "liaison"; airing the (unfounded) theory put forward by Bernard Szarlitt and others that Chopin fell in love with Sand's daughter Solange and that he supported Solange in opposing her mother's wish to marry her to the sculptor Clésinger; explaining that it was Chopin who told Sand that Solange had had a child; and, by way of conclusion, describing Sand as a "hypocrite," calling in as evidence Sand's roman-à-clef of her "liaison" with Chopin, *Lucrezia Floriani*.[31] Now read the *Etude* version:

> There is no doubt that Chopin sacrificed himself in many things, because he felt that his own life was of very little significance in comparison with the high artistic nature that had been given to him. When, however, he was located at Castle Nohant, [or] in Majorca, he was far away from the inevitable noise and din of a metropolis, and where George Sand with her soft hand kept uneasiness away from him, he could transcribe his ideas to paper as they really came to him. His pitiful condition after the breach with George Sand indicated not merely that his pride was unbroken, but also that his haughty and virile strength of character, under such an affliction, was maintained in a manner indicating those characteristics of force which Weismann dwells upon [in his book].[32] Chopin, one day, after the breach, met George Sand at the door of Madame Marliani's, wife of the Spanish Consul at Paris. He saluted her, and when he told her that her daughter, Solange, had a child and that she was feeling well, Madame Sand merely replied, asking Chopin how he himself felt. Although the meeting must have been an extremely painful one for Chopin, the master expressed his thanks, asked the porter to open the door, and refused any overtures for a reconciliation. George Sand apparently thought little of her grandmotherly dignity and thought a great deal of her more or less motherly attitude toward Chopin.

Without knowing the "back story," this paragraph makes quite little sense. There is no explanation of the reason Sand was estranged from her daughter, which is the very crux of the matter, nor of the role Chopin himself played in this family drama. There is nothing about lovers and liaisons. Sand is proud, but not a hypocrite.

For readers interested in seeing the full texts of Rosenthal's lessons, the *Etude* can be located in most libraries. We have opted to give greater weight here to those works of Rosenthal's which have either never been published or translated into English—or both. For the same reason we are not including either the full text of "Franz Liszt, Memories and Reflections," Elsie Braun Barnett's English translation of which was published in *Current Musicology* 13 (1972)—a *pièce d'occasion* written for the centennial of Liszt's birth—or any of the letters Rosenthal wrote to the recording engineer Fred Gaisberg. Their correspondence has been edited by Bryan Crimp and published by APR (1987).

Since Rosenthal's writings were published on both sides of the Atlantic, and across many years, there is no stylistic consistency among them. In the published pieces as well as in his previously unpublished manuscripts (which sometimes are little more than drafts), we have sought to correct errors of fact—both his own (for example, Tausig died in Leipzig, not in Ragaz, Switzerland; Offenbach's operetta is *The Grand Duchess of Gérolstein,* not *The Grand Duke of Gérolstein;* it was Czar Alexander II, not the VI, who was assassinated—there was no Czar Alexander VI) and those of others; spelling (some errors were a charming consequence of the pianist's fluency in several languages: he would attempt to Anglicize German words, for example, or "Germanicize" English ones, with the result that the new word would be misspelled in both languages); translation (the *Etude* in particular was often hard pressed to do justice to Rosenthal's prewar German, which in fact poses distinct challenges to any translator; even the Germans say, "deutsche Sprache, schwere Sprache," or in English, "German language, difficult language"); usage; and typography. (In accordance with the *Chicago Manual of Style,* we have elected in the sections of the book that we wrote ourselves, or that are newly translated, to indicate major keys with a capital letter—A, E, B-flat, etc.—and minor keys with a lowercase letter—a, e, b-flat, etc.)

Where Rosenthal underlines proper names in manuscripts or typescripts, or puts them in italics in published articles, we have elected to leave these names in Roman. We have also normalized the spelling of composers' names (also place names) in accordance with standard English (for example, "Tchaikovsky" instead of "Tschaïkowsky"). And we have replaced the "ff" at the end of most Russian names with "v"; this "ff" being, as Vladimir Nabokov observed in *Speak, Memory,* "an old Continental fad." An exception is Olga Samaroff, who was American, not Russian, and whose name is evidence of that "old Continental fad": she was born Lucy Hickenlooper.

A more aggressive editorial stance has been taken in regard to the presentation of the texts themselves. Rosenthal obviously did not write his articles with a view their eventual publication in volume form; a fact witnessed by his reworking of the same material in different articles and essays (both published and unpublished). For example, he makes the case that it was Chopin, and not Paganini, whose playing caused Liszt to retire in order to consolidate not merely his technique but his ideas, in both "Franz Liszt, Memories and Reflections," written for the Berlin periodical *Die Zeit* on the occasion of the centennial of Liszt's birth, and in "Last of the Pianistic Titans," an interview with Louis Biancolli (*Hi Fi/Stereo Review,* February 1965). Biancolli's framing of the story is superior, and so it is his we have given here. Nor do Rosenthal's famous anecdotes about Bernhard Stavenhagen and Alexander Winterberger need to be retold five times.

In the wonderful article published in English as "The Night Rubinstein Played Bratislava," Rosenthal writes,

While taking leave I thought: "Never again will coincidence or life make it possible for me to see and speak to Liszt and Rubinstein in the same room!" Yet, contrary to all probability, the rare case repeated itself soon afterwards, and I was able to greet the Pressburg triumvirate of Liszt, Rubinstein, and Leschetizky, and Brahms as well, at *one* festive banquet table, and I was permitted to sit again at Liszt's side!

Although he does not describe the "rare case" in this article, he does describe it in "Franz Liszt, Memories and Reflections." We have therefore inserted (in brackets, of course) the account from the latter into the former, just as on other occasions we have incorporated bracketed excerpts from pieces we have chosen not to include in their entirety into some of the selections. By assimilating Rosenthal's writings in this way, we hope to give the reader a richer sense of his life and ideas.

Finally, unless the name of a translator is given under the title of a piece, it is a new translation. The translators are Stephen J. Evans, Barbara Fink, and Margit Grieb.

1 Autobiography

Unpublished

Moriz Rosenthal

The manuscript of Rosenthal's autobiography, some pages of which are written on stationery from the Great Northern Hotel (the pianist's residence in New York), is in the library of the Mannes College of Music, now part of the New School. The typescript, the basis for this translation, is in the possession of Allan Evans.

A photograph of Rosenthal at his desk was published in the Musical Courier *(September 15, 1940) with the following caption: "The Pianist Titan putting the finishing touches on his memoirs, which will have many interesting references to his famous friends including Liszt, Brahms and Rubinstein and which are soon to be published in a translation by Leonard Liebling." This publication did not take place.*

In 1948, two years after Rosenthal's death, his widow, Hedwig Kanner Rosenthal, announced to Robert Breuer, the New York correspondent for Der Bund *(Bern, Switzerland), her intention of editing her late husband's autobiography. The New York Herald-Tribune, which reported this, continued: "Mr. Rosenthal, who died in September, 1946, began to write his memoirs in his youth, and continued his autobiographical writing until the time of the Nazi occupation of Austria in 1938. After that, according to Mme. Kanner, 'he never considered his own life important any more, but tried to help as much wherever help was needed.' The eighty-fifth anniversary of his birth is next Friday."*

> *In order to supplement Mr. Rosenthal's own manuscript, Mme. Kanner would be much obliged if those who possess letters, programs or reviews pertaining to her husband's early tours in this country—he made his American debut in 1888—would send them to her for study. Documents or letters on this subject should be addressed to Hedwig Kanner, Hotel Great Northern, 118 West Fifty-seventh Street, New York. Such material will be returned to the senders after it has been consulted. The tentative title of the biography is "From Liszt to Hitler."*

This publication did not take place either.

On December 7, 1956, the New York Times *printed an obituary notice for Hedwig Kanner Rosenthal, who was in fact alive and well. The obituary had been phoned in as a prank. Mrs. Rosenthal, who was still teaching, said that she was thinking of writing her own memoirs in which she would tell the truth about her husband's career and "not dance around it like a fox." Upon being informed that the obituary gave her age (wrongly) as eighty-three, she admitted, "I'm over twenty."*

Her memoirs were never published. She died on September 5, 1959, in Asheville, North Carolina, at the age of eighty-three.

A word on the text: Rosenthal used chapter headings so erratically (chapter seven begins on page seven of the typescript, for instance, while chapter five begins on page 12) that these have been dispensed with altogether. Like many German writers, for whom reader friendliness is not a consideration, Rosenthal did not break up dialogue in either the manuscript or the typescript of the autobiography. For the sake of the English reader, and in keeping with standard English form, we have cast the texts so that each piece of dialogue is given as a separate paragraph.

"Again?" asked my mother eagerly.[1]

"Again. And even a lot longer than yesterday," answered my sister Rosa, who, being nine years older than I (I was seven), used to pick me up from our father's school.[2] "He walked along nicely until we got to the Frenelgasse, but a window was open on the second floor there, and we could hear someone playing a piano, I think it was Jungmann's 'Ein flüchtiger Gedanke,' and afterwards 'The Maiden's Prayer' by B.[3] Little brother Moriz stopped as if spellbound, and no amount of cajoling could snap him out of it. I could only get him to come along once the piano was silent."

"You must tell your father all this when he gets home," replied mother; "maybe Moriz has a special talent for music."

I wasn't paying much attention to what they were saying, because more important things bounced around in the mind and heart of a seven-year-old Napoleon enthusiast.[4] It was the year 1815, forty-seven years before my birth; accompanied by only my most faithful allies—who, like me, were determined to break the bread of exile no longer—I quitted, one stormy night, the little island of Elba. As early on as the French border we were joined by two thousand bold horsemen. In Lyon I issued a proclamation to the French, which secured for us swarms of followers. Although I had been treated as a rabble-rouser at the border, in Lyon I was celebrated as a victorious general, and so I entered Paris a triumphant Caesar, as emperor of France. At that moment my dear mother entered the room and asked: "Don't you want to come down for dinner?"

* * *

Dinner was excellent. The smell of chicken soup wafted from the table. There were baked chicken livers, then chicken and Polish delicacies, just as resplendent as on the well-stocked tables in Lemberg (French: Leopol, Polish: Lwów), the capital of Galicia. Also red wine, which I wasn't allowed to taste, glinted on the table. I asked my dear father how come Prince Poniatowski had drowned in such a small river as the Elster.[5] He must have been a miserable swimmer. My father answered me very earnestly: "Let that be a warning to you: four-fifths of the earth's surface is covered in water; therefore it is important that you be able to go into the water without fearing for your life. Hence," he concluded, "we'll go swimming at the Palczinsky pond." We set off immediately after dinner, abandoning ourselves along the way to repeating conjugations of French verbs, with particular stress upon the irregular ones. My dear, precious father spoke fluent French; all that I know of this language I learned during walks with my father, whereas I learned English and Italian purely through reading and memorization without any kind of teacher.

A special celebration was underway in Palczinsky. A new swimming teacher had been engaged who had promptly earned a place in the hearts of his young pupils by showing them a few unusual dives. I stayed far away from this noisy crowd of boys because I had decided to learn the art of swimming without the aid of a teacher. Thus, I was rather surprised when I noticed the swimming whiz walking toward me. His first question was whether my father's first name was "Leo." When I answered in the affirmative, he appeared both delighted and moved, and told me that he had learned German from Leo Rosenthal's grammar book, and that the book had been adopted by the Austrian Ministry for Education and was now used in all schools, including the ones where my father taught, of course. He didn't omit to mention that my father, who was originally from Kamieniec Podolski, had spent his first years of study in Zurawno (Poland), where, even in the coldest, bitterest winter, he delighted in bathing in the river, going so far as to have someone break up the ice for him so that he wouldn't miss a single day of his icy baths. My father smiled and proudly verified the teacher's version of the story.[6] Soon thereafter the swimming teacher hastily said goodbye, probably in order to save one of his boys from the destiny of Prince Poniatowski.

* * *

The following days passed relatively uneventfully. However, when I got home from school at the end of the week, somewhat depressed in light of my tragic fate on St. Helena and the beastliness of Sir Hudson Lowe,[7] I saw an object that was as closely related to a concert piano as a newborn foal is to an Arabian stallion. The keyboard only reached F in the treble and contra C in the bass. Above the keyboard gleamed the name "Conrad Graf"; with Streicher, he had been the most famous Viennese piano maker during Beethoven's time. Both manufacturers had had to give way to Erard and Pleyel in Paris. Chopin preferred Pleyel, Liszt Erard. My piano had a rather weak but agreeably singing tone and a worn-out keyboard with yellowed white keys [*Untertasten*] and browning black keys [*Obertasten*]. The instrument had cost fifty Gulden, which was about twenty dollars, and served me faithfully until my final departure from my native town of Lemberg. When I pressed down some of the keys, our cook called out fearfully: "Don't play, don't play. You'll ruin the piano!" And my dear sweet mother said: "I am afraid your other studies will take a back seat to playing the piano."

Then the door bell rang, and a few seconds later Herr Wenzel Galath, viola player at the Civic Theater of Lemberg and my future piano teacher, stepped into the room. "So this is the young scholar," he said as he entered. "Have you already eaten?"

"Yes."

"Then we can get started right away! How old are you?"

"Seven. On December 18th I'll be eight, which is in only six more months."

"And what grade are you in?"

"The fourth."

"How is that possible?"

Here my mother put her oar in. "We let him go to school when he was only five years old, because he was able to memorize every poem or prose piece that we read to him right away. He can recite entire chapters of Noesselt's *World History.*"[8]

"That's fantastic!" Galath exclaimed. Then he began to teach me the notes corresponding to both the piano keys and the lines and spaces of the treble clef; then their rhythmic separation into half and quarter notes. Up to this point he had done nothing to convince potential critics that he was a talented and original teacher; however, shortly before ending the lesson, he said: "Sing me Haydn's *Kaiserlied,* our national hymn!" I sang it to his satisfaction. "Now I will tell you something: Look for it on the keys and then practice it with the second finger of the right hand until you can do it smoothly and without ugly stuttering. Do you think you can do that?"

"Oh, yes," I replied, with all the confidence of youth.

"We will hear the result the day after tomorrow," said Galath. "We will meet three times a week for one hour lessons." He gave me a friendly wave and left the room. I ran over to the piano and, within ten or fifteen minutes, was playing the national hymn for my parents, who could barely contain their excitement. All the next day I rested on my laurels, but the day after it occurred to me that I might play the piece not only in C, but in D, E, and C-sharp, which naturally opened up the possibility of playing it in still other keys. Another teacher would have recommended moderation and restraint. Not so Galath, who encouraged me in my studies with lessons on intervals, offered me a glimpse of the wonderful realm of composition, and delighted me with tales of famous composers.

Napoleon himself stepped into the background when Beethoven came onto the stage. *With Beethoven there was no Waterloo!*

* * *

Whenever Galath was really satisfied with my performance, he would play for me from Beethoven's early sonatas, to which I would listen as to a divine revelation; sometimes he also brought along some sheets of rolled-up manuscript paper on which he had written out in pencil the "Funeral March" in a-flat (part of the A-flat Sonata [op. 26]) with its seven flat notes. At that time, a boy named Sigmund Lilienfeld was boarding with us. He was six years older than I and started his piano lessons with Galath a few weeks after I began mine. He was an exceptionally clever, even cunning young man who amazed the professors at the German Gymnasium he attended with his talents. After his first piano lesson he declared in a breezy, conversational tone of voice that he was determined to catch up with me in a few weeks, and that once he had caught up, I was to be sure to ask for his help if I encountered unexpected difficulties.

A few days later, when I returned from school, I heard him playing a scale slowly and deliberately in the adjacent room where Conrad Graf stood. I called out to him: "You're already playing the G scale?"

He stormed into my room in a state of agitation. "How do you know that I'm playing the G scale?" he asked.

"I heard it," I said to him.

He turned all pale: "Will you let me test you?"

"Why not? With pleasure!"

He began playing single notes, then complicated his questions by adding new notes and chords up to a point where I was identifying eight dissonant notes played simultaneously—calling them out while facing away from the piano. He was especially amazed when I told him to play eight notes and hold them with the pedal. I would come into the room after six to eight seconds and identify the notes as they were fading away. He admitted to me candidly that he was astonished by my aptitude and that, while it was quite possible that I possessed an innate musical talent, it was also quite likely that I would face other problems of the psyche with the rest of humanity against which I would be powerless. I asked him whether he had picked up this lofty language from reading Schiller[9] or through the literary lessons of his private teacher, Professor Urban. He left the question open, but urgently suggested I ought to study with Urban myself, so that I would gain as much pleasure from it as I did from my music. After all, Urban only asked five Gulden (approximately two dollars) a month for teaching one lesson a day.

Urban deemed Schiller's works too highly strung for one of my tender years, but gave me other interesting exercises to do. For example, I had to rewrite the tired platitude "Alle Menschen müssen sterben" ("All men must die") fifty different ways. I could come up with only twenty variations, but the last one amazed my teacher so thoroughly that he stopped counting. I had written: "Der Tod hat manchmal bleierne Füsse, aber stets eiserne Hände" ("Death sometimes has lead feet, but it always has iron hands"). This aphorism met with general approval and even inspired moderate applause from Lilienfeld, leading him later to predict that I could achieve "some glory" in writing were I to follow his lead.

Urban at that time in my life was a dazzling mayfly; but the person to whom I was really drawn, day in and day out, was the musician Wenzel Galath. I will never forget the enchanted hour during which he played Beethoven's *Pathétique* Sonata for me; how he sang the second theme of the first movement with his pleasantly humming voice; and how he revealed and glorified Beethoven's tremendous power over the musical substance of the rondo. He called it an "innocent hussar piano piece" when he played four-handed with me, occasionally stopping to pull out his beloved snuff box and treat himself to a fragrant pinch. This maneuver usually cost him two or three beats, but the important thing was that we were soon able to synchronize our playing again.

Lilienfeld was not part of these vehement excursions; he belonged to the "Fussvolk" [rank and file], the "Impedimentum" as it is called in Latin. His ambition was deeply bruised by the ever-widening gap between his skills and mine. Once, as he listened to me, a thousand disapproving wrinkles on his face, he abruptly asked: "What do you think, could I catch up with you if I studied all of Haydn's sonatas and eighteen of Clementi's?" I answered in the negative, which prompted him to make derisive comments about my conceitedness and overestimation of my own abilities.

* * *

One fine day, while we were taking a walk in the Jesuitengarten, Lilienfeld stopped suddenly. "What's wrong?" I asked.

"A marvelous idea!" he called out enthusiastically. "We'll give a concert every Sunday evening in our apartment. The week before we'll practice assiduously, put together a great classical program, and collect a ten Kreuzer entrance fee from everyone who comes. With the money we take in, we'll buy the complete works of Beethoven, Haydn, Mozart, Schubert, and Weber. It'll only be thanks to the devil's intervention if we don't become famous."

"Okay," I said. "But what shall we play? And two hands or four hands?"

"As many as possible four hands," said Lilienfeld. "The pieces for two hands are generally very difficult." We were now off on a fierce campaign of practicing on my Conrad Graf, which each week had to be tuned anew in order to obliterate the traces of our rivalrous onslaughts.

In the beginning we played our program for Galath in order to get his corrections, but later we let ourselves be guided entirely by our spirits. I will never forget how Lilienfeld handled the excerpt from [Mozart's] *Don Juan* Overture, which he had selected, criminally, to be the opening number on our program. He exhibited a tender devotion to the pedal, lifting his foot from it very rarely. A harrowing chaos was the unhappy effect. Lilienfeld said afterwards that he had regretted the awfulness of this perpetual "pedal sauce," but had feared the sudden onset of "dry" pedallessness.[10] Galath decried this "acoustic bankruptcy," as he called it, but was even more dismayed that I had debased our national hymn by transposing it into a minor key. It was reprehensible to transplant a melody that was supposed to convey good wishes for His Majesty the Kaiser into a key of mourning. By and by he calmed down and praised my sight reading, even though in his opinion Offenbach's Quadrilles on [Themes from] *Barbe-bleue* and *La Grande Duchesse de Gérolstein* were not really suited to a concert performance, the composer's conspicuous talent notwithstanding. But he had to freely admit that my elegant *pianissimo* came as a welcome respite, a true refreshment, for the overwrought eardrums of listeners irritated by Lilienfeld's pedal orgies. At this point in Galath's didactic musings my dear mother's voice could be heard—"Prosze, do kolacji" (Supper is ready!)—and soon thereafter we were all sitting together in a jolly circle.

* * *

We were talking about different peoples and their cultural accomplishments and eventually turned to the Arabs. My occasional tutor Rola Count Bolechowski (Lemberg was full of Polish aristocrats who kept their heads above water by teaching) pointed out that the Arabic numerals were much easier to use than their clumsy Roman counterparts, which were only to be found in official documents or on some buildings as vestiges of a bygone culture.

My dear father launched into an interesting disquisition. He noted that the Roman alphabet derived from a finger alphabet and was therefore based on a decimal system (deka = ten in Greek). One, two, three, four represent the fingers without thumb, each of which denotes "one." The fully extended hand represents the number five (V). The number ten (X) is denoted by two crossed hands. Lower and upper arms, in a right angle to each other, represented an "L," which signified the number fifty, while the "C" (= one hundred) ("Centum") derived from the figure of a sitting body bent over. Everybody applauded as at a concert. Then Galath rose to speak. He declared that he was not a man preoccupied with worldly things and in fact a devout Catholic. Nonetheless, he wanted to tell a somewhat ribald yet historically accurate anecdote. Setting: the golden city of Prague. Time: the early seventeenth century. All the clerical and secular princes were gathered around a golden dinner table. Emperor Rudolf II of Habsburg presides; Cardinal Clesel, an ambitious, splendor-loving man, sits next to him. Everybody begins posing riddles, most of which are easily solved. Then his majesty turns to his princely clerical neighbor and asks the following riddle: "How can one write '150 donkeys' with only one word?" Clesel looks puzzled and makes a dismissive gesture, but Rudolf has already written the word on a slate: "CLesel."[11] The clerical prince leaves the Emperor's dinner table fatally wounded.

We all laugh. Rola Count Bolechowski offers to tell an even better anecdote. MacMahon, commander-in-chief of the French armed forces during the years 1870–1871, has his best officers parade in front of him.[12] He asks each of the officers to mention a few of the battlefields on which he has fought, after which MacMahon casually declares: "Eh bien, mon brave, continuez!" Then an African officer steps forward. MacMahon, surprised to see a black man in front of him, exclaims: "Mais vous êtes nègre!" ("But you are black"). "Oui, Monseigneur!" "Eh bien, mon brave," replies MacMahon machine-like, "continuez!"

A few days after our concert, my father returned home in a somewhat agitated state. He had run into Galath, who had told him plainly that he had nothing new to teach me. He was not a pianist but a viola player; up until this point he had done a lot for me. But now two paths had opened before me: to take lessons from Karol Mikuli, a student of Chopin's, who was certainly very expensive, or from Louis Marek, who as a modern piano virtuoso, and especially through his interpretation of Liszt transcriptions, had created a furor.[13] Marek's honorarium was a lot more reasonable than Mikuli's. After mulling the choice over for a while, we decided to listen to both piano magicians several times.

Marek ran a piano shop, which made it a lot easier to visit him. Destiny was on our side. When we arrived, Marek was sitting in front of a medium-sized piano and attempting to stimulate the interest of two ladies in the instrument to its highest degree by thundering out chromatic octaves while indulging in pedal orgies à la Lilienfeld. In stark contrast to this display of dynamic dynamite excesses, the music stand displayed the title pages of several of Marek's pacific compositions, one of them a "Valse du Boudoir." The playing of this boudoir artist delighted neither me nor my father, and we relayed our disappointment to Galath. He asked, what could one expect from a man and musician who could compose a "Valse du Boudoir" and such things?

Mikuli was held in much higher regard by all pianists and musicians; he had been to Paris and there studied with the famous pianist Chopin, who in spite of his addiction to originality had composed many a work which pointed to a new era.[14] Furthermore, in a few days a concert was to take place showcasing the most famous German royal court pianist, Hans von Bülow.[15] The program was dedicated exclusively to Chopin, probably to flatter the Pole [Mikuli]. Mikuli and Marek were sure to be present. Galath foresaw a piquant intermission from Mikuli. Both as a musician and a critic Mikuli was a man of extremes. If an artist displeased him, he would leave the hall before the concert was over followed by approximately thirty pupils, making a lot of noise so that the entire concert would become disorganized. Yet his admiration was as intense as his displeasure. The day after a good concert, he would be confined to his bed, unable to receive any pupils.

Galath became more and more animated, and he began telling stories of Mikuli's studies with Chopin, of which there were different versions in circulation. Mikuli himself often told stories about how Chopin's lessons almost always exceeded the traditional three-quarter hour—for which an honorarium of twenty gold francs was stipulated—sometimes by as much as four times, at which point master and pupil would be completely worn out and have to call it quits. Supposedly, Mikuli was once invited to a ball at the home of Princess Sapieha (commonly called "Sapiegyna"), where he more than did justice to the excellent champagne.[16] The aristocratic guests gathered around the honored master, and several of them asked to hear in greater detail about his fabled hours as a pupil and squire of the Untouchable. Mikuli banged his fist on the table so that the glasses clanked, and cried: "Leave me in peace with these lessons! *He* would often stand, sometimes the entire three-quarters of an hour, at the fire-place, to warm himself, then adjust his beautiful tie and say: 'One does not play it like that, my dear! It must sound more elegant and rhythmic! Come again next Monday!'" Loud laughter accompanied the punch line of the story. Wonderful as it was, however, no one believed it. Their adoration of Mikuli and reverence for Chopin were so great and unshakable that most abided by the first version.

Galath also believed that version, believed in Mikuli, and mistrusted the dry, polemical intellectuality of the royal court pianist Hans von Bülow. Bülow almost turned his first and only concert in Lemberg into a fiasco. His performance of Chopin's Sonata in b, op. 58 provoked bitter reactions from the melomanes and connoisseurs in the audience. Bülow was no match for the technical difficulties of the last pages of the Finale; he held the tempo conspicuously back without being able to convince anyone that his left hand was not slowing down due to fatigue during the demanding sixteenth-note passages. Most everybody deplored the dry and brittle *cantilena,* and the remark "szkaradnie" ("execrable") could be heard many times.

Mikuli was completely up to this great challenge. A lurch, a rustle and scrape, and he was gone from the scene long before the concert was over. Following him were thirty supporters, their heads held high.

* * *

I was finally able to hear him, . . . revere him, love him! Mikuli had founded a trio in Lemberg which gave weekly public concerts: violin, Bruckmann; cello, Wollmann; pianist and *Spiritus Rector,* Karol Mikuli. The concerts took place in the Sala Ratuszowa (the great room of the city hall) and attracted a large audience whenever a famous virtuoso or Mikuli himself was playing. One night when I was in attendance, Mikuli's trio played Beethoven's Trio in c, op. 1 [no. 3] as well as Mendelssohn's pianistically much more complex Trio in d. Both pieces aroused in me the utmost enthusiasm.

Aside from the profound content of these brilliant works, I was dazzled by Mikuli's consummate performance. I had never imagined that such a round *legatissimo* was possible.[17] "You must study with Mikuli!": this was the quintessence of my father's strong feelings. And when he heard from friends how high Mikuli's honorarium was (and surely it had been reduced by half for me), he nonetheless said: "I must perform my duty."

"Dort, wo die letzten Häuser stehen" [There, where the town frays (into the countryside)], lived Mikuli.[18] He received us cordially and with the best of manners, listened attentively while I played Beethoven's Sonata in c, op. 10 [no. 1], and praised my musical talent, while also pointing out that I held my fingers too high, which hindered me in playing for speed, as well as in my *legato.* [In "The Apprentice Years of a Master" (*Etude,* November 1938), Rosenthal told R. H. Wollstein:

Mikuli realized, perhaps, that my previous studies had concerned themselves more with music than with the piano; and he now set about giving me a purely pianistic grasp. It was he who made me aware of technic.

Technic, to him however, did not mean a mere passion for show or speed. He opened my eyes to the beautiful balance of notes in a scale; to the perfection of clean, clear, orderly playing. I had never realized that such beauties existed (indeed, I never have heard any sheerly pianistic achievement to surpass Mikuli's arpeggios), and I began to make progress at once.]

I had to play the first, very simple study from Czerny's *School of Fluency* [*Schule der Geläufigkeit,* op. 299], first slowly and then ever faster, whereupon I reached a tempo far beyond anything I had achieved so far.[19] Now he put another score on the music stand and had me sight read it. It was a heartfelt piece, Mozart's second Concerto in A [K. 488]. It fascinated me with its mix of intimacy, elegance, and high lyricism.

Mikuli's lessons took place twice a week and continued for almost two years [i.e., 1872–1874]. When I think back to those years today, I cannot contain a certain astonishment at several grave sins of omission from my lessons. I will give two examples: In the above mentioned Concerto, Mozart leads, in an interesting move, the lowest voice of the second theme in the first movement into a descent. Mikuli let this piece pass me by without so much as commenting on the artistry of this terrific section. Even more glaring to me is the following instance: Mikuli noticed my excellent memory right away and by and by assigned me the twenty-four preludes and fugues of the [First Book of the] *Well-Tempered Clavier,* which I was able to play for him from memory in a relatively short period of time. Curiously, Mikuli never said a word about the structure of a fugue, so that its contrapuntal value was utterly lost to me back then. On the other hand, he insisted on specialized instruction in harmonies, which I completed through the conscientious teaching of the theoretician Slomkowski.

He also failed to give me sound instructions concerning the use of the pedals since he himself knew little if anything about the so-called "syncopated pedal." In this case, however, he cannot be found guilty because the first mention of this magnificent discovery appeared in one of the letters from the piano teacher and music critic Louis Köhler of Königsberg to Franz Liszt.[20] It is and remains inconceivable, however, that a genius like Liszt could have failed to rejoice in triumphant cheer at the announcement of this discovery, and instead uttered only reluctant praise. He calls it: especially interesting for ["players, teachers and] composers—especially in slow tempi."

I find it just as unfathomable that Chopin did not teach his pupil Mikuli correct pedal use, indeed, that almost all pedal notations of our classic masters could be improved. Beethoven told Karl Holz, his young friend, while discussing his last five sonatas:[21] "These are the last sonatas that I shall write for the piano, which is and remains an inadequate instrument!"[22] Beethoven would not have said this had he known about the syncopated pedal! (By the way, the master took back his banishing curse on the piano and later composed thirty-three marvelous variations on a waltz by Diabelli [op. 120].)

Mikuli was religious to the highest degree and liked to submit to the customs of the church. I remember that during the Easter holidays he laid out several large tables with delicacies called *swiecone* ("blessed") that had been blessed by a priest. All his good friends would visit with one another and celebrate *con fuoco* the excellent dishes and drinks blessed by the church.

I was present when Mikuli told his very young wife, a charming blonde (he himself was born in the year 1825 (!)), how he had only just returned home after having been detained at the house of the governor, Count Agenor Goluchowski, who had been hosting his own "blessed dishes" event. There Mikuli had eaten several excellent fish dishes and four rolls. This caused his attractive wife and me to break into raucous laughter, in which Mikuli himself joined, an octave lower.[23]

Naturally we started talking about music, in particular about the concert that the great violinist "Wilhelmj" had given a couple of days before, which we analyzed at length.[24] Wilhelmj had brought along his regular accompanist Rudolf Niemann (father of the famous composer), whose beautiful *legato* Mikuli, although usually reticent in his praise, commended highly: "Pan Bōg jemu dał" ("Our Lord has bestowed it upon him").[25] I can remember even today that during this concert Niemann played Liszt's "Tarantella" from *Venezia e Napoli* as his solo piece with grace and elegance, but without any southern verve or turbulence. His performance, but even more his technique, reminded me, to a certain extent, of Mikuli, who, by paying tribute to Niemann, was by extension praising himself.

* * *

The following week brought a singular surprise. The lesson was over, we were alone, when suddenly Mikuli asked: "Can I count on you for something?"

I said with emphasis: "You can be sure of it!"

"Listen then: next Saturday I have to perform a difficult piece on the harmonium in the great room of the city hall. Take a look at the following part! A moron must have arranged, or better yet, *de*-ranged it. I'm supposed to play with both hands in the treble and then suddenly jump into the bass with the B-flat triad. It's really easy to miss it, and I dread the tongue-wagging of Marek, Ruckgaber, and others like them if I do. What I want to ask of you is the following: Will you turn the pages for me? Fortunately the triad is placed so that it comes at the top of a new page. You'll stand up, turn the page with your right hand, and play the chord with your left. The main thing is: you must play the chord cleanly and not tell anyone about it."

I promised both, and kept my word. Today, after sixty-seven years, I am surely allowed to reveal this small, innocent trick cleverly devised by my old teacher.

* * *

Mickiewicz, great Polish poet, your fame will never fade![26] In Lemberg preparations were under way for a Mickiewicz festival, of which the centerpiece and highlight was to be a concert in which only Polish composers and virtuoso performers would take part. Naturally Mikuli's name was featured prominently on all the posters and programs. But there was another, more humble, name gracing the advertisements. I will never forget the sudden, heart-stopping feeling of responsibility that overcame me when I saw the name Maurycy Rosenthal on all the street corners!

Mikuli was a conservative piano diplomat and foreswore all public solo performances. He had therefore chosen to play at the festival Chopin's relatively unknown Rondo in C for two pianos [op. 73], and chosen me as his piano partner, thereby subscribing to the time-honored chamber music formula for such concerts. With what furious seriousness was the study of this piece carried out! Even though we played the Rondo perfectly after only two lessons, Mikuli insisted on repeating it during each of the following lessons, each time inviting new friends in to listen in order, he said, "to get me used to performing in public." He extended his diligence far beyond playing the [second] piano, giving instructions to the tailor to fashion for me a suit of the best Peruvienna material and sending me to the most famous dance instructor in Lemberg, Monsieur Kawecki, so that he might teach me a perfect, elegant bow to perform on the evening of the concert. This was more difficult for me to learn than Chopin's Rondo, and I was practicing taking a bow in the green room right up until my entrance onto the stage. When Mikuli came in to escort me, he called out incredulously: "What are you doing, dancing!?" I told him about my difficulties making a courtly bow, and by way of response had to console myself with his remark: "Let dear God perform his will," and after a short pause the *addendum*: "After all, you are here as a piano player, not as a dancer."

* * *

The Chopin "Pas de deux" was performed gracefully. Mikuli and I were invited into the governor's box where we were met with many questions. My illustrious teacher answered these thoughtfully, which only added fuel to the fire. Even though the governor's approval and applause were important to me, it meant even more to me to receive Mikuli's praise. After all, he was for me the last representative of a mighty piano era.

* * *

During this time my admiration for Carl Maria von Weber evolved into a glowing reverence. How I was able, with my small hands, to play the first movement of the Sonata in A-flat is to me, even today, a mystery. Much easier was the Sonata in C, but only its first movement inspired in me a Dionysian trance. In those days Beethoven, Schubert, and Weber were the gods of music for me. Of Chopin, I knew, apart from the Rondo in C, only his *Variations brillantes* op. 12 [based on "Je vends des scapulaires" from the opera *Ludovic* by Hérold and Halévy] and the posthumously published Polonaise in d. Seldom was serious music played in concerts.

This stagnation was violently disrupted by the appearance of the cellist David Popper and his wife, the pianist Sofia Menter Popper, who was at that time Liszt's most famous (female) pupil.[27] I talked my father into attending the concert [in Lemberg] with me, because I wanted to hear Menter play. I assumed David Popper to be a *qualité negligeable*. But I realized very quickly that Popper was by far the more talented of the two musicians. His elegance and ease, his wonderful tone, and, *last but not least*,[28] some of his own compositions, truly moved me. In later years, both in public and in private, I often saw him, spoke to him, listened to him, and played with him, and I make no secret of the fact that I consider him the greatest and most musical cellist of his time. His wife had extraordinary finger technique but a very small repertoire consisting mostly of Liszt's bravura compositions. In the Lemberg concert she ended with Liszt's "Tarantella" from [Auber's opera] *La Muette de Portici* (in England and America known as the "Masaniello" Tarantella). In St. Petersburg she ended with Liszt's *Don Juan* Fantasie, and in Vienna with a mix of two Hungarian rhapsodies, which were listed as "unpublished" in the program.[29] Beethoven had lived in vain for her; she did, however, play Schumann's *Carnaval* and *Symphonic Etudes* and had a particular liking for Chopin's Mazurka op. 33 [no. 2] in D, during which she always prolonged the initial notes, which threw her rhythm off by an entire octave [*sic;* beat?]. ~~An offensiveness of unrivaled proportions!~~[30]

Some weeks later the pianist Josef Wieniawski, brother of the great violinist Henryk Wieniawski, played a concert in the Polish theater.[31] He was shortly followed by the brilliant, in many ways peerless, pianist Rafael Joseffy.[32]

Joseffy's first concert was a sensation. During the fourth of Mendelssohn's seventeen *Variations sérieuses,* Marek jumped up from his seat and shouted so loudly that the entire hall must have heard him: "He plays even better than Anton Rubinstein!"[33] Mikuli, too, was full of appreciation for his twenty-two-year-old colleague. "With what precision, with what refinement he plays everything. Too bad that he plays all the passage work half-staccato, in so-called *jeu perlé,* and neglects the precious *legato.*[34] He learned that from his first teacher, Carl Tausig,[35] who was an infallible virtuoso but was frequently guilty of neglecting the *cantilena* and the art of *legato.*"[36]

In the meantime Joseffy returned to the stage and played a few short pieces by J. S. Bach with diaphanous clarity, a Chopin mazurka, and the Waltz in c-sharp with considerable piquancy and elegance, then moved on to the well-known Schubert-Liszt *Soirées de Vienne,* during which he displayed an unprecedented *pianissimo,*[37] and concluded with the then still relatively unknown Second Hungarian Rhapsody, with which he set the hall, from floorboards to rafters, so to speak, on fire.

* * *

Because we knew it might mean facing the wrath of my present teacher, Mikuli, my father and I thought it would be a very daring move for me to get to know Joseffy, to play for him, to ask him for lessons, or even just for some tips on fingering. Fortunately we were friends with a rich violin dilettante named Diamant. He knew what to do, and invited us, along with Joseffy, to a fancy lunch. Diamant let me drink a glass of champagne then asked me jokingly if I still had the nerve to play the first fugue (C) of the *Well-Tempered Clavier* by heart. I offered to try at once. Joseffy listened attentively, seemed surprised, and then asked for the C [*sic; c?*] from the first book, which I also played very well. He tested my ear, had me sight read, and at length said to my father: "Send this boy to me in Vienna for six months, and the Viennese will fall over backwards in awe." The thought of Mikuli, however, as well as the painful prospect of leaving my parents' house, stopped us from going through with this momentous step for the time being.

* * *

That summer, when Mikuli went to the country to escape the heat of Lemberg, my dear father decided to take me to Vienna for two months to entrust me to Joseffy. We notified him eight days in advance of our arrival, and reached the Nordbahnhof in Vienna on a very hot morning. We drove to the Hotel Metropole, where in exchange for a large amount of money we were given a small room with two beds that overlooked a small arm of the Danube, the so-called Danube Canal.

After hastily breakfasting and making ourselves more presentable, we hurried over to Joseffy, who lived in a two-room flat at Wipplingerstrasse 45 (which is where the main telegraph station is today).[38] Although he seemed happy to see us, he immediately gave us the bad news that in just two days he would be leaving for the rest of the summer to play concerts in fashionable spas and also to take a much needed holiday. "So what are we going to do now?" he asked rather insouciantly. "All three teachers of the basic piano class at the conservatory, Dachs, Door, and Epstein, are still here, and are likely to remain in Vienna for the summer.[39] But wait! Epstein left yesterday, Door isn't a good teacher, but I would recommend Professor Dachs to you as an excellent pedagogue. I'll tell you what: I'll drive with you to the conservatory right now, or, even better, we'll go right over to his apartment and I'll introduce you personally, I think he lives at Maximilianstrasse 6, just by the conservatory. We'll find the man, not to worry!"

When Joseffy went into the adjoining room to change his casual morning suit for an elegant salon jacket, my father whispered to me: "One can be a genius in art, but at twenty-two, one might still not be dependable. He could have answered our letter and told us that he was about to go out of town. Well, let's hope Professor Dachs is a good teacher!" Joseffy entered the room again, calling: "Quickly, quickly!" and we followed him swiftly down the hundred or so steps that led to his apartment. Once outside, we hailed a "Comfortabel," or "Einspänner," which is what a buggy pulled by only one horse is called in Vienna. (A buggy pulled by two horses is called a "Fiaker," highlighting Viennese elegance, and the passenger in a Fiaker is known as a "Gawaleer" or Kavalier.)

In a jaunty "Allegretto," we proceeded to Maximilianstrasse 6, via the palace-lined Ringstrasse (possibly the most beautiful street in Europe). Even from the stairs outside the apartment, we could hear furious scale-playing. This ceased as soon as Joseffy's visiting card was delivered. Dachs burst in and turned to Joseffy. "So, our prediction has been fulfilled, you have become a fine fellow!" Joseffy humbly tried to avert this compliment, but Dachs went on: "Yes, he plays more evenly and more impeccably than Anton Rubinstein."

Joseffy shook his panegyrist's hand heartily and hurried away from him with the words: "I recommend this young man to you, a colossal talent, most excellent!"

After this sweeping recommendation, Dachs laid down his arms. He agreed with Joseffy regarding my talent, but found that my scales were not up to par. The unavoidable prescription he wrote for me was four hours per day of scales, and afterwards, as "a distraction," one hour of Louis Plaidy's finger exercises.[40] Speaking of his own self-composed finger exercises, Brahms once said to me, somewhat ironically: "I swim in melodies." Certainly they were, compared to my Plaidy, the moving forces of a new theory of melody.

I must also mention here a peculiar twist of destiny: Sixty years after my apprenticeship with Dachs, a young lady visited me, accompanied by her son, introduced herself as the daughter of the late Professor Dachs, and made the urgent request of me to pilot her son faithfully through the labyrinth of advanced piano playing. I accepted her request and was happy to rediscover him a few years ago, a most highly esteemed pianist and first-rate teacher in Los Angeles.

* * *

Warning against excessive scale playing!

Memories of the scale Inferno I had to tread through with Dachs (a promenade from which I much profited, however) obliges me to comment on the "usefulness" of a lifetime study of scales. Undoubtedly one must *practice* them, since one must be able to *do* them. It is a fair question to ask, however, whether—beyond their value as an end in themselves—they lead to technical perfection. And here I say: "No!" I'll go even further and declare: The continual practice of scales, once one has learned to play them at a fast tempo, is positively *injurious*.

As we all know, the hand has three strong fingers: the all-important thumb, then the second finger and third finger. The fifth is much weaker, and the fourth is almost physiologically handicapped. Naturally the two weak fingers, four and five, must be exercised *more* than the strong fingers in order to facilitate evenness in passage work, which, of course, also depends on many other factors, such as a good ear. We also know that the first, second, and third fingers are each used twice in every octave, while the fourth is used only once per octave, and the fifth, in a number of scales, is used only for the highest note; in still others it is never brought into play at all. For example, one can practice the G-flat, D-flat, A-flat, E-flat, and B-flat scales for hours without bringing the fifth finger into action even once. I tend to recommend to my talented students scales in thirds and sixths (with both hands) and point out, with a wrathful smile, that many "famous piano virtuosi" don't even know the finger positions for thirds and sixths.

[Rosenthal elaborates on these matters in "The 'Grand Manner' in Piano Playing" (*Etude,* May 1937):

"I find it best to begin the day's work with something that engages the brain and the spirit rather than merely the fingers. Work at interpretations while your mind is at its freshest, and make yourself think. When those first, most zealous thought processes have begun to cool down a bit, there is time enough left to work at purely technical studies.

"Now what shall those purely technical studies be? There are those masters who advocate scales, scales, and nothing but scales. Saint-Saëns was one of them.[41] I do not hold to this view. Scales are highly important, and must be learned. Not only must they be played, but they must also be felt. They must come to lie naturally to the hand. Certain pieces, by Chopin and Liszt, require fleet, even, perfect scales as part of their performance; and the scales must be there. But they are not the best means of acquiring finger strength.

"This is why. Think of the regular fingering of the regular scale. The thumb, the second, and the middle fingers, which are naturally the strongest, are used twice; while the fourth and fifth fingers, which are the weakest, come into use only once. Indeed, the fifth finger is used only to end the scale; and in scales which begin with a black key it is not used at all. Such a system is hardly helpful in building up strength where it is most needed. Thus, while scales must be practiced, for their value as scales, they should not be regarded as the highest holy ritual of finger development.

"It is a better plan to practice the scales in thirds and in sixths. Thus, the fourth and fifth fingers come into use as much as the naturally stronger ones. It is, of course, much more difficult to play these thirds and sixths; but for practice purposes, they can be begun very slowly. Then even a less well developed hand can undertake them; and it will derive actual benefit while doing so."]

Let's return, in a televisionary manner, to those days far in the past. As I already mentioned, I studied with Professor Dachs and, at his behest, concentrated on scales and Plaidy, which were dreadfully boring for me, but which I practiced conscientiously for five hours a day. Two to three hours a day I spent walking along the magnificent Ringstrasse or in the Prater. I lived with a Dr. Stern, with whom I played chess often and for long periods of time. He also had a small library from which I borrowed a few volumes in order to find some mental distraction from the spirit-killing piano exercises. I reread with delight the "novelistic fragments" of Heinrich Heine,[42] and the fantastic manner in which he sang of Paganini's playing and Mademoiselle Laurence's dancing [*Florentine Nights,* 1837] seemed to me high points of German literature. Included in the same volume was *From the Memoirs of Herr von Schnabelewopski,* which I privately renamed "Symphony of High Spirits."[43] To this very day I find the "Heine" of the newest and last poems, the ones in the *Romanzero,* the most interesting German poet—eagle and nightingale at once—and Nietzsche speaks my innermost conviction when he proclaims dithyrambically: "I seek in vain in all the realms of history for an equally sweet and passionate music."[44] Or when he asserts: "Heine is not a German phenomenon, he is a European one."

Heine and Byron were the spiritual nourishment I drew from the book collection of my landlord.[45] Much less substantial was the bodily nourishment, however splendid my rent was for that time (thirty-five Gulden a month!).

A big role in the menu was played by: potatoes and rice, alternating with rice and potatoes. Meat was served only on important holidays. The doctor's every action, his wife's every action, bore the seal of their stinginess. When, at the end of hot summer days, the shadows of evening fell, the suffering creatures that were the Viennese headed for the cool of the Prater; we hastened from the Glockengasse through dusty streets toward the park, stopping at a small, cheap tavern just outside the Prater which had tried by means of a few flowerpots to raise itself to the rank of a restaurant *in* the Prater. There we sat in the dusty, hot air, ate some of the sausage that we had brought with us, drank beer, and looked longingly at the heavily scented Prater, just as once Moses had looked at Canaan and not been able to enter it.

In the midst of these oppressive days of August, I received a wonderful piece of news: The parliament of Galicia had awarded me a three-year stipend of three hundred Gulden per year for the furtherance of my artistic development. My head was spinning! Just imagine: The highest legislative assembly in my native land, the Galician parliament, had officially declared its powerful interest in my artistic talent and backed it up with a relatively large sum! For the first time since the Dachs era, my scales and exercises displayed a triumphant verve which, alas, gave way to mild depression when Dr. Stern entered the room and reminded me that it was already nine o'clock in the evening and that there was to be no more piano playing.

The dice of destiny seemed to be rolling in my favor in Lemberg; now, however, it was necessary to transplant our entire household, my dear mother and my four younger sisters, to Vienna.[46] (My eldest sister, Rosa, had in the meanwhile married a train station attendant.) At this precarious fork in the road of our destiny, my dear father seemed virtually to multiply himself. Upon mentioning my great honor, he succeeded in obtaining a one-year sabbatical from his teaching position at the high school in Lemberg. He found a capable director as his substitute at the private institute. He secured a good job at a big Viennese life insurance company and, *last but not least*,[47] acquired a concession to open a private teaching institute in Vienna.

We settled in the Schmöllerlgasse 8, in the Wieden [that is, fourth] district [of Vienna]. My father taught "German" and mathematics. In charge of teaching the natural sciences was Emil Ritter von Dunikowski, a favorite pupil of the geology professor Eduard Suess,[48] who later became a writer and journalist. He exercised a magical influence on us young boys. Under his tutelage we walked almost daily through the uninhabited areas of the Prater, until we reached the main stream of the Danube. There we assembled in a circle and listened, in complete amazement, to his disquisitions on Laplace's Theory,[49] on saliva analysis, on the theory of atoms and molecules—in short, sciences which were still in their infancy. But in spite of these powerful incitements, music and piano were on the surface of our consciousness and knocked ever more insistently on mind and heart.

* * *

One evening my dear father entered the room abruptly: "Joseffy is here!" And after a short pause: "You are to meet him Friday afternoon at four o'clock, whereupon you will play for him. He wishes to hear you play Hummel's Sonata in f-sharp!"[50] So this was the longed for prelude to Joseffy's lessons in advanced piano playing!

* * *

It was a glorious autumn day, the fourth of October in the year 1875, when I trekked from the Schmöllerlgasse to Wipplingerstrasse. Urgent office matters had kept my father from accompanying me and staying with me during my first lesson with Joseffy. After a half hour's march, I arrived at the stairs to Wipplingerstrasse 45 and soon thereafter was standing in front of Joseffy's apartment. I pulled the bell and waited with a pounding heart for the opening of the door. Nothing!—Long pause! I rang again and again, to no avail. I saw the Major Domus on a lower floor, the heavy of the building, to make a long story short: the concierge. I harpooned the governor of the house, held him fast by his livery, and asked him whether he knew where "der Herr Joseffy" was. Suddenly a silver piece materialized in my fingers, slid with a "glissando" into the administrator's paw. "Oh, that one's right close, he has his billiards match at the Café Carltheater. That's half an hour from here. Go over the Emperor Franz Josef Quay up to the Aspern bridge, and then it's on the left side of the Praterstrasse." I followed the worthy man's directions, and twenty minutes later I stepped into the Café Carltheater, my master's 'buen retiro.'

* * *

I arrived just at the right moment to see my future teacher execute an exquisitely skillful shot on the green baize. Joseffy looked proudly at the so-called *Kiebitzers* (as spectators are called in Vienna) and by chance noticed me, his forgotten pupil and "champion" of Hummel's Sonata in f-sharp. His first words were: "So, you're interested in billiards, you may watch! But do sit down."

It was a mystery to me how I was supposed to sit since all the chairs were taken by the fanatical *Kiebitzers*. But I was dumbfounded when Joseffy snarled at a young man: "Don't you know that this boy is my best pupil? Get up and give him your place, you jackass!"

Curiously, the young man failed to react either to the demand to get up or to his characterization as a "jackass." Joseffy won his match, was almost carried off by the *Kiebitzers* in triumph, but took refuge with me in an adjacent room, where he immediately became very earnest and explained his absence. It was a match he could on no account afford to miss, he said, and it had been too late to let me know. "Incidentally, what are you doing this evening? I'll tell you what, we'll have a *Mélange* (Viennese expression for a coffee with cream), go over to my place, and you can play 'your' Hummel for me."

Everything went according to plan; Joseffy told me I should be proud that I was being allowed to play Hummel's Sonata in f-sharp. Tausig, whom Joseffy revered, and with whom he had studied for two years, had let him play this difficult piece only in his most advanced class. Liszt regarded the piece as a great compositional achievement. I listened passionately, as I too was enraptured by the Sonata, and everything that I had heard by and about Hummel only deepened my enthusiasm. I thought highly of him, that he, a pupil of the immortal Mozart, had kept away from any sort of slavish imitation, that he had increased immeasurably the possibilities of phrasing and technique on the piano, and attained a height of two-handed playing as perhaps no one since Clementi. His only pianistic rival was Moscheles, who, however, did not possess his enigmatic compositional command over melody. Not until the 1830s, with the advent of Chopin, Liszt, and Thalberg, were unbridgeable dams erected against Hummel's popularity. When Hummel played a concert in Vienna in 1835, some rows were completely empty, which prompted the master to respond with the words: "If this is not a disgrace for the Viennese, for *me* it certainly isn't."

Of etudes, Joseffy had me study from Tausig's edition (with its difficult fingerings) of Clementi's *Gradus ad Parnassum,* which really catapulted my technique to new heights. Unfortunately he only let me work on these etudes for about three months, and so I stood only superficially prepared before the peaks of Chopin's twelve Etudes op. 10. After two more months came the six Paganini-Liszt Etudes, of which I made a cursory study, and presently the idea of a recital before a Viennese audience was raised.

The program that Joseffy chose for me was daring enough! The evening commenced with Chopin's Concerto in f (with Joseffy at the second piano). After that came Beethoven's Thirty-two Variations in c, whereupon, according to the tradition of the times, there was a recital of Lieder, in this case by Richard Schmidtler. At length I returned to the stage and played Mendelssohn's Prelude and Fugue in f, [Chopin's] Etude in G-flat op. 10 [no. 5] and Waltz in e, as well as Liszt's "Au bord d'une source" and "La Campanella." This last piece had entailed tragic consequences, for I'd tried to bridle it as a show horse almost daily. But this time it did what it was supposed to do.

Afterwards, the green room was humming chaotically, as if it were a beehive. Joseffy entered, saw me sitting on the sofa in a very comfortable position, and exclaimed at once: "So, now you're going to take a few years off from giving concerts?" A Frankfurt banker named Hanau, evidently wanting to make amends for a slight against the great artist, held out a package to him and said: "Herr Joseffy, when you were so gracious as to play for us last time, you forgot to take this silver notebook and golden pencil from us. Would you accept it now?" (Apparently it was meant to be a belated honorarium and an attempt at reconciliation.) Joseffy, however, replied dryly, but not without friendliness: "You must be in error, Herr Hanau! I forgot to take a *golden* notebook and a *diamanté* pencil from you."

Another gentleman approached the artist: "Today is the twenty-eighth of April. Where is the Russian-Turkish war? You said that if war had not erupted by the twenty-eighth of April, you would lose the bet and pay me three thousand dollars. Give me a thousand dollars now, and we'll talk about the rest later!"

Joseffy twirled his coiffed mustache and said phlegmatically: "I can give you one dollar straightaway! . . . " The mocked one took off with an air of vengefulness!

In the meantime, the clock had struck eleven. At my request, we strolled on foot into the lilac-scented spring night toward Schmöllerlgasse 8.

* * *

Finally, the day came, or more precisely, the evening, when I first saw him, the great, the glorious, the invincible Franz Liszt! One of his pupils, Frau Toni Raab from Graz,[51] was celebrating her debut in the Bösendorfersaal.[52] Shortly before the official beginning of the concert, which was scheduled for seven-thirty, a murmuring, rustling, and susurration arose. Ludwig Bösendorfer,[53] piano maker, as he likes to be called, appeared at the entrance to the hall, parts the waves of inquisitive audience members, and leads a tall, slender, white-haired man with eagle profile and Jupiter gaze to his decorated seat of honor. A storm of applause rises; Liszt fends it off in a friendly manner and points at his pupil, whose debut he, by his mere presence, has transformed into an occasion of magical glamour. But the jubilance of the audience subsides only after the master has gone up onto the stage four times, each time taking a thankful bow. Now Frau Toni Raab appears, at first discomposed, but soon fully in command of her very respectable means.

What really surprises me about her playing is her round, soft *legatissimo;* she plays as if under the spell of the "Chopin-Kalkbrenner-Mikuli-School." She plays, among other works, Liszt's "Tarantella" from *Venezia e Napoli,* a piece which possesses more musical subtleties than strict classical musicians suspect, and ends her program with Tausig's seldom performed "[Ungarische] Zigeunerweisen." Joseffy applauds demonstratively, and his friend, Dr. Eduard Schiff, whispers to me: "That piece is by his teacher. That's why he's applauding so much. If she repeats the 'Zigeunerweisen,' I'll die!" I laughed at this unbridled hyperbole, but had to agree with him in principle, and was glad when Toni gave a short *bluette* as her encore instead.[54]

I heard [them] tell again, with fabulous ardor, of Tausig's tireless work at the piano. That he practiced ten hours a day, until his fingertips became numb, and that the piano manufacturer Bechstein built a new keyboard for him with *rough* ivory and ebony keys. All this was confirmed for me two years later in Warsaw by the pianist Paul von Schloezer, composer of two excellent and very well-known etudes.[55]

* * *

Even Richard Wagner could not stop Tausig's piano fanaticism, as the autobiography of the great music dramatist reveals. Liszt sent off Tausig, then his sixteen-year-old pupil, to Wagner [in Zurich, in May 1858] as one gives a dear friend a costly present. Carl was supposed to perform all time-consuming tasks for him—commissions, the copying of notes—but also to accompany him on walks, dine with him, etc. Presumably the youth could not tolerate Wagner's white-hot company, felt trapped by the sovereign nonchalance with which Wagner laid claim to his time. He felt seriously impeded in his studies, and resolves to defend his piano playing. He invents a Polish countess with whom he has begun having an affair and who hinders him in seeing Wagner as often as Tausig, from the bottom of his heart, wishes and longs to do.

In Wagner's autobiography, it says that the Master never had the slightest doubt as to the authenticity of the Polish aristocrat. But I ask: "How is it possible that a woman who moved in intellectual circles would not have demanded that Tausig should introduce her to his phenomenally interesting master?" No! Tausig courted no countess, he courted the much more difficult passions which the piano held for him. And what a terrific *argumentum ad hominem* the sixteen-year-old chose! Had he hidden behind his studies, he would have reaped much derision from his great friend! But where Brangäne mixes her potions was for Wagner holy ground.[56]

* * *

You will forgive me if I linger a while longer on the glowing image of Tausig. I spoke about him much with his almost fanatical appreciator [*Schätzer*], even overappreciator [*Überschätzer*], Rafael Joseffy, then with W. Lenz, the famous Beethoven worshipper, and with Vladimir von Pachmann, the important "pianissimist," as Liszt characterized him with epigrammatistical marksmanship; but I learned most about him from his Etude in F-sharp and his five Strauss paraphrases: "Nachtfalter," "Man lebt nur einmal," "Wahlstimmen," and two untitled ones, the refinement of which one can elude only with difficulty.[57] The titles are coming to me now: "Pessimistische Walzer" and "Strauss und Schopenhauer." What refinement in the chiseling of the passage work, what elegance in the harmony! Here the earthly bonds fall away, and the aristocracy of artistic mastery triumphs. Never has anyone made such a reverential bow to Strauss as was done in these transcriptions. I once asked this great giver of joy what kind of an artistic and personal impression Tausig had made on him. He answered without delay: "The most astonishing thing about him was his great humility." I took the liberty to remark: "Before you, dear master, anyone would show his humility," which Strauss dismissed with a laugh.

Tausig died in July of 1871 of typhoid. His female friends sat by his deathbed in Leipzig. Liszt or Wagner might have transfigured his earthly farewell, but neither of the great masters appeared.

Tausig's death shattered a pillar of the pianistic world at that time. The greatest technician of his age departed, but not without inspiring Brahms in his Paganini Variations. These remained: Liszt, the most universal, spiritual, and still the innovative piano poet; Rubinstein, the most temperamentally glowing, melodically richest, the piano hero mightiest with tone; finally Bülow, the quick-witted, but often technically deficient, and more amusing than spiritual piano analyst; and, from a younger generation, Rafael Joseffy, of fairy-like elegance, and Alfred Grünfeld, who set himself apart as a virtuoso through his rhythm and his magnificent right-hand octaves.[58]

The pedagogical element was represented predominantly by the Vienna Conservatorium. The most advanced, so-called training classes were taught by the aforementioned professors: Anton Door, Josef Dachs, and Julius Epstein. Yet there was a whole host of composers who, regardless of their lesser or greater fame, instructed trusting youths in the piano without giving concerts themselves. Here I should mention Johannes Brahms and Karl Goldmark.[59] The value of their instruction for the pupil may have been immeasurable; its price was five guilders per lesson. Even if Brahms was not a pianist in the elevated sense of the word, many of his compositions do display complete familiarity with the most difficult problems of piano technique. It was different with Goldmark, whose usual instrument was the violin. When I came to Vienna in 1875, both masters were only moderately recognized. In a small music society, where the music publisher and composer I. P. Gotthard had the leading voice, he hazarded the following conclusion: "It appears that nothing will become of Brahms! The eight *Klavierstücke* op. 76, are Mendelssohnized, Schubertized, Chopinized in an unprecedented fashion." The others formed a chorus of agreement.

At this time Joachim Raff still had a phalanx of supporters.[60] Anton Rubinstein splashed and bathed in hot melodies, but often strode through glowing desert sand. Saint-Saëns gained the liveliest successes through his chamber music and witty Death Dance [*Danse macabre*], and Norway sent us warm light from the cold north [in the music of Edvard Grieg]. But everything paled before the enormous sensation caused by Wagner's *Ring of the Nibelungen.* The Festspiele were held in Bayreuth, and one listened, partly with delight and partly with revulsion, to the miracles of tone from the magician of sound. Only a few noticed the weak points in what Wagner referred to as the "eternal work," like the eternal repetition of the same harmonic and melodic expressions. The diminished seventh chord, hunted to death by the classics, took a backseat to the augmented triad, which took up a kind of autocratic rule. I shall give one of many examples: when Siegfried is about to forge the Notung anew, Wagner has the augmented triad sparkle in the orchestra about 120 times consecutively.

Oddly, the numerous assembled musicians and critics did not notice how Wagner had left himself spectacularly open to attack. They did not realize that Chopin had first used the "augmented" in the Sonata op. 35 and in the Nouvelle Etude in A-flat and that Wagner used it in the piece fully but excessively about 10 years later. Some opponents indulged in shallow scolding, for example, Ludwig Speidel, critic of the *Wiener Fremdenblatt,* who called the *Ring of the Nibelungen* "a musical monstrosity." Eduard Hanslick, in his post at the *Neue Freie Presse* in Vienna, was not much more cultivated, although his judgment was of a higher level.[61] Slowly the critical atmosphere was evolving for an antithetical high priest to Wagner—for Johannes Brahms.

In October 1876 two extraordinary violin virtuosi appeared before the Viennese public. Pablo de Sarasate, who seemed to have been blessed by nature with everything but a deep musical sensibility, and Henryk Wieniawski, a surprisingly big-toned violinist and composer.[62] Sarasate concluded his concert, amid tumultuous applause, with a suite by Raff; Wieniawski, with his own somewhat long, but very effective *Faust* Fantasia.

2   Review of a Concert by M. R. in Vienna

1884

Eduard Hanslick

In his weak, unprepossessing outward appearance Moriz Rosenthal recalls Tausig. Nor is that the end of the similarity. He also resembles Tausig in the extraordinary brilliance of his playing. Through many years of acquaintance with modern piano virtuosity I have almost forgotten what it is to be astonished, but I found young Rosenthal's achievements indeed astonishing. His technique scorns the most incredible difficulties, his strength and endurance the most inordinate demands. I need recall only two offerings which, in respect to technical difficulties, represent the ultimate in the piano literature: Liszt's *Don Juan* Fantasie (which he played for the first time with the uncut ending) and Brahms's Variations on a Theme of Paganini, op. 35.[1] In this last piece Brahms, not content with the obvious tests of dextral strength and velocity, has added latent (particularly rhythmic) difficulties hardly perceptible to the listener but enough to drive the player to despair. Although not comparable to the wonderful Handel Variations as a composition, the Paganini Variations comprise a noteworthy contribution to the piano literature and reveal an interesting and little-known aspect of Brahms's creative talent. The piano virtuoso can as little afford to overlook them as the various Brahms studies (without opus number), his arrangements of Chopin's Etude in F Minor in thirds and sixths, Weber's Rondo in C Major (with the sixteenth-note figure transferred to the left hand), and Bach's Chaconne (for the left hand alone).

The Paganini Variations (on the last of the twenty-four Capriccios) suggest a bold campaign of discovery and conquest in the field of piano virtuosity, an experiment in the capacities and possibilities of the instrument. To report that Rosenthal mastered them faultlessly, and with utter security and freedom, is to rank him automatically among the first pianists of the time. Less satisfactory was his performance of Schumann's Novelette [op. 21] no. 2. The element of virtuosity was intrusive, not only by way of fast tempi, but also by way of certain liberties (slighting of certain notes, separation of melodically related notes and

From *Hanslick's Music Criticisms,* translated and edited by Henry Pleasants (New York: Dover, 1988), pp. 236–237.

phrases, etc.) which here and there gave a stilted effect to the melodious middle section. I was unfavorably impressed, also, by too frequent recourse to the pedals and by the unlovely violence with which the keys were pounded in fortissimo passages. And yet, these are details characteristic of all the youngsters of the Liszt-Tausig school. Such impetuosity may well subside with the years, as it did with Liszt and Tausig, and make way for more tenderness and warmth. Rosenthal's modest bearing and his quiet and unaffected manner at the piano merit special praise.

3   Letter to Lilli Lehmann

circa 1899

M. R.

Rosenthal's letter is explained by the fact that Lehmann had agreed to step in for an indisposed singer in Das Rheingold, *an opera she had not previously sung. Lehmann prefaces the letter thus:*

"I resolved to look at the *rôle,* and to learn it if it were possible. A piano score was not at hand, and had first to be borrowed from van Dyck, who lived nearby, a conductor had to be fetched, and then the work began. I knew much of the text, of course, and I had the music by ear, but as soon as I had to sing it accurately and from memory, all that I knew was wrong, and the right seemed unfamiliar. My hair rose on my head! The performance was to begin at eight o'clock, I had begun at half after four, and the time ran away as though it were paid for it. Reizl was again my blessing, as she sang everything to me when I rested a moment. I worked out also the acting of the part at the same time, and, about six o'clock, I knew it up to the finale, which I could commit to memory at the opera-house during the changes of scene. Now it was necessary for me to rest a little before I went to battle, but I had hardly lain down before our neighbor, evidently an artist, began to play exercises, cadenzas, and single measures a hundred times over and over. I was desperate. We sent hurriedly below to enquire who was the virtuoso. Moriz Rosenthal! Now wait, I thought, you will stop at once, and I wrote him a nice little note, begging him to have regard for my nerves of hearing as I had to sing an important rôle, and I promised to leave the field to him at about a quarter to seven. The playing stopped. When I returned late from the opera, I found the following *billet-doux* pushed under my door:

HIGHLY ESTEEMED PATRONESS:

I am venturing to approach you with a request. You yourself have to-day set forth the high consideration due to and the importance of undisturbed sleep, and I have reduced my annoying activity to a minimum. To-morrow I have a

---

Lilli Lehmann (1848–1929), German soprano. Rosenthal's letter is quoted in her autobiography, *My Path through Life,* translated by Alice Benedict Seligman (New York: Arno Press, 1977), p. 444.

very complicated recital, and my sleeping-room is distinguished by being directly next to yours. You will return home late to-night. It is unnecessary for me to quote the words from *Macbeth*—"Do not murder holy sleep!" As supreme mistress of nuances, will you execute the modulation from Orpheus to Morpheus *pianissimo* and *con dolcezza* (still to-day, after many years, every tone of the Chopin *Mazurka* that you sang once in the great hall of the Musikverein at Vienna is sounding in my ear and heart), and to-morrow, after so many nights of travel, I shall be able to express my thanks to you with feeling, and above all, following upon a good sleep.

With sincere esteem for you and your sister,

Your most devoted, [etc.]

Rosenthal was famous for needing sleep, and sometimes left hotels in the middle of the night when his sleep was interrupted; on occasion he would even cancel the next day's concert in consequence. In order to give himself the best chance of getting a good night's rest, he was known to rent the rooms on either side of his own as well as the ones above and below it.

4 Review of a Concert by M. R. in Manchester

November 23, 1900

Arthur Johnstone

An exceedingly remarkable performance of Schumann's Pianoforte Concerto was given by Mr. Rosenthal and the orchestra. In no other performance that we remember was the balance between orchestra and solo part so well preserved. Mr. Rosenthal played with his usual perfection of technical mastery; his phrasing was beautifully intelligent, and the distinction of his style was to be noted no less in the homely sweetness and graceful fancy of the Intermezzo than in the rich and complex Allegro. Again, in the finale, his marvelous accuracy and fine phrasing enabled the hearers to enjoy every *nuance* of the composition, notwithstanding a tendency to hurry that was perceptible at certain points. The tremendous *Don Juan* Fantasie, for pianoforte alone, gave Mr. Rosenthal an opportunity of exhibiting his technical powers in one of the most audacious *bravura* compositions that exist. In many persons the fine frenzy that rages through the middle and latter parts of this piece awakens no sympathy. It has, nevertheless, a legitimate place in the Palace of Art, being nothing more than the logical development to the highest possible point of the *bravura* style that originated with Liszt. The latter of the two variations on "Là ci darem"—that section which precedes the entry of the champagne song—is the most bewildering and repugnant part of the piece to the general public. For that reason, and also on account of its heartbreaking difficulties, the variation in question is often omitted. But Mr. Rosenthal omitted nothing yesterday. He hurled forth the Dionysian declaration of war against all the chilly conventions and proprieties, the priggeries and pruderies of Mrs. Grundy, that forms the real content of the piece, with that technical power in which he is surpassed by no living performer. After many recalls he was constrained to play once more; and, by way of the sharpest possible contrast, he gave Chopin's Berceuse, bringing out all the delicate moonshine filigree of the right-hand part with infinite subtlety.

Collected in *Musical Criticisms of Arthur Johnstone* (Manchester: At the University Press, 1905), pp. 165–166.

5 Rosenthaliana

The Musical Courier, November 6, 1901

Leonard Liebling

Probably nowhere is the deadening inactivity of the dog days felt more keenly than in the offices of a large daily newspaper. At least, so young Barthmann had just said, sitting at his desk in the reporters' room of the Berlin *Mittagblatt* and tapping his nose rhythmically with a loose wrist and a long lead pencil.

"A nice profession for a man of ambition, I must say," he continued to complain; "nothing but dog bites, sunstrokes, and accidental drownings to write about."

"What did you expect to do when you came here?" queried grizzled old Boetticher, laying down his pen and looking quizzically at his younger colleague.

"Interviewing," replied Barthmann, enthusiastically; "the interviewing of great personages. That's where I could show my real powers. Studying a man's face and character, divining the hidden meanings in his answers; matching my wits against his; questioning, probing, counter-questioning, dodging, fencing, sparring, and wading forth from the encounter with the truth triumphant, the armor of reserve, the bulwark of deceit, the breastwork of prevarication shattered and banged to bits, the naked facts standing forth—"

"Clothe those facts at once and come in here, Barthmann," suddenly spoke the managing editor, appearing in the doorway of his private room. Sheepishly Barthmann followed him.

"I happened to hear something of what you said," began the managing editor. "Those are admirable sentiments for a young newspaper man. You should succeed with such principles. You complained of a lack of opportunity. I shall give you a chance. You've done some good musical articles for us. Moriz Rosenthal, the pianist, is in town; at the Reichshof Hotel. Do you think you could get an interesting review for us; draw out some new facts?"

"I'll try, sir."

"Find out what he thinks of his colleagues. Get his opinions on modern men and things in music. He is keen and caustic and spares no one. Lead him on to the bitterest outbreaks against everybody and everything. That will make some spicy reading in the *Mittagblatt.*"

"Yes, sir," said Barthmann, and left the room. Like a true reporter, he went to work at his assignment the moment he received it. Already he was preparing in his mind some of the shrewd questions that would force important musical truths from the caustic Rosenthal.

"It's awfully easy," reflected Barthmann as he neared the Hotel Reichshof; "like all great artists, Rosenthal will be only too glad to talk. In my hands he'll be like wax. I'll mold him as I please."

"Herr Rosenthal is dining on the terrace," announced the stately portier. Barthmann sent a card advertising himself as the *Mittagblatt*'s representative.

Some moments later our young journalist, with his most engaging smile, faced his unsuspecting victim, who, seated before an elegantly appointed table, seemed absorbed in the X sharps and Y flats stirred up by the strenuous performance of Vörös Miska and his celebrated band.

"An interview for the readers of the *Mittagblatt*?" asked Rosenthal, good naturedly. "Take dinner with me. Waiter, another cover. Double the order I gave you. And get that dinner here with the speed of a hunted tortoise. If you do, I'll include you in my evening prayer—or give you a tip, whichever you prefer. Now I'm at your service, Herr Barthmann."

"Um-ah, oh, yes," hastened the young man, asking his last question first. "Do you think a true artist should be bound by tradition? Should he not have an opinion of his own?"

"Some have several, suitable to various climes and times," answered Rosenthal.

"Should one practice scales?"

"One should not practice scales—one should play them perfectly."

"Whom do you consider a great modern composer?"

"Strauss."

"Johann or Richard Strauss?"

"Why be particular about such a trifling detail as a Christian name? Let us hold to the main questions."

"What do you think of 'Till Eulenspiegel'?"

"A most valuable book for young and old. A pure source of innocent delight, of healthful merriment."

"Well, then, what do you think of the *Fledermaus*? (*The Bat*.)"

"A very unpleasant animal, commonly supposed to have predilections for one's hair."

"Should pianists compose?"

"A thousand times one resolves never to write down a musical idea, then one happens to hear a pretty melody somewhere, and instantly one composes it."

"What do you think of some of our younger artists—Hofmann, Kreisler, Hambourg, for instance?"[1]

"I consider Johannes Kreisler one of the happiest delineations of that wonderful author, E. T. A. Hoffmann.[2] Hamburg, too, I like; but my favorite harbor town is Genoa."

"Do you consider D'Albert a great composer?"[3]

"I know his opera, *The Departure* (*Abreise*). What varied thoughts are suggested by the very title! A cold, dreary day, for instance; lovers bidding each other farewell, perhaps forever; tears, kisses, vows, more tears—the mere idea is heartrending."

"Idea is heartrending," stenographed Barthmann. "But how would you classify Busoni?"[4]

"Busoni?" cried Rosenthal, enthusiastically. "How Italian sounds the very name. Truly, Italy is the real home of beauty. The Levantine Riviera, and the surroundings about Lago Maggiore are among the most enchanting spots on earth. And Lower Italy, Sicily, stately Vesuvius, with its crown of smoke, and at its feet three ghostly, buried cities. Pliny, the ancient and celebrated historian, wrote: 'For a while one could hear subterranean rolling almost as loud as thunder—'"

"I believe I read that in Bulwer's *Last Days of Pompeii*.[5] Pardon me, but I'd like your opinion on Godowsky's arrangements."

"I think he has made arrangements for a winter tour through Germany."

"I see; but how does De Pachmann's left hand impress you?"

"It is small, white, and well kept."

"Do you consider Franz Liszt the father of modern piano playing?"

"Certainly of some of its chief exponents, were I to believe all I hear from them."

"Whom do you regard as the greatest living composer?"

"Frédéric Chopin."

"And the greatest dead composer?"

"My friend, Max Breitenfeld, of Vienna.[6] He is one of the teachers at the Conservatorium there."

"What do you think of *The Musical Courier*?"

"He is certainly to be preferred to an unmusical one if he possesses the other necessary qualifications."

"What form of composition do you like best?"

"Square, thick print, flexible cover."

"Should a composer print his opus 1?"

"No; he should induce a well paying publisher to print it."

"Where is the most intelligent public to be found?"

"At my concerts."

During the last few questions and answers Barthmann's face had gradually assumed a vacant, then a pained expression. He drew forth his handkerchief and mopped it nervously across his forehead.

"Aren't you well?" inquired Rosenthal, regarding the young man anxiously; "you haven't touched your dinner."

"I—I'm quite well, thank you. I don't care for any dinner. I—I think I'll go."

"Are you sure there's nothing else you'd like to know?" urged Rosenthal, almost eagerly.

"N—No. Except that I intended to ask you for an autograph. I wanted to ask you to write only a line—something characteristic in one line."

"H'm! Let me see," mused the great pianist; "in one line. Suppose I write the repertory of some of my brother pianists?"

Rosenthal's leave taking of the young reporter was in truth fraternal. "Goodbye, my dear young man," he said; "whenever you'd like information about music, information unadorned, frank and free, without pitfalls or prevarications, always come to me. I shall be only too happy to do everything in my power for you and your esteemed paper."

Later the portier found Barthmann wandering up and down the corridor, murmuring: "De Pachmann reminds him of Italian scenery; Liszt has a small hand; Busoni has a thick, flexible cover; Chopin is alive—"

When the portier politely asked him where he was going, Barthmann rather rudely replied that he didn't know, and what's more, he didn't give a damn.

6 The Diémer Competition, Paris [1903]

Unpublished

M. R.

The international [triennial] competition for the prize of four thousand gold francs, endowed by Professor Louis Diémer of the Paris Conservatoire, had once again drawn the French capital into the spotlight of musical interest.[1] Above all, the names of the twelve judges appeared like a shooting rocket: there they all appeared in the judges' box of the Conservatoire, Massenet, Saint-Saëns, Paderewski, Fauré, Planté, De Greef, Paladilhe, Wormser, Pugno, Philipp, Chevillard, and little me.[2]

On the first day we all listened to Beethoven and Schumann ("Appassionata" Sonata and *Etudes symphoniques*), Chopin on the second (Fantasie op. 49 or Ballade in f, then mazurka), and either "La Campanella" by Paganini-Liszt or the "Etude en forme de Valse" by Saint-Saëns to finish.

The Spaniard Malats, the "star," and Diémer's crack student, Lazare Lévy, were the odds-on favorites.[3] As Diémer and I were exchanging greetings, he took the opportunity to put in a good word for Lévy by exclaiming: "Oh, this poor Lévy, he has such a terrible fear. He is quite sick with it!" I was more than a little shocked by this shameless propaganda, but determined to allow nothing to influence me in my judgment.

I sat next to Paderewski, and we got on to the topic of famous concertists, and I jokingly offered him a simple means by which to measure the greatness of a success by asking a simple question of his colleagues. One should not ask how he had performed, but rather what public appreciation and the local critics are like. The level of success could be measured from the answer, just as from a thermometer. At this moment we heard a melodious, powerful baritone, that of Pugno, who called to De Greef: "You ask me, my dear fellow, what appreciation the Milanese have of music? Here is my answer: They are vulgar, ignorant, and incapable of grasping true greatness!" Paderewski and I broke out into hearty laughter, whilst Pugno and De Greef looked on in astonishment.

Now Malats began the "Appassionata" and led it to its conclusion with a serene disposition. It was a polite, peaceful, domesticated "Appassionata," an "Appassionata" of the restrained zone, with a little stab at the Faubourg St. Germain.

He was also successful with the *Etudes symphoniques*, although it cannot be denied that the main emphasis lay on the etudes and not on the symphonic. Lazare Lévy had specialized a little too much on the Etude by Saint-Saëns, but demonstrated quite brilliant pianism and much love for his instrument.

The vote resulted in a resounding victory for Malats.

Terrible excitement: what will Diémer say? In vain, I searched for Massenet among those present. Finally, I found him deep in thought on a square near the Conservatoire. Had the birdsong brought him a new, wonderful *cantilena?* Was he thinking of his friend Diémer, upon whom he had just inflicted a gaping wound? With the exception of Saint-Saëns's, all of the votes had been cast against Lévy, that is, against Diémer. [Massenet's] ancient Roman sense of justice aroused my enthusiasm. Nothing could shake him. I said to him: "You have often enchanted me, as a fifteen-year-old I was inspired by your *Hérodiade*,[4] but today you have climbed to your summit!"

"But why?" asked Massenet, astonished.

"Well, Diémer is an old, close friend of yours and was probably hoping for your vote, which, with a keen sense of justice, you gave to Malats."

—Pause: Then a true wail from Massenet's breast. (Oh, etc.)

The dinner began without the principal character, who was letting his indisputable success be acclaimed by his Spanish and Catalan journals. The twelve of us on the jury, however, were astonished by the delirious ovations in Barcelona, such as torch-lit processions, fireworks, public speeches, etc., until exact reports made clear to us that the correspondence and telegrams from Paris had contained one small error: We on the jury had served not as judges but as rivals. Saint-Saëns, Massenet, Paderewski, etc., had competed at the piano and had all —all—succumbed to Malats's genius.

None of us cleared up the truth of the matter, and thus Malats was able to bask in his glory undisturbed. To his credit, let it be said that he launched the twelve pieces of the *Ibéria* by our great friend Albéniz splendidly, in spite of all the revelry.[5] And when I came to Barcelona after about a year to give a series of concerts and picked up the main paper, *La Vanguardia*, I found a hymnically spirited article of three printed pages about me. The signature read: Joaquín Malats.

7 The Bane of Virtuosity (excerpt)

Harper's Weekly, December 1, 1906

Lawrence Gilman

The following excerpt from Gilman's article provides evidence of the right-wing strain in music criticism with which Rosenthal and other virtuosi had to contend. At the same time, Gilman shows himself to be rather myopic: Rosenthal's arrangement of Chopin's "Minute" Waltz was a calling card left (usually) at the end of his concert, and not its substance. In any case Rosenthal's arrangement did not stop other pianists from playing Chopin's original. This is a point detractors of works in the virtuoso tradition are reluctant to concede.

It has long been more than a suspicion with many of us that our voracious New York musical public, which can approach with enthusiasm a season offering several hundred concerts and almost as many performances of opera, cares relatively little what music is offered for its consideration, but a great deal for the manner in which it is offered. It is, one means, largely a worshipper of personalities—of the conductor, singer, and pianist of genius or marked peculiarity. Its concern with the mere composer, the mere musical producer whose function it is to furnish a convenient vehicle for the virtuoso, is almost, as it seems at times, wholly negligible. The opening weeks of the current season have furnished some striking instances. For example, there is Mr. Moriz Rosenthal, the pianist. Now it is a perfectly recognized fact that Mr. Rosenthal is one of the two or three most complete masters of the technique of the piano now living. His command of the mechanism of his instrument is uncanny, necromantic, almost incredible: the ear refuses, at times, to credit the fact that mere human fingers and wrists are accomplishing what they seem to be accomplishing. Mr. Rosenthal is almost as infallible, as sure and precise and imperturbable and unerring, as one of those marvelous piano-playing machines that amaze the modern world. This is not to say that he has not much besides: for he commands, at times, a lovely quality of tone color, and he plays often with tenderness, dignity, and repose, though not with impeccable taste. But Mr. Rosenthal is capable—and this illustrates the point that one would make—of butchering a charming and inoffensive little waltz of Chopin's (the one in D-flat which is played daily by several million schoolgirls throughout the civilized world) to make a pianistic holiday. He has accomplished this notable end by tricking out the gracious and unpretentious little melody with every variety of vulgar pianistic ornament that his ingenuity could suggest. The result is, of course, that Chopin is quite buried out of sight—smothered in cheap embroidery and made unlovely by rouge and patchouli. It is an astounding achievement—an achievement that causes many persons who should know better to sit up very straight in their seats and applaud hysterically when it is done; but from the point of view of any one who owns to the most rudimentary sense of artistic rectitude the thing is atrocious. It betrays an incurable flaw in the artistic constitution of its perpetrator: it is an unmistakable index of the quality of mind and taste which made possible its accomplishment, and it vitiates and renders ludicrous any pretensions which its author chooses to make on the score of musical taste and appreciation. It cannot be too positively asserted nor too inflexibly reiterated that no sincere and sensitive and scrupulous artist could possibly be guilty of exploiting such a barbarism, much less of being responsible for its existence. Mr. Rosenthal has played the piece for years, and will doubtless continue to do so as long as he finds it profitable; but there is a certain consolation in the fact that he is probably the only pianist in the world who can so perform it as to make its marvellous vulgarity completely apparent.

It is an infinite pity that a musician who has so perfectly mastered the expressional medium of his art, and who has such undoubted potentialities of fine and sincere accomplishment, should be content with the things that now satisfy and sustain him.

8   From *Music, The Mystery and the Reality*

1955

Paul Roës

Even among those nearest to him, including some of his students, [Liszt] was often misunderstood. One of his disciples understood him profoundly; that was Moriz Rosenthal. We must give Rosenthal credit for having communicated, without keeping anything secret, his rich experiences to all those who had the pleasure of approaching him.

Member of a group of students of which, besides him, the most famous were Eugène d'Albert, Alexander Siloti, Emil von Sauer and Frédéric Lamond[1]—all of quite different characters—Rosenthal appeared among them as the most objective observer. Self-confident, he approached Liszt in a complete freedom of spirit. He told with pleasure how much his master appreciated this independence: "Above all no imitation; it is better to find for yourself, after mere suggestions on my part," he had the custom of saying. A perfectly free admiration resulted from it.

Rosenthal did not have Liszt's religious conceptions; for this reason, his words of admiration were strictly objective, the least contested. Another reason for his objectivity was the ease with which Rosenthal developed his technique. Effort never obscured his spirit. "The vexation of an obstacle," he said, "begins when one imagines that it is insurmountable." Provided with the easy technique of a Godowsky, having a keen sense of analysis and synthesis, he belonged for a long time to the elite of pianists. His memories, rendered precious by the intimate contact that he had with Liszt, merit more attention than the writings of the whimsical chroniclers.

One day, speaking of his master, after remaining deep in his memories for a moment, he supplied a key to the enigma of this misunderstanding of which Franz Liszt was the object: "Liszt was not a man like others. One always felt that his suggestions came from a mystical thought. He saw further than we did, and when he spoke, his thoughts were so well-considered that he gave the impression of seeing with the eyes of a creator . . . "

Paul Roës, *Music, The Mystery and the Reality,* translated by Edna Dean McGray (Chevy Chase, Md. : E & M Publishing, 1978). Originally published as *La Musique Mystère et Réalité* (Paris: Henry Lemoine et Cie., 1955).

9 On Liszt's *Don Juan* Fantasie

Unpublished

M. R.

Beginning with Tirso de Molina, many of the greats of poetry and music have engaged with the titanic revolt of Don Juan against moral law.[1] To name but a few from the ranks of the poets: Corneille, Molière, Byron (who created a highly un-Byronic Don Juan, depicting him as merely the plaything of an inordinately merciful destiny), E. T. A. Hoffmann, Grabbe, and Lenau, all of whom captured the hot-blooded and heroic Spaniard with all the power of their smoldering imagination.[2] Mozart, Liszt, Richard Strauss, and many others have crafted Don Juan musically. Mozart, with the unconscious recognition of genius, not only depicted the seducer, who scorches women's hearts with his gaze, but was also the first to have a feeling for the hero in *Don Juan,* who defends his claimed rights with a dagger in his fist. In the *minore* of the champagne song, Don Juan goes for his sword. In his *Don Juan* Fantasie, Liszt raises this proud act of daring to a peak and thereby equals Grabbe, if not surpasses him. Don Juan's triumphant affirmation of life, in contrast to the revolt of hell and heaven that threatens him, swells up into an heroic, violent expressiveness in and after the triple crescendo of the champagne song; the musical force causes two worlds of distanced, opposing principles, like Christian and heathen morals, to collide suddenly—all this bears irrevocable witness to Liszt's fiery imagination and creative power.

Our friend Ferruccio Busoni, untimely departed, draws his own conclusions in his analysis of his own edition of the *Don Juan* Fantasie. It stresses that Da Ponte "has depicted Don Juan as not victorious enough," that the knight's gallant successes in the piece "are not brilliant," and that, furthermore, he became "more suave than demonic." However, here Busoni seems to forget that the rather outrageous censorship of ancient Austria would have dealt Da Ponte a painful rap on his writing fingers had he dared to portray the victories of this *dissoluto punito* on the stage. Da Ponte had no other option than to let Leporello make an epic pronouncement of the "Don's" fame. But do we not also encounter what Busoni reproves as Da Ponte's "flaw" in the works of much greater poets, against whom Busoni takes care not to level such critical expositions? As Don Juan is the titan of sensuality, so Faust is the titan of the questing spirit, thirsty for knowledge, a much more elevated type! But must we not accept in good faith, especially in the first part of Goethe's drama, the lonely height of Faust's spirit without being able to follow its motivation in the dramatic events? Does Faust, who after all has over time made the almost omniscient Mephistopheles his own through a bloody pact, ask about the remaining mysteries of reason, as would seem to befit a gloomy romancer of truth?

No, he lets himself drift in the current of life and is stranded for the rest of the play on the isle of blissful love. Does Wallenstein, in Schiller's drama, show musical genius? But if we were to surrender all of Da Ponte, where would Mozart be, who depicts Don Juan in a battle with death and hell, while Busoni prefers to find, in the story and music of the champagne song, worldly mobility, "insouciance, bubbling zest for life," and even a characteristic "non-sens(e)uality"?[3] This conception seems to be in sharp contrast to Liszt's, who elevates the Don Juan of his Fantasie to a symbol of nature's power in battle with dominant morality.

Whoever breathes in the heady, fiery air of Mozart's or Liszt's enthusiasm will see Don Juan as being as inseparable from his unbridled affirmation of life and audacious glorification of death as, say, Napoleon is from his battle roar.

10 A Stroll with Ferruccio Busoni

Unpublished

M. R.

The letter from Count Seilern-Aspang concluded with the following words:

> "Tomorrow evening Busoni will be dining with us, and will perhaps play a few
> miniatures afterward. It would be delightful if you could come. I have just heard
> that you are in London; please do join us."

The evening approached. The count's head chef in London did the noble
family credit, even more so the "butler" who, with a sanctifying hand, poured
red and blond alcoholic drinks into the glittering glasses. The conversation soon
moved on from the initial *mezzopiano* to disembogue into a sonorous *fortissimo*.
The red and violet flecks on the faces of the highly dignified guests, along with
their numbed, somewhat glazed gazes, were quite remarkable.

And now to our friend Ferruccio Busoni, who approached the piano with a
light step and enticed Beethoven's solemn, ethereal Sonata op. 109 out of the
instrument. Naturally he repeated all of the final movement's variations. Whoever believed that his honorable obligations had been fulfilled and that one now
had to conjure rather more approachable gentilities out of the piano was sorely
mistaken, for Busoni mercilessly let rip with Schumann's *Etudes symphoniques*,
performed six lesser known *Lisztiana*, and rounded off the gastronomically and
musically festive evening with three longish pieces from Chopin's musical treas-
ure trove.

It goes without saying that Busoni performed everything with technical perfection and wit, and that the audience, accustomed to lighter fare, were not in
a position to keep up with him.

We stepped out into the spring night and, captivated by its magic, decided to
make our way home on foot. We had been silent for a long while, when Busoni
finally decided that the time had come to subject the somewhat cool behavior
of the aristocratic company at Count Seilern-Aspang's to indirect criticism by
pitting his own greatness against the illusory splendor of society. He began with
an inspired gesture:

"Oh, my dear friend, there is something so magnificent when one is neither
restrained by any technical ties, nor inhibited by any difficulty, and is completely
given over to the deepest feelings when proclaiming the word, the spirit, of the
composer as a gospel to the lumpish world at large!"

I appeared shaken to my core. There followed an uneasy pause. Then, with a determined step, I approached my school friend, shook him warmly by his limply hanging right hand, and said to him in a trembling voice:

"I thank you from the bottom of my heart: you will get there one day too."

Our laughter rang out in the spring night.

> Busoni's essay Sketch of a New Aesthetic of Music[1] *contains a passage about transcendental interpretation akin to the one he shared with Rosenthal after they left Count Seilern-Aspang's, making one wonder if Busoni had published the essay at the time of this after-dinner conversation or was still formulating his ideas for it—and trying them out on his colleagues:*
>
>> *If Nirvana be the realm 'beyond the Good and the Bad,' one way leading thither is here pointed out. A way to the very portal. To the bars that divide Man from Eternity—or that open to admit that which was temporal. Beyond that portal sounds music. Not the strains of 'musical art.'— It may be, that we must leave Earth to find that music. But only to the pilgrim who has succeeded on the way in freeing himself from earthly shackles, shall the bars open.*

11 Mahleriana

Unpublished

M. R.

Lunch at Prof. Julius Epstein's, the doyen of the piano professors in Vienna, was very lively. Opposite me sat a man who was still young with sharply cut features and nervous, distracted gestures. Epstein introduced him: "Gustav Mahler, composer, conductor, and my piano pupil. He will play his [first] symphony for us after lunch." I suddenly felt a mental jolt while two of Prof. Epstein's colleagues looked as though they would have liked to exchange the promised symphony for a gentle afternoon nap. There was no chance of that, however, because Mahler began his symphony with a verve and gusto that were reminiscent of the "grand style" of our youth. Trumpets radiated, heroes under official Valkyrian protection presented themselves for battle. A funeral march spread sadness, but was consolingly called "ironic" by the composer. There were contradictions enough, melodic inventions did not exactly celebrate orgies, but a clear will and a strong imagination were clearly knocking on the door. In between there were some drops of Liszt's Italian sweetness. In all of it something [illegible] of Brahms. My feeling was: There is someone up and coming here. Epstein too was impressed in his own way. The gist of his verdict was always: "And people claim that I only teach pupils to play the piano quietly!" (Which Mahler consistently ignored.)

Young Richard Epstein, J. Epstein's son and heir, then attempted to create a diversion by insisting that I play Brahms's Paganini Variations for Mahler,[1] Mahler too wished to get to know the piece and the player more closely, and so I suddenly found myself sitting at the Bösendorfer. During the octave glissando Prof. [Anton] Door called out: "Some opera glasses!" During the second finale I suddenly heard Mahler call out loudly: "Two pairs of opera glasses!"

After I had played, Mahler said to me: "You are the pianist that interests me the most, I hope to hear you again many times, we should meet more often." My heart went out to him! I felt that I had made a close friendship that was very valuable to me.

In the meantime Mahler had been made director of the [Court] Opera [1897–1907]. One of the following summers I was in Toblach [now Dobbiaco] in the Südbahnhotel. One day Mahler arrived, distraught, dejected. He had been sent to Toblach for recuperation by *Primarius* Gersung after a somewhat complicated operation.[2] With my friend Max B., who was visiting me there, we actually formed a [illegible] trio in which we dined together every evening and spoke mainly about music and literature.[3] Mahler said: "You played Scharwenka's Concerto in b-flat this morning. It is an amusing piece. I have selected it as the final test piece for the conservatorium."

At that time he was very fond of Dostoyevsky, whose *The Brothers Karamazov* he claimed to be the best novel in world literature. He did not much agree with my admiration for Chopin, thinking him too *en miniature,* too modest in manner. I said: "In a distinguished society you cannot legitimately demonstrate the wit and depth of your conversation as a man of the highest degree (as Heinrich Heine called him) with such manners. It's a poor man who needs to put his feet up on the table to legitimize his reputation." [Mahler] seemed cross about this temporarily, but it was only a little summer cloud that was quickly dissolved by the sun.

We often discussed Hugo Riemann's phrasing reforms that were rightfully causing feelings to run high.[4] To my amazement [Mahler] even claimed one evening that the phrasing depended on the disposition and current attitude of the conductor (singer, pianist, etc.). He overestimated the bar lines, which became apparent in the allegro theme of Beethoven's Third *Leonore* Overture, and was perhaps jointly responsible for Richard Heuberger reporting with a sneer in the *Neue Freie Press* about a genuinely French *Leonore* Overture decorated with the most delicate Parisian nuances.[5]

These memories should not form part of a historical work in which the dates become hypertrophically important; therefore I would like to mention one evening that I spent in Hamburg in the house of Mayor Sigmund Hinrichsen and that took place before the Toblach episodes. Here I played Beethoven's Sonata op. 111 and some pieces by Chopin and Liszt. Even before I went to the piano, M. whispered to me: "I am sorry for you that you have to play to these coffee sacks!" That verdict appealed to me quite strongly then (in the year 1891!), but today seems all too superficial to me. What if an Einstein, a Marconi, a great painter or poet had been present? Might he have been labeled a coffee sack too?

After the Sonata op. 111 Mahler expressed his warmest admiration for the Arietta con variazioni. In my place and with my technique he would have thundered down all the thematic pairings in the first movement in octaves. (And this sonata consists only of these!) He was very much in favor of such [octave] doublings because they made the composer's intentions much clearer. [Illegible.] Unfortunately, I could not agree with him in the case of the [Beethoven] Ninth Symphony either when he advocated doubling.

These improvements were characteristic of Mahler, with their somewhat forced heroism, and had a strange effect on Hans Richter, also a good friend of mine, who was already engaged in Manchester at that time and enjoyed almost divine honors there.[6] One morning I arrived at the local Queen's Hotel and went into the breakfast room where Hans Richter was already sitting at a heavily laden little table! A steak, a melon, a bottle of white wine completed the simple but hearty meal. Hardly had I entered when Hans Richter called out to me very loudly: "Dear Rosenthal, is it true that you are improving Beethoven?" I replied: "Not at all! Who told you that?" "Well," he said, "Mahler told the whole orchestra in Vienna last week, 'Of course I don't improve or correct Beethoven, I double the important passages just like my friend Rosenthal.'" I told Richter calmly and coolly: "This must be a misunderstanding. Apparently M. believed in good faith that I had accepted and followed a doubling that he once recommended to me for the Sonata op. 111. But he was wrong." Only now did H. R. begin to thaw and voiced the most bitter complaints about M.'s impiety.

Then came my American tours. I spent a lot of time away from Vienna and saw Mahler only very infrequently; he was usually sitting at a little table in a Ringstrassencafé with his—in the true sense of the word—faithful paladin, Ludwig Karpath,[7] and always seemed engrossed in newspapers. One evening—I had not seen him for years—he came toward me on the terrace of the Café Imperial, very agitated and dejected. "I have," he said (without further preliminaries), "eaten something bad. Can you tell me what I should do now?" This trust in my medical abilities electrified me. I jumped up, led him into a pharmacy, and there started a well-considered thorough strategic battle of pills with the cooperation of the apothecary.

Somewhat calmer, M. returned to the café with me, and we sat town at a little table to wait for Bruno Walter and Gempler, who was standing in for M. as the conductor in [Verdi's] *Ballo in Maschera*.[8] After a quarter of an hour the expected persons arrived, and M.'s first ironic question was: "The singers of course got the biggest applause?" Walter replied without a trace of bitterness: "Of course!" The discussion turned to America, to the material chances of an American artistic tour, and unfortunately I gave him favorable news.[9]

Half an hour later Mahler got up, took his leave of me with great deliberation. I accompanied him part of the way, not knowing that I would never see him again.

12 Czar Alexander II

Unpublished

M. R.

Often I have been asked by interviewers: "Before which sovereigns have you played during your career?" Then I always thought of the uncrowned kings of my acquaintance who honored me with their friendship or their friendly interest, like [Albert] Einstein, Liszt, Brahms, Anton Rubinstein, Turgenev.[1] Afterward my memory would recall from stygian darkness the worldly crowned ones, Czar Alexander II (torn to pieces by nihilists' bombs), King Alfonso [XII] and Queen Christina of Spain, and especially that most genial monarch Franz Josef I, who made me his Chamber Virtuoso (*Kammervirtuose*) of Kaiser and King. Vividly do I remember a Court concert given before him, at which appeared beside myself also Fritz Schrödter, Marcella Sembrich, and Toni Schläger[2]—the last named setting a world record for nervousness. She crossed herself and prayed before her performance. I do not remember whether or not the gods were responsive to her entreaties.

After the concert, the Emperor held a reception and thanked the artists in rather impersonal fashion. However, I was surprised at his technical question to me: "It must be difficult to conquer those intricate pieces with so much ease?" When had the Emperor found time to busy himself with the nature of pianism? Or had the *Spiritus Rector* of the concert, old Hellmesberger, told His Majesty something in praise of me?

About twenty years prior to the foregoing happening, I had played, as a fourteen-year-old boy, before Czar Alexander II, the mightiest monarch of Europe. This was at the time of the Turkish War, when allied Russia and Romania had defeated Osman Pasha, the Lion of Plevna, and captured that place after a long siege. The Czar left his headquarters and want to Bucharest to visit his ally, Prince Karol. I was Court Pianist to the poetess, Carmen Sylva, then Princess and later Queen of Romania.

This city was brilliantly illuminated to greet the Czar, and rapturous masses of people, carrying torches, marched through the streets. The following day brought a Court Concert and Ball in honor of the royal visitor. Carmen Sylva arranged the musical program, putting me down for five pieces. As I approached the piano (an excellent Bösendorfer), I was presented to the Czar and heard him say: "Si jeune?" (So young?) Before and after I played I found occasion to study his truly classical features. His face had—at least on that evening—a remarkable color, which I have never seen on any other person. It seemed to me a rusty, dark silver. His manners were altogether royal, nay, imperial. Pressing around him, ambitious, lovely women, in daring décolleté, fluted their honeyed flatteries. I could not hear much except the word "Majesté." In fact, the word was batted about in the manner of a shuttlecock.

Carmen Sylva gave a sign, silence ensued, and I began to play. Hardly had I sounded the first *fortissimo* grace-noted C-sharp, when the Czar, with a strong Russian accent, said: "Rhapsodia." Satisfied murmuring resounded through the hall, for Liszt's Second Rhapsody was at that period at the zenith of its fame and popularity. After that I played mazurkas and waltzes by Chopin, *Soirées de Vienne* by Schubert-Liszt, and the *Campanella,* and was delighted at the applause which sounded by no means merely courtly and formal.

The Czar offered me his hand, which ruled 150,000,000 Russians, and said that he hoped to hear me often, and also in St. Petersburg. Grand Duke Serge asked the courtiers whether he or I had the larger hands. The question worked to my detriment, for my hand, still exceedingly small then, disappeared completely in his enormous bear-paws. The next day I received a document from the Court Chamberlain which attested "que le jeune Maurice Rosenthal a joué devant l'Empereur etc. d'une manière vraiment élevée etc." (that the young Maurice Rosenthal had played before the Emperor etc. in a manner truly elevating etc.).

At the banquet after the concert I was introduced by his charming Secretary, Baron Fredericks, to the Russian Chancellor, Prince Gortschakoff, uncrowned king of diplomacy. He invited me to tea the following day, when piano-playing, Chinese-Russian Zakuski, and a Muscovite buffet were enjoyed with an obbligato of frenzied shouts and howls serving as counterpoint, and coming from the victory-drunk mob in the streets. Gortschakoff requested a mazurka, but every few moments he was compelled, despite his venerable age and the wintry weather, to show himself on the balcony in order to acknowledge the dinful greetings of the crowd. Torchlight processions, red fire, Bengal lights, illuminated the early darkness and the face of Gortschakoff, who threw his fur coat coquettishly over his shoulders and glanced quickly into the mirror before each exit to the balcony. In the intervals he would call out to me: "Another mazurka!" Baron Fredericks took me into a corner, winked and said: "Do you believe that he really likes the mazurkas, really values them? You see, he has the undeserved reputation of the Poles, and he protests against the charge by manifesting his appetite for mazurkas.

"Yes, most of his colleagues might well have sat as pupils at the feet of Gortschakoff, eminent admirer of Talleyrand. Dissimulation was Gortschakoff's passion and (paraphrasing Talleyrand) he might well have—like so many other composers—looked upon music as a means of concealing his thoughts."

13 Review of a Concert by M. R.

The Times (London), December 5, 1921

H. C. C.

We reached the Wigmore Hall on Saturday in time to catch Mr. Rosenthal maltreating Brahms's Piano Sonata in F Minor [op. 5]. The sonata is an early work, badly written from the point of view of piano effect. Mr. Rosenthal does not make it more effective by playing fast and loose with the rhythm of the Scherzo and indulging in explosive *sforzandos* with additional notes packed into the chords to increase the percussion. Moreover, this treatment obscures the fact that, whether well written or ill, this sonata is a piece of very beautiful music. The "Rückblick" does not look back over a murky past, but dreams over the innocent aspirations of a romantic youth, but Mr. Rosenthal apparently can perceive nothing of these finer aspects of Brahms. Similarly, he could make nothing of the little Intermezzo in A flat (from op. 76), though the Capriccio in B Minor gave him an opportunity for the display of his wonderful staccato touch, which he took to the full. A selection from the Paganini Variations, taken without regard to sequence from the two books, showed off many other sides of the pianist's accomplishment and further illustrated his supreme disregard of the composer's intentions.

14 Letter to the Editor

The Times (London), December 14, 1921

M. R.

Sir,—Your highly esteemed musical critic asserts in your issue of December 5, commenting on my seventh recital of the historical series, that in performing the Paganini-Variations by Brahms I showed my "supreme disregard of the composer's intentions."

The question arises: Who could give us documentary evidence on the master's intentions respecting this work? Probably only the master himself! Alas! he is dead; but his words remain. I am in the happy position to quote his judgment about my performance of the Paganini-Variations *verbatim*. Richard von Perger, his lifelong friend, Director of the Conservatorium in Vienna, wrote in the *Allgemeine Kunstchronik* in the year 1886 the following words:—"But as the greatest success of Mr. Rosenthal must be regarded that Brahms himself was present, and that he bestowed unreserved and unrestrained praise on this bold pianist." Allow me to mention also a work of Theodor Helm, entitled "Fifty Years of Musical Life in Vienna," which appeared in the Viennese periodical [*Der*] *Merker*.[1] Helm mentions my first performance of the Paganini-Variations, which took place in the year 1884, and observes:—"Those Paganini-Variations, of which Brahms used to say that nobody could play them as this 21-years-old Rosenthal." It seems, therefore, that your esteemed musical critic cherishes ideas about this work which differ entirely from the ideas of Brahms himself. As a matter of fact, Brahms not only approved of the selection I made out of the two sets, but heard them five times in my concerts at the old Bösendorfer Hall in Vienna and twice at the Tonkünstlerverein without diminishing the cordial praise he bestowed the first time on me.

But your esteemed musical critic disagrees not only with Brahms; he quarrels also with—Beethoven. In commenting on my reading of the so-called "Appassionata," he asserted that I played it in a dramatic way, whereas all sonatas by Beethoven are "mainly lyrics," where one "single thought" should be chiseled out. Quite apart from the well-known fact that the sonata form is built not on one, but on at least two contrasting themes, and that most of the sonatas are full of red-hot dramatic life, force, and passion, we can just in this one instance rely on the words of the immortal composer himself. When his friend, secretary, factotum, and biographer, Schindler, asked him which poetic idea filled his mind, when he wrote the "Appassionata," Beethoven answered: "Read Shakespeare's *Tempest!*"[2] Now, as everybody knows, Shakespeare's *Tempest* is not a lyrical poem, but a drama, full of stress, storm, shipwreck, and love. There was all to be found in my reading, happily, except the shipwreck. Should the *Tempest* have frightened your esteemed musical critic I wish to apologize. I wish also to confess openly, that I always derive much pleasure from his masterful essays. They may boast of all those qualities which make a critic prominent. They have only the one shortcoming, if I may venture to say so, that they seem not particularly adapted to the specific performances about which they are written. Your esteemed musical critic reminds me in this respect of my famous compatriot, the great Polish painter Matejko.[3] When once he delivered a portrait of the Countess Zamoyska, and the unfortunate husband, almost paralyzed by astonishment, exclaimed: "But this portrait does not look in the least like my wife," Matejko answered calmly: "Your wife ought to look like my portrait." (I heard the story in 1890 from the Count himself.)[4]

After all, Matejko was perhaps right. The individual is perishable, art remains. Perhaps performing artists ought to look like their "portraits"; they should try to adapt their playing to the criticisms passed upon them. If they succeed, then will have come a new era of musical life, where we will derive the most pure, the most intoxicating delight from the essays of your highly esteemed musical critic, to whom I wish to express through these humble lines my gratitude for all the kindness bestowed upon me and my art.

I am, Sir, yours most sincerely and obediently, [etc.]

London, Dec. 7.

15 As Others See Us: H. C. C.'s Response to M. R.'s Letter to the Editor

The Times (London), December 17, 1921

Mr. Rosenthal's letter has shown his skill in defense and counter-attack with a good story for a weapon. I grudge him nothing but the weapon, the story of Matejko, the painter. That should have been in my hand, though I might not have wielded it as deftly as Mr. Rosenthal has. For what I set out to tell him was what his friend the Count told the painter, that his portrait of Brahms may be very fine, but is not a bit like Brahms, to which he replies that my portrait of his piano playing may be highly estimable, but is not a bit like his piano playing.

So we stand confronting one another and awaiting the verdict of an arbitration board. Mr. Rosenthal professes to produce a final arbiter in Brahms himself, but a correspondent has been quick to point out the flaw in this argument of which no doubt Mr. Rosenthal is already conscious. "The flowers that bloom in the spring, Tra-la, have nothing to do with the case."[1] Apart from the fact that my strictures were directed primarily towards his performance of a very different work from the Paganini Variations (the later movements of the Sonata in F Minor) what Brahms said of "the 21 years old Rosenthal" may have only the slightest bearing on a performance given a fortnight ago. No doubt after Brahms's elderly commendation of his youth Mr. Rosenthal would not in elder years wittingly maltreat the youthful Brahms. But he knows, as every sincere artist does, that a thousand conflicting circumstances have operated on him through nearly 40 years of strenuous toil and travel, enlarging his vision in some directions, contracting it in others—quickening certain sensibilities and deadening others, shattering early ideals, and awakening (let us hope) the consciousness of new ones. Mr. Rosenthal would not be the alive man he is if his playing to-day were a replica of his playing in 1884. So when a hearer in 1921 exclaims, "But this portrait does not look in the least like Brahms," it is at least conceivable that the artist has lost something amongst all the gains of an international celebrity.

So much for his portrait of Brahms; his objection to mine of him reminds one that great artists are like ordinary people in one respect. Given two portraits of themselves they have a natural tendency to choose the better-looking one, and declare it to be the only faithful portrait. The other may have caught a fleeting likeness which the subject is sorry to own. Mr. Rosenthal is not above the rest of humanity in this. He has found the pen-portrait of his playing which he likes, and was so obliging as to enclose a copy of it with his letter, a cutting from another paper, in which he had underlined these words:— *The natural successor of Anton Rubinstein in the royal line of pianists. We have not his like to-day in any land.*

No wonder he prefers this as a portrait for general distribution to either of the two sketches which appeared in *The Times,* two entirely distinct sketches, it may be noticed, one of his Brahms the other of his Beethoven, drawn by different hands. This portrait, set in his own italics, is the fulfillment of the pianist's dream just because it is so general, and his real objection to our sketches (I must drop back into the plural pronoun here) is possibly less that they contradict anything which Brahms or Beethoven said about the interpretation of their works, than that they were rather too "particularly adapted to the specific performances" under discussion, and therefore not suited to italicized reproduction.

Granted that Brahms liked the selection from his Paganini Variations, and that the whole of the drama of *The Tempest* (not excluding the shipwreck) is packed into Mr. Rosenthal's reading of the Appassionata Sonata, it does not follow that the listener need accept either without question on his own part. If Mr. Rosenthal thinks that the phrase "disregard of the composer's intentions" lays claim to certain knowledge of the composer's mind, I renounce it at once and substitute for it "disregard of what the composer wrote." For the listener to any well-known music must be prepared to receive impressions differing widely from those which he has previously formed of the same music; indeed, he hopes to discover some fresh aspect of the composer's intentions in every rehearing of the work. These impressions are conveyed in different ways, and for the sake of convenience they may be described in the form of four questions. The listener asks himself, Is this what I came to hear, the music which the composer wrote? If not, are the alterations improvements, that is of the kind which ignore the letter for the sake of the spirit? Does this player express those qualities which have given the music enduring value in the past? Does he discover in it something unrealized before, which makes his performance a new revelation of its beauty or its force? The first three are applicable alike to the playing of a Rosenthal and of a tyro from the music schools. The last only gets posed when an artist "in the royal line" is at work. Then it supersedes the other three, and the affirmative answer to it is his hall-mark. He is a creative artist. He takes a work which perhaps the composer left rather in the rough, as Brahms left his F Minor Sonata, strips off its encumbrances, moulds it to triumphant completeness. Or, again, in an acknowledged masterpiece, he discovers depths which even the composer himself never plumbed and heights which the most faithful disciple can never scale. When that happens we ask nothing of "the notes," of how it was done, or whether it accords with any previous idea of the composer's intentions or our own desires. The artist is not called on to produce his credentials; he could not if he would, for he may know as little of the how or the why as the least sophisticated of his hearers. He and they only know that it is done. A miscellaneous collection of people, sensitive and insensitive, willing and unwilling, is seized with the artist's message, so that every man hears him speaking in his own tongue wherein he was born.

Mr. Rosenthal has produced his credentials in these instances, and they are not to be lightly dismissed, even by those who accept them with some reservations. But perhaps he will do this greater thing for which none are required. I hope so. Indeed, far from asking Mr. Rosenthal to look like his portrait as drawn by me, I would beg him to look as unlike it as possible, so that someday I may have the pleasure of drawing another one in which he can both recognize and approve the likeness.

16 The Korngold Scandal

Wiener Sonn-und Montags-Beitung, July 10, 1922

The Blood Vengeance of the House of Korngold

Herr Julius Korngold has responded to accusations of tactlessness and impropriety by trying to besmirch Richard Strauss with a "critique"; he has also assured us of his being a just father to his composer son and furthermore promised to ignore the "loutish behavior" directed against him.[1] It is not our intention to examine which is the greater about him—the insolence with which he greets his public or the art of misunderstanding that manifests itself in the father—whom we reproach for his tactlessness—doggedly insisting that he is a critic. But one has to remind him once again that the side of the matter that he studiously puts forward has long been resolved. Only completely uninitiated or naïve readers can still consider taking Korngold seriously as a "critic"; all others have known for over fifteen years that the name Korngold is not given to a critic passing his more or less meaningful judgments, but rather that the composer's father is using the office granted him by coincidence for the sole purpose of promoting his son. Korngold's trick of putting on a pained expression and sighing: "I have a son—how difficult it is for me to be a strict critic, and yet my duty, my conscience, I must, I have no choice . . . " For this trick to have any credibility, it would have to have a different past, a different mindset, a different style, a different person as its prerequisites. Employed by Korngold, whom one has known about for years, it appears as an ungraceful attempt to deceive. It is all too obvious; this state of affairs, documented hundreds of times, requires no further light cast upon it in my opinion. It is simply more a question of whether one can still tolerate the Korngold family's craving for vengeance when it becomes dangerous to all. Voices by the thousand say no and approve of the tone that, however "loutish" it may appear to Korngold, is the only appropriate one. This rejection of the "tone" comes too late; it works as poorly as the trick of misunderstanding. His son's agent, masquerading as a critic, previously could not even be bothered to hide the true nature of his office; whoever did not do the son's bidding, whoever did not do what the old man told him to do, was met with the curse of blood vengeance. It was only the greatness of Strauss that forced the vengeful man, crazed by his paternal vanity, to conceal the vengefulness somewhat. But the case is clear: above all, what we have here is an attempt to pass off the revenge of the father as the duty of the critic, as a serious duty. He has no choice, God help him . . . [2] But it is strange that this duty arises when the family's well-worn vanity is not satisfied.

To illustrate the nature of the "critic" using an old case, let us refer to the sworn statement of a Viennese artist of the highest order who has brought Korngold's vengeance upon himself. It suffices to mention the name of Moriz Rosenthal and allow the tale to be told. The statement, upon which Rosenthal has sworn an oath, reads:

Sworn Statement.

I first met Dr. J. Korngold in a music criticism context on the occasion of a concert I gave on January 5, 1905. Back then he composed an arts commentary in which he celebrated me enthusiastically. (See Korngold's review in the *Neue Freie Presse* of January 6, 1905.) In his later reviews, for example, the one from the year 1909, Dr. Korngold still wrote of me with admiration.

When his son's talent began to stir, Dr. Korngold often permitted suggestions regarding my program to make their way into his reviews of me. Indeed, he often gave as much consideration to my future programs as to those I had just performed.

The psychological explanation for this odd behavior became [clear] to me in the summer of 1911. I met Dr. Korngold and his son in the Stadtpark, and, after exchanging greetings, and while pointing at his son, Dr. Korngold said to me:

"Do you know what he is writing at the moment? A Rosenthal Sonata!"[3]

In reply to my question as to what he meant by that, Dr. Korngold said verbatim:

"He imagines how you would play his work, with such force and power."

Some days later I availed myself of an opportunity to hear the young composer's work, though in skeletal form, for myself. I enjoyed the first two movements, but the third, with its intentionally prickly-poisonous harmony, displeased me—of which I made no secret at all. Having made up my mind that I would not decide to play the "Rosenthal Sonata" in public, I let some weeks pass before enquiring after the work. This, in conjunction with my critical remarks on the harmony in the Largo [: Con dolore], made Dr. Korngold so angry that he told me on the telephone that he would do without hearing the Sonata performed by me. According to him, fifty great pianists had applied to be allowed to play the Sonata, but he did not wish to entrust it to anyone. Thus, I had fallen out of favor. Finally, Artur Schnabel was entrusted with performing the Sonata, although Dr. Korngold had by no means been exactly full of praise for his playing previously.[4] (Review in the *Neue Freie Presse* of December 4, 1909.)

On November 13, 1911, Schnabel launched the Sonata, and on November 14 the review appeared in the *Neue Freie Presse,* dripping with praise and admiration for the work and the pianist. This dithyrambic review was continued when Schnabel gave a Beethoven evening. The same Korngold who had emphasized many an error in Schnabel's playing (inability to captivate, a meatless *forte,* etc. . . . See the *Neue Freie Presse* of December 4, 1909) was now writing his review as an apotheosis (see the *Neue Freie Presse* of December 8, 1911). Thus it was proved how right I had been with my harmless remark that young Korngold's Sonata was "thankless" though by no means was the father.[5] Dr. Korngold was particularly piquant in his review when writing of me in the same article, characterizing me as a mere virtuoso. Even if this *volte-face* can still be explained psychologically as damaged pride, it is certainly inexcusable that Dr. Korngold attempted to turn other critics against me.

Dr. Korngold's partiality and arbitrariness had reached such a level at this time that old Leschetizky considered proposing a complaint to the *Neue Freie Presse*, which both I and Godowsky supported. We sent a promemoria to the *Neue Freie Presse*, and when this received no satisfactory reply we submitted a detailed complaint cosigned by E. Gaertner and Dr. Heinrich Schenker.[6] Upon this, we received a reply that the case would be investigated thoroughly. However, we have received no further sign of life from the *Neue Freie Presse*.

The statement goes on to show, with illustrations, the manner in which Korngold continued to exact revenge upon the Viennese artist who had fallen out of favor with him. Moriz Rosenthal had to experience being treated like any old novice by the newspaper at Korngold's disposal. Too cowardly to show his hate in public, Korngold exacted revenge in the manner of a malicious reptile; it was petty, base, how he tried to wound with a bug's sting the great artist who has performed in Vienna for 45 years and enjoys world renown . . . Rosenthal continues:

. . . this outrageous audacity characterizes the dark and yet so clearly transparent machinations . . . I declare: I share the general conviction held both at home and abroad that such an abuse of the office of critic in Vienna's greatest newspaper represents a terrible impairment of our cultivation of music and the standing of musical life and music criticism in Vienna.

I hereby attest to all of the above in a statutory declaration,

     Moriz Rosenthal,

    Chamber virtuoso and court pianist.

17 From *Franz Liszt*

1911

James Gibbons Huneker

"You ask how [Liszt] played? As no one before him, and as no one probably will ever again. I remember when I first went to him as a boy—he was in Rome at the time—he used to play for me in the evening by the hour—nocturnes by Chopin, études of his own—all of a soft, dreamy nature that caused me to open my eyes in wonder at the marvellous delicacy and finish of his touch. The embellishments were like a cobweb—so fine—or like the texture of costliest lace. I thought, after what I had heard in Vienna, that nothing further would astonish me in the direction of digital dexterity, having studied with Joseffy, the greatest master of that art. But Liszt was more wonderful than anybody I had ever known, and he had further surprises in store for me. I had never heard him play anything requiring force, and, in view of his advanced age, took for granted that he had fallen off from what he had once been." ("Liszt Pupils and Lisztiana," 367–368)

* * *

Setting aside Tausig—and this is only hearsay—the word "pianism" has never matched Rosenthal for speed, power, endurance; nor is this all. He is both musical and intellectual. He is a doctor of philosophy, a bachelor of arts. He has read everything, is a linguist, has traveled the globe over, and in conversation his unerring memory and brilliant wit set him as a man apart. To top all these gifts, he plays his instrument magnificently, overwhelmingly. He is the Napoleon, the conqueror among virtuosi. His tone is very sonorous, his touch singing, and he commands the entire range of nuance from the rippling *fioritura* of the Chopin barcarolle to the cannon-like thunderings of the A-flat polonaise. His octaves and chords baffle all critical experience and appraisement. As others play presto in single notes, so he dashes off double notes, thirds, sixths, and octaves. His Don Juan Fantasie, part Liszt, part Mozart, is entirely Rosenthalian in performance. He has composed at his polyphonic forge a Humoreske [on Strauss waltzes]. Its interweaving of voices, their independence, the caprice and audacity of it all are astounding. Tausig had such a technic; yet surely Tausig had not the brazen, thunderous climaxes of this broad-shouldered young man! He is the epitome of the orchestra and in a tonal duel with the orchestra he has never been worsted. His interpretations of the classics, of the romantics, are of a superior order. He played the last sonatas of Beethoven or the Schumann Carnaval with equal discrimination. His touch is crystal-like in its clearness, therefore his tone lacks the sensuousness of Paderewski and De Pachmann. But it is a mistake to set him down as a mere unemotional mechanician. He is in reality a Superman among pianists.[1] ("Modern Pianoforte Virtuosi," 431–432)

18 The Old and the New School of Piano Playing

St. Louis, March 21, 1924

M. R.

By some musical writers of high rank I was most flatteringly alluded to as "one of the most distinguished" or even (in some instances) "the most distinguished" representative of the older school of piano playing. I began to meditate about the difference between the older and the new schools of pianism. The conclusions I reached, founded on partly unknown facts which throw some new lights on the history of piano playing, I submit to musicians, musical writers, and the large musical public.

One hundred years ago: The modern "Hammer-Klavier" came to the forefront. Ludwig van Beethoven celebrated the new invention by his "Grosse Sonate für das Hammer-Klavier" op. 106 and by his following piano works, opp. 109, 110, 111, and 120. Happily enough, Beethoven promoted the piano to the highest extent by his compositions and did not concentrate his unique musical powers on the reproductive side of his art. The true piano virtuoso of this epoch was J. N. Hummel, Mozart's pupil and rival of Beethoven, of course not as a composer (in spite of his wonderful Sonata in F-sharp Minor) but on the battlefield of "Eros," in a love affair, where both masters were deeply interested in the same "damsel," which severed considerably their mutual friendly relations.

[Ferdinand Hiller:[1] "On March 13 [1827] Hummel took me with him a second time to Beethoven. We found his condition to be materially worse. He lay in bed, seemed to suffer great pains, and at intervals groaned deeply despite the fact that he spoke much and animatedly. Now he seemed to take it much to heart that he had not married. Already at our first visit [March 8] he had joked about it with Hummel, whose wife he had known as a young and beautiful maiden. 'You are a lucky man,' he said to him now smilingly, 'you have a wife who takes care of you, who is in love with you—but poor me!' and he sighed heavily. He also begged of Hummel to bring his wife to see him, she not having been able to persuade herself to see in his present state that man whom she had known at the zenith of his powers" (1046). On March 23, Hiller, Hummel, and now

---

The text here follows Rosenthal's original typescript, rather than the version published in *The Journal of the American Liszt Society* (autumn–winter 1985), pp. 129–132.

Hummel's wife visited the composer. Hiller: "Not a word fell from [Beethoven's] lips; sweat stood upon his forehead. His handkerchief not being conveniently at hand, Hummel's wife took her fine cambric handkerchief and dried his face several times. Never shall I forget the grateful glance with which his broken eye looked upon her" (1047). Beethoven died on March 26.]

Hummel's art, which for decades held the musical world spellbound, can be safely characterized as the bygone old school of piano playing. He banished every movement of wrist and forearm from his playing, despised the pedal (he used to call it "Der Sündendecker"—the "sin coverer"), and favored almost exclusively difficult finger work, which he played in finished style and at lightening speed, but without strength or splendor of tone. It is true that he was hampered by the scant sonority of the instruments of this time (the so-called spinet), but he did not alter his style after the invention of the "Hammer-Klavier." Little wonder that in 1835 Hummel had already lost his spell over the masses! At his concert in Vienna at this date, he played before empty benches. When the great composer emerged from the artists' room, he was overheard to say: "If this is not a disgrace for the Viennese, for *me* it certainly isn't."

It speaks much in his favor that he was more progressive in composition than in piano playing. When Chopin, then twenty years old, came to Vienna, the fifty-three-year-old Hummel paid him the first visit (quite an uncommon thing in Europe, where the newcomer calls first), which visit Chopin relates to his parents with unconcealed pride.[2] Hummel died in Weimar, the later residence of Franz Liszt, whom he had once refused to take as a pupil because the child prodigy could not pay the high fee Hummel asked for (one gold ducat for a lesson; about two-and-one-half dollars).

From about 1833 until 1848, the very quintessence of piano playing seemed to be embodied in three names: Chopin, Liszt, and Thalberg. Thalberg was a wonderfully correct and brilliant player, but without great musical distinction. His most conspicuous trick consisted in declamating [i.e., declaiming] a melody with the thumb and surrounding the theme with most brilliant scales, *arpeggios,* passages, etc. Even this device he took from Parish Alvars, the famous harpist, who deserves lasting memory, as even the great Richard seems to have used it, translating this musically effective scheme for grand orchestra in his *Tannhäuser* Overture.[3] What a contrasting, nay inverted, scheme is this to Liszt, to introduce the grand orchestra, or at least orchestral effects to the piano! A Hungarian instrument, the cimbalom, inspired him to the invention of interlocking octaves, with which he achieved his greatest effects.

What Chopin did for his instrument is too well known to dwell upon it. He was the seraph and the demon of the piano, he opened a new range of human and superhuman emotions, he invented a new world of harmonies and was besides one of the very greatest melodic inventors of all times. He also invented new passages compared with which all others sound a trifle commonplace, and he played them in the most refined, finished style, for which he used the velvetlike, delicate *legatissimo,* which secrets his pupil, Mikuli, my teacher, held [i.e., took] from him and which he imparted to his pupils.

This *legatissimo* sounds infinitely more dignified, elegant, aristocratic than the commonplace half-staccato (*jeu perlé*) which is now almost generally used and abused, and of which already Beethoven had made fun, speaking derisively of "dancing fingers."

My teachers, Mikuli and later Joseffy, delighted my ear with their almost infinite dynamic range from *piano* to *pianissimo* and *pianississimo,* but they left my thirst for big orchestral effects unquenched, which I sought, found, and learned first when I was fourteen years old from the old thunderer in Weimar and Rome, Franz Liszt. But I learned much more from him than mere piano playing. In spite of a sometimes surprising pedantry as to pianistic cleanness and accuracy, he saw all with the eye of the composer, and made us feel the same way. These were unforgettable days at Weimar and Rome, and we drank deeply from the intoxicating draughts the old wizard and alluring composer brewed for us. But in spite of all these splendors, after seven years I grew weary, like Tannhäuser at the Venusberg. A new desire, a new thirst tormented me! I had heard Anton Rubinstein!

In the "Triumvirate" of Chopin, Liszt, and Thalberg, Chopin holds easily the place of Caesar Octavianus, Liszt the place of Antonius (with many Cleopatras!), and Thalberg of Lepidus.[4] We could easily dismiss Thalberg from his exalted position, replacing his name with that of Anton Rubinstein. It is true that Rubinstein was lacking in finesse of execution and even to a certain extent of interpretation, and that his passages were often blurred beyond recognition, but the heroic vein of his style, his colossal climaxes, and in the first place his compositions gave him claim to true greatness. Moreover, he was to my knowledge the first pianist who introduced the syncopated pedal to his readings.

This may sound incredible to the younger generation of pianists who learned the right use of pedals almost in their cradles, who were told almost when they began to study that one should not strike keys and pedal simultaneously. They were told to come down with the foot on the pedal at the very moment when they raise the hands from the keys in order to avoid blurs and to keep a continuous flow of the melodic line, keeping the sound ringing now with the hands, now with the pedal, without break. I can prove it by a letter which Liszt wrote to Louis Köhler, the well-known piano pedagogue and musical critic, in July 1875. When Köhler sent him a copy of his technical studies, where he introduced some exercises for the syncopated pedal, Liszt answers with the following lines (I omit the beginning of the letter as not pertinent to our theme): "Best thanks for your kindly letter and for sending your Opus 147: 'Technische Künstler-Studien.' And although I am more disposed to turn away from than toward Methods and Pedagogics, still I have read this work of yours with interest. *The entrance of the pedal after the striking of the chords as indicated by you at the beginning of page three, and as consistently carried through by you almost to the utmost extreme, seems to me an ingenious idea, the application of which is greatly to be recommended to pianoforte players, teachers and composers—especially in slow tempi.*"[5]

This letter proves beyond any doubt that Liszt, the supreme ruler over the piano, did not use the syncopated pedal, but not only this: It proves that he did not even grasp the immense importance of the discovery when it was brought to him by Louis Köhler.

Who invented the syncopated pedal? Mikuli, and consequently Chopin, did not know it. Köhler does not put forth any claim for the discovery, nor did Rubinstein.[6] The great benefactor and inventor deserves to be immortalized. I consider the syncopated pedal to be one of the most important discoveries because it promotes music and makes true musical readings possible. It constitutes the high-water mark between a glorious past and a more glorious future. No more painstaking fingering for *legato* chords, no more dry playing without pedals and without overtones, in order to avoid blurs. The syncopated pedal signifies the emancipation from dry or blurred tone, the emancipation of wrist and arm from sticking to the keys; it constitutes true orchestral playing; in its unbroken *cantilena,* it is superior even to other musical instruments and to the exhaustible human voice.

I called this discovery one of the most important in the history of piano playing. Alas, it was also so far the last one! The methods of Breithaupt and others are not only for the most part distressingly erroneous, they are also derived from the methods of Deppe, Caland and others, published about fifty years ago.[7]

After having stated the merits and the shortcomings of the methods of Chopin, Liszt, Thalberg, and Rubinstein, it seems very easy to answer the question: What progress has been made by and what are the characteristics of the *new* school of piano playing; that is, the school of the younger generation of pianists? The answer must be the following: There is no such thing in existence as a "new school of piano playing." The mere fact that one has not studied with Liszt, that one has not heard the Chopin school, and that one has never been privileged to listen to Rubinstein is a colossal drawback and can never constitute in its helpless negativity any claim to distinction or greatness. Having missed the great Triumvirate Liszt-Chopin-Rubinstein, the pianists of the younger generation are bound to learn from those of us who had the great privilege to study directly or indirectly with these pianistic and musical giants. If they choose to turn away from us they will not harm *us,* but *themselves.*

They may boast of their youth! But who is really young? I may turn for an answer to my favorite philosopher, namely to myself. I gave long ago the following definition: a man is *young* if a lady can make him happy or unhappy. He enters from the age of the stage lovers to the *middle-aged* bon vivant class if a lady can make him happy but no more unhappy. He is *old* and gone if a lady can make him neither happy nor unhappy.

Well, after all, I am still young!

19 Review of a Concert by M. R.

The New Age, August 5, 1926

Kaikhosru Sorabji

I know no great pianist of Rosenthal's rank and importance who is more unsat-
isfactory, uneven and so curiously deficient. In the last Beethoven Sonata and
the Chopin B Minor, one was irritated almost beyond endurance at the flabby
shapelessness of his phrases, the floppy, sagging rhythm, the general looseness
of texture of the playing, and the lack of grip and clear-cut conception of the
work as a whole, to say nothing of the false emphasis, magnification and exaggeration of subsidiary and secondary matter, almost complete loss of sight of
ground-plan, noisy muddy climaxes, degenerating into mere welter, a dead,
hard, dry tone—due in a certain measure to a very indifferent piano and an
almost entire lack of living, vital quality in the playing generally. This is, as far
as I am concerned, no new experience with Rosenthal's playing, and every time
I hear him I am more confirmed in my original opinion of him, formed some
fourteen or fifteen years ago, as the salon-player *in excelsis,* but in no sense a
great interpretative artist. In light elegancies he is matchless; and the polish,
grace and charm of his playing in things like his own delicious and monstrously
intricate "Carnaval Viennois," for instance, in debonair *désinvolture* are inde-
scribable. His sense and feeling for the lilt of the Strauss waltz-rhythm are incomparable, and scarcely is it possible to sit still under the buoyant intoxication
of the thing at his hands. In these things and his own "Papillons" he is enchanting beyond words—his qualities of miraculously clear, rapid and crystalline
finger work and his urbane aristocratic style are seen at their very best. Singularly enough, his playing of "Triana" of Albéniz was stiff and stilted; for one
had imagined that this music would have suited his style to perfection.

Kaikhosru Shapurji Sorabji (1892–1988) was a Parsi-English composer, critic, and writer on music
famous for allowing performances of his music only upon his consent, which he almost never gave.
His collected published writings have been brought out by the Sorabji Archive (Bath, England,
1995).

Karol Mikuli.

Rafael Joseffy.

Liszt and his pupils, on his 73rd birthday, October 22, 1884: Front row: Saul Liebling, Alexander Siloti, Arthur Friedheim, Emil von Sauer, Alfred Reisenauer, Alexander Gottschalg. Back row: Moriz Rosenthal, Viktoria Drewing, Mele Paramanov, Franz Liszt, Friedheim's mother, Hugo Mansfeldt. Photo by Louis Held, Weimar.

Moriz Rosenthal, 1888.

Silhouette by Hans Schließman, ca. 1890.

Moriz Rosenthal playing chess, 1930s. Photo courtesy of *Musical America*.

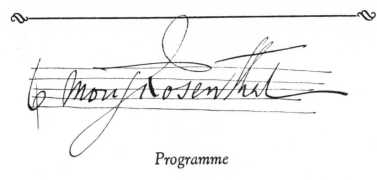

Programme

✍

LUDWIG VAN BEETHOVEN.....Sonata in E major, Opus 109
          Vivace ma non troppo
          Prestissimo
          Andante con variazioni

FRANZ SCHUBERT..........Wanderer Fantasy, Opus 15

FRÉDÉRIC CHOPIN ....Nocturne in D flat major, Opus 27,
          No. 2
          Barcarole in F sharp major, Opus 60
          Two Etudes
          Mazurka
          Waltz in A flat major, Opus 42

ISAAC ALBENIZ.............Triana

FRANZ LISZT ....Hungarian Rhapsody, No. 2

MR. ROSENTHAL uses the KNABE Piano

Program performed at the Curtis Institute of Music, Philadelphia, on
February 8, 1928.

Moriz Rosenthal, 1938.

Seventy-fifth birthday concert, December 19, 1937, during a reception after performing
with the NBC Symphony: Rosina Lhévinne (wearing brooch), Josef Hofmann, Adele Kanner
Rosenthal, Moriz Rosenthal, Ernest Schelling, Josef Lhévinne.

20 Letter to Herbert Hughes

September 9, 1927

M. R.

My dear friend,

I was very happy to receive your charming letter, which I will answer immediately in spite of being confined to bed for several days. Kindly excuse my handwriting! First of all: Many hearty thanks for your kind intention to dedicate to me such an important work, as your Chopin-book will undoubtedly turn out. I regard this as a most fascinating and convincing proof of your friendship.

Let me now try to answer your both questions, from several points of view:

1) Who of all Chopin pupils was the most important one? Chopin himself was easily influenced by personal predilections. Very likely no pupil could satisfy such an incomparable master. It is very queer that he confined himself in his teaching strictly to piano playing, that he never discussed with his pupils the merits or shortcomings of his or others' compositions, contrary to the teaching of Liszt, who dwelled more upon the music itself than the manner how it was interpreted. His love for piano technique was so outspoken, that he writes in the last year of his life: Nothing has come forth from my efforts except my long nose and my badly cultivated fourth finger!

This seems to me a proof that he did not think much of his pupils in a musical way. On the other hand, it is reported by all his friends and contemporary musicians that he was hugely interested in the art of piano playing, where he was a worthy rival of the greatest pianists, whereas as a composer he certainly was without a peer, namely after the year 1828, in spite of Schumann's greatness. Wagner belongs to quite another type. (Beethoven died in 1827, Schubert in 1828.)

His favorite pupils were: Gutmann, and "La princesse" Marcelina Czartoryska from Kraków, Poland.[1]

Gutmann was not only his pupil, Chopin treated him as a friend. He was also on terms with G.'s family. It is reported that he was the guest of the G. family and that they treated him like he would have been a King or an Emperor. (Only?!)

When Moscheles came to Paris (around 1839) Chopin was very anxious:

Herbert Hughes (1882–1937) was an Irish-born composer and critic. At this time he was writing a biography of Chopin, but on May 1, 1937, he died after a short illness, with the work unfinished.

Moscheles should hear the titanic Scherzo op. 39 in C-sharp Minor. Being too weak then (it was, if I am not mistaken, shortly after the trying Majorca episode) to play it, he conferred this honor to Gutmann.

Gutmann had only one day's time to prepare it but came off, if not with flying colors, nevertheless in a decent way. He excused himself with the short time of his preparation, but Chopin declined his excuses with the words: "Of course, if you will play it better than anyone else in this world," etc.

Wilhelm [von] Lenz, the biographer of Beethoven and for a short time one of the lesser pupils of Chopin, told me in St. Petersburg, where I concertized as a boy in 1879: Gutmann had no poetry nor "finesse." He pleased Chopin by his mere strength (!?) The first chord in the C-sharp Minor Scherzo (left hand) was only possible for the prize-fighter fist ("Klopffechterfaust" in German) of Gutmann. Therefore the dedication to Gutmann.[2]

So far Lenz, who printed also this nonsense in a short study on Chopin. As a matter of fact, this chord is only difficult or rather impossible with the fingering Lenz seems to have employed [5–4–3–2–1] but becomes very easy for normal hands with the fingering Chopin has very likely invented and Liszt has taught. It is the following: [5–4–2–1–1].

It seems and stands to reason that Chopin dedicated the Scherzo to Gutmann for his artistic services in the affair with Moscheles. On the other hand, it is reported that Chopin, asked if Gutmann makes good progress, coolly answered: "Yes, he makes an excellent [hot] chocolate" (referring to some breakfast, taken in company with Gutmann). The success of Gutmann as a concert pianist seems to have been rather mediocre. Surely the world has judged him less favorably than his great teacher and friend.

Marcelina, Princesse Czartoryska! Here I can speak *as an eye- and ear-witness.*

When I concertized in Kraków (Poland) as a 13-year-old boy, Director Skarzynski introduced myself to the Princess, who dwelled in the suburbs in a palace. I remember her "Erard," which had a very light action. I played for her the "Campanella" and then the first movement of the E Minor Concerto by Chopin. The Princess was good enough to give me a bit of "true tradition" in playing for me a part of the concerto beginning at the second theme in E. The *cantilena* seemed to me a little too slow and a bit too stiff. When the difficult passage part began, the noble Lady resigned from further playing with the Polish words "i tak dalej," which means "et caetera."

It is sure that the origin and the illustrious name of the "grande Dame" had considerable influence on Chopin's judgment.

There was *one* pupil of Chopin, whom the Master mentions only once with the words: "*Mikuli* will present you my letter." Or something like.

I must confess that I consider Mikuli as the most important of all pupils of Chopin. I made his acquaintance or rather was introduced to him when I was a boy of *10*. I studied under his personal care and guidance for two years and heard him very often. I never heard such a perfect *legatissimo*. It was an inheritance of his great master, and he gave me the secret, how to study it, at the beginning of his teaching. The roundness and elegance of his passages were admirable. He refrained from any *forte* and *fortissimo*. His musical insight he proved by his edition of the works of Chopin (Edition Kistner, Leipzig). There is only one other pupil of Chopin who edited the works of his master: Tellefsen, a Norwegian.[3] But after all, I cannot refrain from thinking that the pride of place amongst all pupils of Chopin belongs to Charles Mikuli, Director of the Conservatory in Lemberg (my native town).

By the way: Mikuli was not a Pole! He was born in Bukovina, a province situated between Galicia (a part of Poland) and Romania.[4] Other pupils of significance were: Jeanne Stirling (Scotland) with her big heart and her immortal love for Chopin. The most beautiful "Delfina Potocka," then: Schulhoff, the composer, (Brinsley [sic] Richards?), Stamaty, Edouard Wolff, the composer, and many others known by the dedications of Chopin (Miss Caraman, Miss Maberly, and others). Hallé heard and saw him often, but was not his pupil.[5]

2) *George Sand!*[6]

Facts known: She was an offspring of the Maréchal de Saxe, her maiden name was Aurora Dudevant [sic], she married the writer Sandeau, got a divorce (unless I am mistaken), and took the name of George Sand. She wrote a multitude of Romances, Novels, and Dramas (*Lélia, Consuelo, La Comtesse de Rudolstadt, François le Champi, Lucrezia Floriani*) and the autobiographical *Histoire de ma vie*. Her lovers were quite numerous and belonged often to the highest aristocracy of genius. The most famous was naturally Chopin, then came Alfred de Musset,[7] whom she betrayed (when he fell ill in Venise) with his physician. Liszt and Heine were her friends (*platoniquement!*), and Heine defended her against malevolent gossip. It was, I believe in the year 1837, when George Sand expressed her wish to Liszt to make the acquaintance of Chopin. Liszt fulfilled her request, and Chopin seemed somewhat repelled by her appearance and manly manners. Later on he accepted her invitation to the castle of Nohant, where she resided, and a "liaison" began, which lasted until 1844 (error possible as I am far from all books in this village!). In 1838 G. S. went to Majorca, one of the Balearic Islands under Spanish Dominion. She took with her her children, "Maurice" and "Solange" (daughter), and—Chopin. Utmost secrecy prevailed. They met at Marseilles and took the ship together. The *cargo* were mainly pigs, which annoyed Chopin very much. They found at last (after changements) some quiet quarters at the old monastery of Valdemosa. Here in those unsheltered damp dwellings Chopin caught a terrible cold, was badly treated by some stupid physicians, and nearly escaped death 10 years before his real *exitus*. In the spring of 1839 he returned to Marseilles, where he was very wisely treated by Doctor Corvisart and returned with G. S. to Paris. It seems that from the date of his illness her feelings for him died slowly. She called him jestingly "mon cher cadavre," which joke seems to me of bad taste and worse augur. Their love cooled down more and more. There are Polish writers like B. Szarlitt, who even pretend that Chopin fell more or less in love with Solange, the daughter of G. S. I looked up the whole correspondence of Chopin with Solange and with other people about Solange, but could not find a single word justifying this bold and queer assertion. The truth seems to be that Chopin disagreed with G. Sand's plans, to marry Solange with the sculptor Clésinger,[8] that later on he sided with Solange against "George," and that he stopped further relations with her after she had not answered his letter or letters. It seems that he saw her the last time, when he met her at the staircase of Mme Marliani. He was able to give her the news of her "grandmothership" as Solange had had a child without informing her mother of this event. He congratulated her and left her after bowing very politely. And this was the end!

[Chopin, letter to Solange Clésinger, Paris, March 5, 1848:

> Yesterday I went to Mme Marliani, and as I left, I met your Mother in the doorway of the vestibule; she was entering with Lambert. I said good day to your Mother, and my second phrase was: had she had any news of you lately.—"A week ago," she replied.—"You have heard nothing yesterday, or the day before?"—"No."—"Then I can tell you that you are a grandmother; Solange has a daughter, and I am very glad that I am able to be the first to give you this news." I bowed and went downstairs. Combes the Abyssinian (who has tumbled right into the Revolution on arriving from Morocco) was with me, and as I had forgotten to say that you are doing well, an important thing, especially for a mother (now you will easily understand that, Mother Solange), I asked Combes to go up again, as I could not manage the stairs, and tell her that you are *going on well*, and the child too. I was waiting for the Abyssinian at the bottom of the stairs when your Mother came down with him and put to me, with much interest, some questions about your health. I answered that you had written me a few words, *yourself, in pencil,* the day after the birth of your child, that you have suffered much, but that the sight of your little daughter has made you forget everything. She asked me whether your husband was with you, and I replied that the address of your letter appeared to me to be in his handwriting. She asked me how I am; I replied that I am well, and asked the *concierge* to open the door. I bowed, and found myself in the Square d'Orléans on foot, escorted by the Abyssinian.[9]]

As my opinion G. Sand understood to a high degree the true greatness of Chopin. She was fully conscious of his unlimited powers of thematic invention and of the dynamic or dynamite-force of his musical ideas. But she was hypocrite to a degree, spoke to her lovers of her "maternal" love, and in *Lucrezia Floriani* she reaches the pinnacle of her selfish *hypocrisia*. In this Romance she painted herself as "Lucrezia" and gave the picture of Prince Karl, her lover, some Chopin-like traces. "Lucrezia" is so chaste that it needs a third person, who closes his arms around the loving couple, to bring them together!! As far as my knowledge and conviction goes, Chopin loved only once, and the object of his love was Constantia Gladkowska. He did not love G. S. with his fervent imagination! He had learned to like her presence, he loved Nohant for the quiet time it gave him for his work, and after all: his greatest and unique love was devoted to his creations. Think of the sublime happiness which uplifts us, when we hear his music, and you may conceive what storms they caused in *his* the creator's heart and brain! There has not been left much for George Sand, Maria Wodzinska, especially after the honey-moons and honey-years of their "liaison."

I have answered your both questions explicitly. Here at Bagnoles I am far from any books about Chopin, and I have to rely on my memory, which is not quite so faithful as that of some contemporaneous composers.[10]

The resort, where I am now, is called in full: Bagnoles de l'Orne, France (Orne) and I live at the "Grand Hôtel." You may get this long letter in two days (11th of Sept.), and I may get a line of you, say the 13th Sept.?

I send to you both my loving greetings and to Angela my "respectueux hommages." [etc.]

21 Moriz Rosenthal–Emil Sauer: and Modern Pianism

1927

Edward Prime-Stevenson

Mr. Moriz Rosenthal, unobtrusively confident of bearing, *dégagé* as ever, occupies local musical attention lately, to no small purport. Since Mr. Rosenthal's previous pianistic campaign hereabouts, where has he roved, busily? Has he been touring not only the Far East, and Australia, but also Mars, Jupiter, the Solar System, the Great Nebula in Andromeda?—always being—probably—best (or next-best) advertised virtuoso of this world. Meanwhile a good deal of water has streamed under the pianistic mill-wheel. That effulgent artist, Mr. Paderewski, not to mention Mr. Vladimir de Pachmann, particularly will be thought of, as planets newly swum into our ken—two potent rivals. But Mr. Rosenthal has not to fear comparisons with anybody. His reputation has been attaining only greater breadth, confirmation on merits. Time has added to him more than one indispensable trait of a superior pianist, including fuller interpretative authority. Yet Mr. Rosenthal, so far as concerns his largest public, probably comes back to notice from connoisseurs and setters-up of standards, in the aspect of the grand demon of the clavier, the arch-technicist of an ever intractable and defective instrument!—as the one man alive who seems to find nothing so hard to play that he cannot make us think it trivial of his effort. He is the pianist whose ten fingers appear to be able to function as twenty; as the almost superhuman artist, concealing his art to the degree of suggesting that there is only fluent, elegant recreation in a player's dealing with difficulties to appall the majority of his profession. Once on a time, an excited Italian swore that he had seen Satan behind Paganini, guiding the violinist's bow and doing some of his "double-stoppings" for him. When a certain great coloratura singer, of the last century, was warbling away, one evening, in *cadenze* and floridities that seemed beyond the powers of mortal larynx, a gallery auditor called at the end of a trill,

From *Long-Haired Iopas: Old Chapters from Twenty-five Years of Music-Criticism* (Florence: Privately printed for the author by the press of *The Italian Mail*, 1927; based, in part, on an article published in *Harper's Weekly*, November 28, 1896). Edward Prime-Stevenson (1858–1942) was an American writer known chiefly for his novel *Imre: A Memorandum* (1906), which has been brought out by Broadview Press in a new edition by James Gifford.

"Damn her! She has a nest of nightingales in her—stomach!" When Carl Tausig, the steel-fingered and infallible Carl Tausig, was playing a Liszt Polonaise, in the presence of its author and of Peter Cornelius, Cornelius exclaimed that Tausig kept on "knocking us all down with his superhuman octaves."[1] A Polish concert-goer went about declaring that Liszt possessed "a secret machine" of some sort, hidden in his pianoforte, to manage with a prodigious readiness the effects of execution demanded by Liszt's more intricate show-pieces.

Ideas of the same sort may well come to the imagination of one who listens to Rosenthal. There is nothing whatever suggesting, as was the case with Paganini, an unearthly physical personality. Quite the contrary. This fattish, comfortable-looking, matter-of-fact type of Teutonic, or Magyar, Hebrew, crosses the platform. He sits down, not behind a ledger or exchange counter, but before a pianoforte. What agreeably everyday, inartistic, unassuming demeanor! But after a few minutes, we realize that the ancient demoniac virtuosity is there! Busy before us with such a thing as Ludwig Schytte's Concerto in C-sharp Minor; or with the player's own arrangement of Chopin's Waltz in D-flat Major, where Rosenthal's thirds and sixths and octaves take the place of most of the original single notes; or with his own stupendously effective adaptation of Johann Strauss's dance-themes, concerted into a fabric of gossamer lightness and terrific difficulties,—taken at lightning-dash speed,—he amazes the hearer, first and last. One has the impression that eight hands, instead of two, are delivering those wonderful coruscations of sound. And the wonder grows with each such exhibition. This plump wizard of the Danube-region appears not even mundane. . . . Are his hands really rather like the pair in your lap? Like hands that never play the piano at all? Apparently so. Yet Rosenthal seems a creature who has his fingers everywhere and anywhere at once; hands without right or left to be differentiated. It is the veritable ambidexterity, and far beyond. The most intricate pianoforte writing is mocked by them. Octaves are counted technical stubble, as were clubs by Job's hippopotamus.[2] So are details much more bothersome than octaves. Is he executing that limpid, crystalline trill by way of *four* of his fingers of the same hand?—a double trill in thirds? Quite likely—you cease to guess, to wonder. Every shade of dynamics is heard. Everything is equalized, kept in exquisite proportion. There is seldom great excess of sound. The pedaling is perfection. The fact that the player's hands are so separated that right may be excused from knowing what the left is doing, while at the same time one gets the impression that something besides may be in activities between them, reminds one of the old story of Weber, with his long nose; and of the bet which Weber won from a brother-pianist, resourcefully striking a certain absurd "middle-note," with his olfactory organ, when both arms were extended at opposite ends of the pianoforte. But there is no trickery in Rosenthal. Within an hour or so of his pianism, we believe the impossible, because of what we ourselves have thus seen and heard.

It must not, however, be gathered that Mr. Rosenthal is a mere human machine at his pianoforte—an incarnated firework. Rosenthal is today, as ever he was, a superior intellect in his art; often is a delightfully poetic, even *simple* pianist. He is a great music-interpreter, as well as a great executant. Beethoven, Liszt, Schumann, Brahms are delivered by him with impeccable analysis, as well as unsurpassed technic. He has varied and magnificent tone. Few pianists play Mozart more purely, with more delicate sentiment—with as much of what Germans call *innig* quality.[3] In Bach's music Rosenthal is a luxury. And in the more romantic and temperamental composers, as might be expected, he constantly shows his fine insights. Still, it is to be particularized, today as yesterday, that Mr. Rosenthal is a playing-king in the demesne of the great technicists in music-writing. By such pianoforte-music flashes out his individuality. Therewith is Mr. Rosenthal unique, or nearly so, among contemporary pianists of the first rank and genius. If tomorrow he should retire from public work, there is but a single pianist or so, in as general recognition, all the world about, who could, in the language of the Arabian romancers, "warm himself at his fire." In technique, Mr. Rosenthal occasionally can be even closely approached; but he is still une-qualled, supreme, unique, as a sort of changeless phenomenon of virtuosity. . . .

22 Schumann's *Carnaval*

M. R.

Part 1
Etude, November 1932

*This work was one of Rosenthal's specialties, for he rightly under-
stood it as "not only a musical but also a literary conception, a
kind of esoteric autobiography in sounds." Philip Hale, one of
the most sympathetic and enlightened of American critics, wrote
that a performance of the work by Rosenthal in 1898 "was
throughout the most satisfactory of all performances of this
much abused work heard here for the last ten years."*

> *For once you did not watch the program—dolefully when the pianist was
> not beyond "Coquette"—hopefully when he arrived at "Promenade"—
> thankfully when the march against the Philistines began to thunder. The
> work for once seemed as though it were one inspiration; with all the
> varying moods, you were conscious of a firm and coherent design. There
> was a true carnival, and the maskers were sharply characterized. You
> never mistook Eusebius for Florestan, and when Chopin appeared, the
> strange apparition searching for his ideal and singing that unearthly
> melody, you were not obliged to ask, "Who is that gentleman?" (Un-
> dated clipping)*

> *Into the program booklet for his recital at Carnegie Hall in No-
> vember 1906, Rosenthal had inserted an extra page containing his
> own poetic program for Schumann's* Carnaval. *We do not know
> when Rosenthal wrote the program, or if he included it in other con-
> cert booklets; probably he did. In any case, excerpts from this note
> included in reviews of Rosenthal's performance suggest that it is
> both better written and more interesting than the "lesson" on the*
> Carnaval *that Rosenthal published in the* Etude.

. . .

We spoke of the worship of Schumann for Chopin, for Clara, and for
Ernestine, who all three were implicated and celebrated in *Carnaval*. But there
was one man, a colossus among poets, whom Schumann extolled to the stars,

and whom he placed side by side with Ludwig van Beethoven, his hero among musicians. The name of this incomparable writer was Jean Paul Friedrich Richter (pen name, Jean Paul) who was born at Wunsiedel, 1763, and who died at Bayreuth in 1825. His imagination, his humor, his poetry created a sensation in Germany. Even such men as Goethe and Schiller said of him that he would be worthy of their admiration if he would dispose of his richness "with the same care as other writers did of their poverty."

When Schumann, at a congress at Vienna, gave a toast praising two great men as supermen of the German people, Beethoven and Jean Paul, an immediate protest, not without basis, came from Grädener against the coupling of these two names, the infinite superiority of Beethoven being pointed out.[1] Schumann, offended and wounded in his love for Jean Paul, left the assembly precipitately without further word.

The masterpiece of Jean Paul is a romance called *Flegeljahre*, which title, not literally translatable, means "years of hot, impetuous and stormy youth."[2] Schumann admired this work to such an extent that he wrote to Clara, "Read the *Flegeljahre*! It is a book like the Bible!" The influence of this work on Schumann is obvious. It is a tale with two heroes who, by the way, are twin brothers named Vult and Walt. Like Goethe's Faust, Jean Paul felt two different souls in his bosom; he divided his "ego" into two parts. Vult is the brilliant one, full of humor, witticism, and sarcasm, a widely famous virtuoso on the flute, a seducer in the grand manner, full of poetry but ruling over his poetic sentiments by means of his enormous intellect. Walt is wholly the poet and is extricated and saved from the nets of this bad world by Vult's greater knowledge, wisdom, and experience. Both the flutist and the poet love the same girl, Wina, the daughter of a general, but Wina gives her heart away to Walt. Vult, becoming aware that he has lost on the highest stake of his life, decides to leave Wina and Walt. So when, one night, Walt consults his brother, Vult, about the significance of a wild dream he has just had, Vult answers that he (Walt) will hear the meaning of this dream through his (Vult's) flute, a meaning which will pierce even into Walt's new dreams. Vult leaves the house and Walt hears soon the sounds of the flute from afar without knowing that those melodies carry away his beloved brother forever. The romance comes to an end at this point.

I have had to dwell so explicitly on Jean Paul and his *Flegeljahre* because here we find the literary key to the innermost musical feelings of Schumann. Some of his first works he edited under the assumed names, Florestan and Eusebius. These figures also appear in *Carnaval*. Florestan is the musical personification of Vult, but it must be confessed that he remains very much behind his fascinating model. He seems, in comparison, clumsy, lawless like the University students of Schumann's time, a little noisy, and without the grace of Jean Paul's Vult. On the other hand, we feel the highest enthusiasm for Walt's descendant, Eusebius. Out of the ballroom and the dancing crowd he steps into the moonlight, dreaming of beauties which are not of his world. And it seems characteristic of the poet and dreamer, Schumann, that the exquisite lyrical moments of Eusebius have a more masterly portrayal than the wild moods of Florestan.

Carnaval... was played in part for the first time at Leipzig by my teacher, the great master, Franz Liszt, at his concert in this city [in 1840]. Liszt played it practically at first sight in spite of the dissuading of Schumann who expressed his fear that the public would not be pleased by the piece. But Liszt's confidence remained unshaken and, sure of his own great and entrancing powers but taking care nonetheless not to tire the public, he played only a few selected numbers from the composition.[3]

Yet, in spite of all his efforts, the audience would not grow enthusiastic, but remained so frosty that Liszt gave up the playing of Schumann in all his recitals thereafter. For instance, when Schumann dedicated to him his standard work, the *Fantasie,* Liszt acknowledged the honor by dedicating to Schumann in return his great Sonata in B Minor, but he did not perform the *Fantasie* in public.[4] Later on, after the death of Schumann, Liszt apologized in a letter to Wasielewski, the Schumann biographer, for his neglect which bore bad fruit among Liszt's imitators.[5]

But even without this example, Schumann and the average virtuoso would always have remained somewhat distant strangers. Schumann's *Fantasie,* his *Kreisleriana,* his *Humoreske* are from intellectual and soulful points of view three high snow peaks which remain inaccessible for the ordinary climber. It is much easier to captivate the larger public through the medium of the *Etudes symphoniques* and, of course, our *Carnaval.*

* * *

Part 3
Etude, January 1933

. . .

21. "Marche des 'Davidsbündler' contre les Philistins":[6] The two words "Davidsbündler" and "Philistins" should be explained. Let us begin with the latter. *"Philister"* as it is called in German has a double meaning. In the first place it alludes to the old notion of the Philistines of Phoenicia who were continually fighting against the Israelites. But the German students called everybody a "Philistine" who cared only for his purely physical needs and joys, who held ideals in contempt, and who strived for low pleasures and personal welfare rather than for transcendental ideas and high poetry or art. In the opinion of Schumann, who was for a long time a student at the University, every musician who did not strive for high ideals belonged to the crowd of old-fashioned Philistines. He imagined therefore an alliance, a confederacy of enemies of the Philistine crowd, and nominated as members of this ideal club Florestan, Eusebius, himself, great progressive musicians and poets. As the Biblical King David was the enemy of the Philistines and killed the Philistine giant, Goliath, Schumann called his alliance (in German called "Bund") "Davidsbund," and its members "Davidsbündler." It is now clear that his "Marche" depicts or illustrates a decisive battle of the flaming, youthful music against the oldish, out-fashioned art of bygone days.

The proof that this is not a true march, but rather a warlike assault, a battle, is demonstrated by the fact that every march before it was written in double or quadruple rhythm, whereas this one is in triple rhythm. Furthermore, after majestic and tremendous marching, the tempo becomes faster and finally about three times as quick as in other marches. The "Philistines" are characterized by the eighteenth-century melody: "When Grandpapa married Grandmamma." They are knocked on the head by the "Davidsbündler," who seem to use, anachronistically, cannon. The climax Schumann reaches in this flamboyant piece is astonishing! He, the tender lyric poet, becomes a hundred-armed giant, a true hero, a Napoleon of music. Of the greatest climaxes in the literature of the piano, three belong to Schumann: the Finale of the *Carnaval,* the Finale of the *Symphonic Etudes,* and the Finale of his *Fantasie,* second movement. In this respect only Chopin and Liszt can be regarded as his rivals, and nobody as his superior. The execution of this piece requires a fire of glowing temperament, imagination, and much sheer strength and technic, besides a peculiar art for bringing forth a perpetually rising climax—qualities which we find seldom combined.[7]

Robert Schumann considered his *Carnaval* more as a temperamental outburst, as poetically interesting, but he preferred by far his tender moods as they appear, for instance, in the *Davidsbündlertänze* or in the *Kreisleriana.* In his letters to his bride, Clara Wieck, whom he married five years later, he exhorts her to concentrate herself on those pieces rather than on the *Carnaval.* But at other times when "old Wieck" called him phlegmatic,[8] he revolts against this (ridiculous) judgment and writes to Clara, "*Carnaval,* Sonata op. 11, and phlegmatic?" He knew probably very well that the *Carnaval* was one of his important steps toward the heights of immortality.

It seems amazing that this most popular piece, played by thousands of amateurs and performed publicly by hundreds of pianists, should remain for almost all of them a riddle, a literary enigma. The names of Eusebius, Florestan, Chiarina, Estrella, are for them empty sounds. But Schumann is never to conquer by fleet fingers and a loose wrist alone. For him your worship and love and the flights of your soul! (If you have them.)

In his highest moments Schumann is as deep, as solitary, as ecstatic, as exalted and exalting as Beethoven in his last works, and, as long as music is heard and loved, he will be admired and worshipped as one of its noblest heralds and prophets.[9]

23 Anton Rubinstein's Concert in Pressburg

Neue Freie Presse, April 23, 1933

M. R.

In 1885, a memorable concert took place in a city that was not yet called Bratislava.[1] It was still the historic Pressburg where Empress Maria Theresia, before her wars with Frederick the Great, appeared before the Hungarian parliament pleading for help, and where the valiant Hungarians, in exuberant enthusiasm, broke into the heroic shout: "We shall die for our Queen." It was in Pressburg that Johann Nepomuk Hummel was born in 1778, the man who—with his splendid Sonata in F-sharp Minor—thought himself worthy of a contest with Beethoven. Now, in the loyal city of his birth, a monument was to be erected to him, and Anton Rubinstein had agreed to contribute to it in a concert that would include his monumental piano playing.

One fine morning [in Vienna], my friend and guardian, Ludwig van Bösendorfer the Piano Mogul, as Bülow called him, asked me: "Would you like to go to Pressburg with me this afternoon? Rubinstein is going to play there for the Hummel monument, and (here his voice sank to a *pianissimo* whisper) *Liszt is also going to be at the concert!*" Overjoyed, I accepted and hurried home to rummage in the drawers of old desks until I found a letter of introduction addressed (in Cyrillic characters) "To Anton Grigor'evich Rubinstein" and signed "Ivan Turgenev."

I had met Turgenev, together with Saint-Saëns and Gounod, at the Paris home of that most musical of all singers, Mme. Pauline Viardot-Garcia, when I played for her as a so-called child prodigy and brought her the compliments of Franz Liszt.[2]

Armed with my letter of introduction and an overnight bag, I picked up Bösendorfer at his study on the Herrengasse and drove to the East Terminal, where we found Rubinstein in a first-class compartment. The titan of the piano greeted us with kindness and took some pains to make room for us in the compartment, which was virtually stuffed with admiring traveling companions. He then read with interest the letter from Turgenev (who had recently died), all the

---

Fritz A. Kuttner's "free translation" from the German was published as "The Night Rubinstein Played Bratislava" (*Stereo Review,* August 1971).

while asking questions about my concerts in St. Petersburg and my studies with Liszt. From his subsequent remarks, I learned that he, of course, admitted Liszt's enormous merits of technique, brilliance, and pianistic virtuosity, but conceded him less musical quality in general.

In Pressburg Rubinstein was led in triumph by the Monument Committee to the Hotel Palugyai, while Bösendorfer and I stayed at the railway station to wait for Liszt, who was coming from Budapest. When the master put his snow-white head out of the compartment window and waved to us, Bösendorfer exclaimed enthusiastically: "Now comes the King!" And I, who had traveled with Rubinstein from Vienna to Pressburg, was now riding with Liszt, whose good will touched me as we drove from the station to his quarters.

Reflecting on Liszt's conduct toward Rubinstein, I feel that it was an act of magnificent kindness and *esprit de corps* that he, at the age of seventy-three, undertook the four-hour trip from Budapest to Pressburg, spent the night in unfamiliar surroundings, and returned the following day to Budapest—he did all that to hear Rubinstein and to show his admiration. But not everybody seemed to feel likewise. I overheard two elderly gentlemen saying that Liszt would now hear, for once, a rival of equal or possibly even superior rank. But Liszt had merely to appear in the hall to be overwhelmed by hundreds of shouts of "*Éljen*" [Hungarian: *Viva!*] and enthusiastic cheers.

After a short while, the evening's lion, Anton the Great, stepped out on the stage, flanked by six trusty musicians, for Hummel's Septet was to open the evening. After this came Hummel's Sonata for Four Hands, in which Rubinstein left the treble part to his boyhood friend Leschetizky while he limited himself to the bass. "Limited" is perhaps the wrong word, because here Rubinstein showed himself, even more clearly than in the preceding Septet, not just as the *master*, but rather as the *despot* of the music and the piano. Bösendorfer whispered to me uneasily, "Is there a treble part in the world that could hold its own against this 'orchestral' bass?" Rubinstein, indeed, tore so mightily into the keyboard with his lion's claws that Leschetizky, in the treble, was only visibly at work, not audibly. One *saw* him playing as if his life depended on it, but one did not hear him.

During the following intermission, which was planned as a "calm before the storm" (the storm being Rubinstein's solo performance), Leschetizky bitterly reproached his friend Bösendorfer for what he erroneously believed to be an inadequate treble on the piano. I remembered that Bösendorfer, red-faced, bowed at every new rebuke but made no reply. He probably made allowance for Leschetizky's grief over the unfortunate outcome of the piano-four-hands expedition, and he knew that Rubinstein would now make the treble sound and sing.

The first of the solo pieces was Handel's Suite in D Minor, one of the climaxes of the evening. I still recall the steely tone of the aria, the grand declamatory style of the variations, the magnificent octaves of the left hand (added to the original by Rubinstein), and also the atrociously speeded-up finale, which Rubinstein treated as a "grand *stretta*." Leschetizky remarked wittily to me after the piece: "What technique you must have to mess up the finale that way!"

With a lion's leap, Anton Grigor'evich next attacked the trembling gazelle of Mozart's Rondo in A Minor. He played it with a much too turgid tone, but technically and musically it was beautiful, with innumerable fine details; it earned him a series of loud bravos from Liszt, who came from the virtuoso epoch when no consideration for the composition itself restrained any applause during a performance. And then came Beethoven's Sonata in C-sharp Minor, the so-called "Moonlight Sonata."

The faces of Rubinstein and Beethoven resemble each other amazingly, but, as I said to Leschetizky, Rubinstein looked *more* Beethovenian. And what went on at the piano? Did Rubinstein know that the sentimental name "Moonlight Sonata" did not originate with Beethoven, but with Ludwig Rellstab, a poet and an enemy of Chopin?[3] It appeared that he did, because "glowing radiance" seemed to blaze from the keyboard; the dynamics didn't sink below a *mezzo forte* at first, kept to an undifferentiated *piano* in the second movement, and burst all bounds in a truly volcanic finale.

In Chopin's Sonata in B-flat Minor, which followed, Rubinstein used a very different approach. In the first movement, where the hero grabs fate by the throat, Rubinstein oddly enough played with an intimate, poetic style. (This strange musical interpretation was explained to me seven years later when Rubinstein told me, over dinner at the Hotel Hauffe in Leipzig, that in the first [demonic!] movement of the Sonata in B-flat Minor he found Heine's poem of the young page and the queen![4]

[There was an aged monarch,
    His heart was sad, his hair was grey;
Alas, poor fool, he took him
    A wife that was young and gay!

There was a handsome page-boy,
    Light was his heart and gold his hair;
The silken train he carried
    Of that queen so young and fair.

Dost thou not know my story,   .
    So sweet, so sad to tell?
Death was the lovers' portion
    Because they loved too well.]

It was a good example of how destructive a poetic program can become for supreme music.)

He played the second movement, the Scherzo, phenomenally, both technically and intellectually; the Trio in G-flat Major was virtually the conception and execution of a genius. And then came the "Funeral March" to which all of us were feverishly looking forward. But—what was that? This was not Chopin! Four crashing B-flat Minor chords in the deepest bass region of the piano! Were they perhaps funeral knells? But there was no time for solving puzzles, since the "Funeral March" had already started in a distant *pianissimo*, which then swelled through *piano, mezzo forte, forte,* and *fortissimo* with an orchestral power. The funeral procession came to a halt. A melody of pious childhood faith rose (how dreadfully it is betrayed in the inferno tragedy of the fourth movement!), and then again the "Funeral March," but now in triple *fortissimo* which descended uniformly, all too uniformly, gliding into *piano* and *pianissimo*. No doubt this was a funeral cortège passing. [From Rosenthal's lesson on the Funeral March (*Etude,* March 1935):

> Without any doubt (and he explained it in this way) [Rubinstein] imagined a procession coming gradually nearer and afterwards passing and dying away. This proceeding has been imitated by many great and small artists; but it seems, to me at least, a very superficial interpretation, and a wrong one besides. Suppose, for a moment, the listener to the procession's music should not remain at the same place until the music dies away, but, giving way to a very human sentiment, should follow the procession, then this whole interpretation loses all meaning. Still, there is a wonderful impression, if the last twelve measures are played *diminuendo*. Then it sounds rather as if even the power to feel loss and grief would vanish.][5]

And once again four merciless B-flat Minor chords, a proclamation: *tragoedia finita est.* After that the hushed horror of the unison finale! Strange and incredible as it may seem, Rubinstein did not master it technically. Once more he had invented for himself a rather external program ("the wind over the graves"), although the extreme economy of chromaticism in this movement contradicts such an interpretation. Protected by this program and under the cover of thick pedaling, he let the tones fall pell-mell in wildly convulsive crescendos. The result: unparalleled delight on the part of the audience. In fact, a musician sitting next to me informed me that for the first time he had understood this usually unpalatable movement!

I believe, however, that Rubinstein must have immediately realized the nature of this wholesale blunder, because without announcement he canceled four further Chopin pieces listed in the program, among them the Barcarolle op. 60 (that bible of a new high Romanticism!), for which he substituted a series of his own compositions, concluding them with his "Valse allemande." What he presented here in glorious tone, daring virtuosity, and grandiose musicality (one is not a great composer for nothing) was simply unprecedented. It was a pianistic and musical champagne orgy which I remember to this day with delight. There were cheers from the audience, and then an encore of Liszt's *Etude de concert* in D-flat Major, which was played with a virtuosity which miraculously (and quite deceptively) covered the misinterpretation of the occasionally intimate and perfumed mood. Liszt expressed himself about it, as he did at times, somewhat enigmatically, mixing words that showed various degrees of praise: "Splendid, superb, quite good, hm, hm!"

The concert was followed by a banquet during which Rubinstein made a speech, saying roughly the following: "Did you ever see a private drilling before a field marshal? All the time I could not rid myself of the feeling that I was the private. The field marshal is and remains Franz Liszt!" Everybody rose from his seat. There were embraces, kissing of hands, amorous glances from beautiful women, scenes of sincere frenzied enthusiasm *à l'hongroise*.

The next day Rubinstein returned to Vienna, while Liszt remained in Pressburg. I called on the master in the morning, and he subjected Rubinstein's program to a thorough but generally benevolent criticism. He found fault with Rubinstein's having compressed four sonatas (he included Hummel's Septet in this group because of its length and sonata form) into *one* program. With charming urbanity, he continued: "I don't have to tell you that the Chopin Sonata, especially the Scherzo, was the high point of the concert. The interpretation of the Funeral March was full of effects, but quite superficial, and by subordinating the contents to an arbitrary dynamic principle, it became musically less interesting than it would have been had he followed Chopin's carefully considered nuances. Toward the end of the march, a diminuendo could be better justified even before the entry of Chopin's corresponding specification."

I volunteered: "The grief is lost in sleep?"[6]

"Something like that," said Liszt, nodding. "You are coming to Weimar again this summer, aren't you?"

"With the greatest pleasure!" I exclaimed.

While taking leave I thought: "Never again will coincidence or life make it possible for me to see and speak to Liszt and Rubinstein in the same room!" Yet, contrary to all probability, the rare case repeated itself soon afterwards, and I was able to greet the Pressburg triumvirate of Liszt, Rubinstein, and Leschetizky, and Brahms as well, at *one* festive banquet table, and I was permitted to sit again at Liszt's side!

[Rosenthal gave a detailed account of this "case" in "Franz Liszt, Memories and Reflections" (*Die Zeit* [Berlin], 1911):

The scene is the Tonkünstlerverein in Vienna, in the year 1885, I believe. Rarely had a small salon seen a meeting of a triumvirate of such significance: Brahms, Liszt, and Rubinstein at one table. And since they were sitting near one another, a stimulating and interesting conversation could have developed easily, but for reasons [then] unknown to me it did not. When in the course of the evening a neighbor of Rubinstein's asked him for an autograph, the titan of the piano drew from his pocket a calling card and handed it to her. The peculiar "autograph" was passed on to Liszt, who wrote below the printed name of Rubinstein: "et son admirateur F. Liszt." This was only a *lever de rideau* [curtain raiser]. A very pretty and well-known pianist [Annette Essipov], whose ambitions were higher-reaching still, and who was eager to cut a lock from each of the three "world-famous" men as a souvenir, approached Rubinstein, clanked her scissors, and uttered her request persuasively in the most tender sounds of their native country. Rubinstein, who in his opera *Nero* had already proved his aversion to any cruel emotion and the extreme kindliness of his character, bent his head to the beautiful petitioner. With the sails of hope billowed by fresh breezes, she turned to Liszt, who said with an indulgent bow and a sardonic smile: "Samson and Delilah! But do not fear, Madame; I shall not knock down the pillars of your conjugal happiness." Somewhat derailed but still not quite crushed, Delilah intruded vehemently on Master Brahms. But he wholeheartedly declined such antiquated homage of faded clichés and tried to fend her off with words and gesticulations—and hurt his finger on the curl-guillotine. Embarrassed silence followed, and a chilly breeze blew over the assembly. Presently the music publisher Albert Gutmann hastened along with a glass of water, caught a few drops of blood, and exclaimed with pathos: "Whoever tastes of this blood will understand Hanslick's language!" The situation was saved.[7]]

After the memorable evening in Pressburg, I heard Rubinstein again in about thirty public concerts and several times in private. The general opinion was that Rubinstein sometimes played divinely and sometimes all too humanly, depending on his mood or even his whim. This judgment is wrong. The greatness of his playing depended, in large measure, on his choice of program. He had in his repertoire some 180 pieces, a number of which he had mastered to perfection, while in the others he was sometimes severely handicapped by technical considerations. If there was a large number of such "dangerous" pieces on the program, the result was a bad evening. His tone was always extraordinary, about three times as large as that of Bülow, for example, and many other cautious pianists. His powers of persuasion, his abilities of enhancement, and his triumphant reentries of main themes worked to thrilling effect. He was like a great battle leader of Napoleonic audacity. But suddenly a cloud would drift in front of the telescope, and when it moved past, you saw instead a Russian cavalry general charging up a steep hill and trampling a lot of delicate blossoms under the hoofs of his horses.

Above all, Rubinstein's playing was orchestral. His most intimate effects were achieved in the small Schumann pieces and in the *Moments Musicaux* of Schubert. His Chopin was drawn with too inflated a line, and technically, as well, it was anything but perfect. He lacked the ethereal *pianissimo,* and he also lacked the necessary fidelity to the composer, whose melodic ornamental passages were frequently changed by Rubinstein. But I shall never forget his Polonaise in A-flat Major, which he played with an unprecedentedly heroic power of expression. There you heard revolution, death-defying audacity, cavalry clashes, battle, and proclamation of future victory.

After Pressburg, my path crossed Rubinstein's at Dresden and Leipzig, and he attended my concerts in both of those cities. In Dresden, after the final item on my program, he climbed onto the stage, shook my hand, and said loudly enough for everybody in the hall to hear it: "Quite memorable!" Josef Hofmann reports that Rubinstein told him: "I never knew what technique was until I heard Rosenthal."

Rubinstein was underappreciated as a composer. It was taken as a joke and retailed as such that Rubinstein considered himself to be first a great composer —and a great pianist only second. The most remarkable thing about this is that he was correct in his self-assessment. Themes of grand and songful character kept flowing to him in amazing abundance. His numerous chamber music works, operas, symphonies, oratorios, lieder, and, last but not least, his piano compositions, colored by a characteristic Oriental splendor, all bear witness to this gift. In triumphant consciousness of his melodic wealth, he once allowed himself to utter the following phrase: "Si j'avais cultivé la presse, on ne parlerait pas de Brahms, ni de Wagner." (If I had cultivated the press, no one would talk of Brahms nor of Wagner.)

I saw him for the last time during a walking trip to the Italian lakes. I arrived with my friend Max Breitenfeld in Bellagio on Lake Como, at the hour when the sun slowly loses its glow. The picturesque scenery—the lake with its purple radiance—enchanted me so much that I decided to stay on for a few weeks. I inquired of the hotel manager whether he could get me a piano from Milan. "Certainly," he said. "Another pianist is staying on the other side of the lake, in Cadenabbia, and he also ordered a piano for himself."

"What is his name?" I asked curiously.

The answer was: "Anton Rubinstein."

We were electrified. "What ferry can we take to get across?"

"Unfortunately," said the manager, "there are no more ferries today."

But here my determination became overpowering. "Listen," I said to my friend, "I want to get to Rubinstein *today*. You row the hotel's boat, I'll take my bathing suit and put my clothes in the boat. You row straight to the Grand Hotel in Cadenabbia, and I'll swim across."[8]

"Isn't it too far?" my friend asked apprehensively.

"It is an hour and a half," said the manager.

Within fifteen minutes, we were on our way to Cadenabbia; we arrived around 9 P.M. After dressing appropriately, we asked to be announced to Rubinstein, who received us most graciously.

After a brief conversation, Rubinstein asked me: "Why is your hair all wet?" I told him of my swimming feat, which seemed to interest him enormously. "Indeed, a second Leander!" he exclaimed in his pleasant bass voice.

We took our leave most cordially, and the next morning I sent my card to Rubinstein with this dedication: "Leandre à son Hero." Soon afterward I heard that Anton the Great, through a severe attack of angina pectoris, had been summoned to the immortal heavenly symphony orchestra.

24 My Memories of Johannes Brahms

Neues Wiener Journal, May 24, 1933

M. R.

Whether "My Memories of Johannes Brahms" was written before or after "Brahmsiana" (unpublished) is unclear. However, two anecdotes, one about Bülow and the other about Alexander Winterberger, appear in both pieces. These alternate tellings present an editorial challenge, as do other details in "Brahmsiana."

That the Bülow anecdote is better told and taken farther in the unpublished piece suggests that this piece came later. To avoid repetition, we have therefore deleted the Bülow anecdote from "Brahmsiana," incorporating into "My Memories of Johannes Brahms" those passages from the version in "Brahmsiana" that do not appear in the published piece. These insertions are bracketed.

As for the Winterberger anecdote, the version in "Brahmsiana" is so much fuller and more detailed that we have elected to omit the telling in "My Memories of Johannes Brahms" with the exception of the occasional insertion and the last paragraph, which we have appended to the version in "Brahmsiana." Again, these insertions are bracketed.

On January 7, 1884, I played in a concert in the Bösendorfersaal, alongside the "Appassionata," a set of Chopin compositions; alongside Liszt's *Don Juan* Fantasie, Brahms's Paganini Variations, which in those days were very seldom performed in concert halls. Max Kalbeck told Brahms all about it.[1] About two weeks later, Professor Julius Epstein came to me bearing the message: "Brahms wishes to meet you. Come to the Tonkünstlerverein tomorrow, I will introduce you."

At that time Brahms had not yet reached the zenith of his fame, but I can say today that even then I had been convinced of his greatness for a long time and had many a time fought on his behalf. I had also heard about his sharp interjections and his sarcastic wit and anticipated the meeting not without anxiety. But finally I thought with Mephisto: "Stab away, Doctor, I will parry,"[2] and went on my way. But something happened that I had hardly dared hope for. Brahms welcomed me with entrancing kindness. He even left the official round table and led me to a small table where an older musician was having his dinner.

At the beginning the conversation turned on the Paganini Variations, and I asked the Master whether he approved of my selection, approximately twenty of the twenty-eight, and how one should treat the prescribed repetition of the theme before the Second Book. Then, for the first time that evening, his wit flashed. He answered, self-mockingly: "Your selection is good. But you can also do what I do. I play the First Book, and then wait to see if the applause is stormy enough, in which case I play the second one. But so far this has never happened."

[In the foregoing, Rosenthal's performance of the Paganini Variations is a fait accompli when he talks about them with their composer for the first time. However, Rosenthal wrote in a letter to Joseph Bennett dated March 23, 1898:

> May I still say one word about the variations of Brahms' (Paganini)? I asked the master, fifteen years ago, which set of the two he wished me to play in public, the first or second? (Both together would give an anticlimax, as there are two long Finales.) He told me to make a choice from both, and I did so, and he agreed with my selection, hearing it four times in public, and very often in the Tonkünstler-verein. Allow me to state this, as I would not seem to take liberties with such a great master as Brahms.[3]]

Now the musician who was sitting at our table entered into the conversation, and I was more than a little appalled that in his speech he showed not the slightest respect, not the slightest civility, toward the Master. Brahms got up angrily and said to me: "Come to another table. I cannot speak with this person. He is insufferably crass." I was amazed at how differently things can turn out from what one expects: Brahms taking flight from the affronts of an insignificant musician . . . This picture did not fit in with the image that I had created of him.

* * *

[In general, Brahms was not receptive to praise or, for him even worse, flattery. He always seemed to be asking: "Who are you? What rank are you vested with that you presume to decorate me? Am I a merely a general and you a war minister?" Brahms's rapport with Bülow, with whom I saw him more than once, was singularly odd. This interesting, spirited pianist and conductor, who certainly didn't disdain promotional drum-beating on his own behalf, had via "Johannes the Great" found his way back from the Hörselberg and the music of Venus to absolute music.[4] Bülow chronicled his return from pre-Brahmsian sin in his correspondence and articles alike. He went after his former father-in-law, great teacher, and protector, Franz Liszt, with especial vehemence. On the positive side of his musical account were his brilliant interpretations of Beethoven's and Brahms's orchestral and piano works.

One evening of chamber music which Bülow devoted wholly to compositions by Brahms stands out as particularly interesting. My friend [Albert] Gutmann had undertaken the arrangements for the evening and assigned me a seat in the first row, so that I could observe the course of this peculiar concert at close range.]

It was an unforgettable evening, during which my admiration for the composer Johannes Brahms soared into adulation. His super-brilliant and yet rigorously masterful Quintet in f was played, with Bülow at the piano. Contrary to his habit, Brahms sat very close to the stage. (The scene I will be describing was played out in the jam-packed Bösendorfersaal.) The applause for the first two movements was tremendous, and swelled to gale force after the third, the Scherzo. That was the moment for which Bülow had prepared. He stood up and walked as close as he could to the audience. [He points again and again at the master Brahms, pleading with him to come join him on the stage and accept the audience's thanks, and at last Brahms assents. When Brahms has gone back to his cushioned seat, Bülow returns unexpectedly, and indicates that he wants to speak.] He gave one of his famous concert talks: "*Meine Herren und Damen!* The last Austrian poet, Franz Grillparzer[5]—I call him the last Austrian poet (long pause, in order to let the insult to all *living* Austrian poets really sink in!)— anyway, Franz Grillparzer once said: 'The most difficult thing is this: to be great.' (Parturiunt montes, nascetur ridiculus mus!)[6] There is the one who knows, there he is, there he sits, the Master Johannes Brahms! [Let's offer our admiration and show it by standing up from our seats!" Most people rise.] Here Bülow tried to kiss Brahms's hand, but Brahms pulled it out of his grip and said: "Ach, stop this foolishness!"

[What a cold shower! The next scene shows the deathly pale Bülow straining to play the Finale of the Quintet and succumbing to its mounting thirds and octaves.]

. . .

> Rosenthal's anecdote about Bülow and Brahms fails to show the complex relationship between the two men: his characterization of Brahms as a man indifferent to praise is totally false, as is his characterization of Bülow as an inept flatterer. In fact, Bülow conducted the world premiere of Brahms's Second Piano Concerto (the composer was the soloist). He wrote to his daughter, Daniela (December 9, 1881): "On the 4th, 5th, and 6th of January [1882] there is a cycle of Beethoven concerts in the Singakademie, on the 7th a Mendelssohn evening, and on the 8th and 9th two Brahms concerts with the composer, who is playing one of his concertos, with me as conductor, and conducting the other, which I am to play." The offices Bülow performed for Brahms were considerable.
>
> Although Brahms lived simply, he was intensely ambitious, and hungered for praise and recognition, particularly imperial patronage. Bülow knew this very well. In another letter to Daniela (January 10, 1882), he wrote of Brahms, "So he has a heart, you see; not so big as his head, but far bigger than that of most great men, your unique grandfather [Franz Liszt] excepted."[7]

25 Brahmsiana

Unpublished

M. R.

A delightful summer evening waned in the Vienna Woods, luring one irresist-
ibly out of doors.[1] But a great name was buzzing through the balmy summer air
like a bass note: Johannes Brahms! I hastily left my apartment, at Wollzeile 25,
which Brahms had blessed with several visits, to go to the restaurant of the
Vienna Tonkünstlerverein. And I was joyful and thrilled to spot the master at
his rightful place of honor among his trusted and not so trusted friends and
acquaintances. When he saw me enter, he briskly put away his napkin, got up,
walked toward me, and shook my hand cordially. "How splendid of you to come
here," he called out. "You're not out of touch with the '*Chronique amoureuse*' of
our time, and know how little one can trust [the Parisian boulevard authors].
I've just now proposed the thesis that all the erotic conquests of which our
young Casanovas boast are nothing but tales of Münchhausen[2] and impertinent
humbug." I had already known for some time how shy Brahms was around
women and how he tried to hide that shortcoming behind excessively rustic behavior, coldness, even rudeness. I gladly did the revered master the favor of
agreeing with his daring thesis, and switched from the role of actor to that of
spectator when Brahms darted off toward a violinist [who had not been blessed
with much that inscrutable nature has to bestow] who had just entered the
room. Grace and charity were not this man's long suit. "Say, my dear Baspitzer,
I hear you have colossal success with [married] noble women. How do you do
it, you lucky dog?" Baspitzer was flattered to the highest degree, believing that
he had discovered something akin to envy in Brahms, and really pulled out all
the stops! He feigned discretion, [stammered something like "Can't complain,"]
then proceeded to assert that an immense and interesting individuality was the
primary basis for victory in the trials of love. Unfortunately, I must concede that
Brahms let his mask drop and erupted in convulsive laughter. [The violinist was
surprised by the hilarity that his words had inspired.]

At this point the attentive hostess of the establishment sent over a "Giardi-
netto" (an ostentatious Viennese dessert, made from cheese, butter, and both
common and tropical fruits). Brahms, who was evidently becoming more re-
laxed, arranged to have the dessert brought into a small adjacent room for himself and some especially close friends, and invited me, Kalbeck, Ludwig Rottenberg,[3] and my longtime friend Max Breitenfeld to follow him. He refreshed

himself with delicious, cool Pilsner beer, of which he customarily drank four to five glasses before heading home, all the while dipping into youthful memories of his first Vienna period. But even in speaking of his youth he didn't repudiate the symphonic design shown in his present-day themes.

Suddenly he asked me: "Do you know the pianist and Liszt pupil Alexander Winterberger?"[4] I answered: "Personally, I know him very well, *but not by reputation*," which was very amusing to Brahms. "Fine, imagine this," he went on. "Winterberger had announced a small piano recital in Vienna, playing Bach and Brahms, death and devil ["Tod und Teufel"], and on the day of the concert I listened to him play a few of my own pieces for me so that I could teach him the correct tempos. [Suddenly the door was thrown open and a middle-aged lady stormed in.] And guess who it was? *She*—Winterberger's '*inamorata*.' His undying love of the last three months, [she sunk onto the tuxedo vest that provided the only fragile armor for Winterberger's chest and cried out solemnly: 'Here I am, I have left my husband, now I am all yours!'" Brahms made a dramatic pause and then resumed his tale. "Of course, the concert was a shambles, Winterberger] naturally played like a pig [and received the most crushing reviews." We listeners shuddered dutifully.] "He gives up his career in Vienna. That's a telling example of adventures in love! By the way, dear Rosenthal, when we pass Baspitzer on the way out, say a couple of friendly words to him!" This was a typical Brahmsian modulation!

I gave Baspitzer a friendly pat on the shoulder: "I hear that about fifteen years ago you had great success with your concerts in Europe and in America under the pseudonym Pablo de Sarasate!?" Baspitzer bowed in a machine-like fashion. Envied by Johannes Brahms, treated as an equal of Sarasate by me, effectively at the high point of his entire existence, he staggered triumphantly into the summer night, off to his house, while I accompanied Brahms to his apartment in the Karlsgasse.

[This episode, which wanted for the master's usual kindheartedness, came to mind when, a few years ago, the assertion was put forward that Johannes Brahms and Clara Schumann were bound to each other by a very earthly love. Notwithstanding the touching shadow of the noble, great Robert Schumann, how could Brahms have spoken as he had in the Tonkünstlerverein had he been having a love affair with Clara? No, their love was as pure and chaste as the snow on the Alpine peaks, which the sun imbues with rosy colors but does not melt.]

* * *

On my summer trips, on which I often embarked with my friend Breitenfeld, I generally spent a few days in Bad Ischl, where Brahms and Johann Strauss, "the Second and Only," took their summer holiday, Strauss in his luxurious villa, Brahms in two humble rented rooms.[5]

Musicians from England and America would show up there in July and August to see the two famous men and to extend to them their heartfelt admiration. The musical city of Boston punctually sent out its world-famous quartet.[6] Among the Austrian musicians who turned up were operetta composers with a lot of Hungarian flair, but also the very serious Ilona Eibenschütz,[7] the highly talented student of Clara Schumann, widow of the great Robert! Ilona was an exceptional piano talent, while her mother was esteemed as a genius in the kitchen by dyed-in-the-wool gourmets. Brahms willingly surrendered to her magic when she invited him to try her garlic-scented Hungarian goulash. Light Pilsner beer and Hungarian red wine flowed, as did Brahms's memories of playing Hungarian gypsy music with Reményi and Joachim.[8] Obviously the goulash provided the theme for the conversation!

Kneisel, the first violinist of the Boston [i.e., Kneisel] String Quartet, reminded me during an early morning breakfast with Brahms on the Ischl Esplanade of a good line that I had come up with recently. I had been engaged to play a chamber music concert with the Kneisels in Boston, arrived in the bitter cold of the early morning, and happened to meet, to my delight, dear Kneisel, who was waiting for me at the train station. With him was an old gentleman who squinted as if from the age before Beethoven at the snowy winter landscape. Kneisel cast a critical eye over the evening program and asked with apprehension: "Do you think that the audience will like the [Trio in] B-flat, op. 97?" I replied amiably: "You can rest assured that there aren't ten people in all of Boston who could compose such a piece!"

Brahms suddenly asked: "What was the story with your Weimar colleague Stavenhagen?"[9]

"May I tell the anecdote as an eyewitness, dear master?" Breitenfeld asked.

"By all means!"

"Stavenhagen gave three piano recitals in Vienna and caused quite a stir, even though he played the same pieces at each concert and only modified or changed their titles. He made much effect with Schubert-Liszt's *Soirées de Vienne* no. 6. In the second concert he played the same piece, but called it the 'Valse Caprice' by Schubert-Liszt, and at the third concert, he named it simply and refreshingly 'Valse-Schubert.' Rosenthal wants to congratulate his colleague in the artist's room, but in order to do so has to cut a swath through a phalanx of young female pianists. One lady in particular seems to appear everywhere with her autograph book. 'Just one line, precious master!' she implores, 'but something characteristically you.' Stavenhagen turns to Rosenthal. 'You are not easily cornered. How should I solve this problem? *One* line, and it must be characteristic of me as a man and as an artist!' After Rosenthal had contemplated this for a moment, he retorted: 'You know what? Write your repertoire!'"

* * *

Brahms appreciated a good joke told by others, but he didn't merely repeat them, he was also a productive artist in this arena. The number of ideas that he had was not overwhelming, but their quality was often extraordinary. I remember the "brilliance of his dagger in the sun," when his just published chamber work, the Quartet in c, was played by Bachrich.[10] The performance lacked confidence, sharp rhythm, in short, any hint of artistic perfection, and Brahms sat there with closed lips—no criticism, but no praise, either. This deathly silence outlasted the piece! Finally, Bachrich decided on a daring offensive! And in his mouth welled up the worried question: "Say, dear master, were you pleased with our *tempi?*"

A short, fateful pause—then the stupendous answer: "Of course, of course, *especially with yours!*" (There was one tempo for Bachrich, another for his quartet companions!!)

* * *

Some time later: Brahms, accompanied by the extraordinary musician Ludwig Rottenberg (later conductor of the Frankfurt Opera), comes to my first piano recital of the season in the Bösendorfersaal. I begin with Chopin's Sonata op. 58. On the stage, close to me, Mrs. S. W., the famous, very ambitious pianist, takes her seat. In the middle of the sonata, Brahms gives Rottenberg a friendly dig in the ribs. "See, now she believes she can play as well as Rosenthal, *but she is wrong.*"

End of the Sonata. Pause. Rosenthal reappears. And for the first time in Vienna, Brahms's Paganini Variations, Books 1 and 2. At the tremendous "crescendo" of the Finale and its demonic jumps, Brahms shouts into Rottenberg's auricle: "Now she can't believe it herself anymore!"

(Rottenberg told me that at the same concert, Brahms warmly praised Rosenthal's rhythmic treatment of Chopin's Waltz op. 42.)[11]

In England, as in America, the Brahmsian muse was noted and cultivated with the greatest enthusiasm, yet the master did not return these sympathies wholeheartedly. He was even angry that Joachim gave frequent concert tours in England. The excellent writer Bonavia, in London, tells of a visit that Hans Richter and the famous composer Stanford made to Brahms one lovely morning at his apartment in the Karlsgasse.[12] Brahms came in after a short delay with his cigar case, and first offered one to Hans Richter. Then it should have been Stanford's turn, as he worshipped the ground Brahms walked on. Instead of which, Brahms clapped the box shut with the venturesome assertion: *"Englishmen don't smoke!"*

But the nicotine-craving Briton was not about to acquiesce. He opened the box himself and took out a cigar, remarking: "On the contrary, we Englishmen are very fond of smoking, *and many of us even compose!*"

* * *

The attentive reader will have noticed how differently Brahms treated Richter and Stanford. There are reasons for this! First of all, Richter controlled all the programs of the Philharmonic, as well as other important concerts, and therefore, more or less, he controlled Vienna's relationship with Brahms. But Richter was also important for England. He conducted not only the most important concerts in London, but also in other large English cities. With a nod to Shakespeare's *Richard III*, Brahms could exclaim: "A kingdom for a cigar!"

Things were different with Stanford! A fellow musician and devoted Brahmsian, he did not have to be handled with kid gloves; not like Hans Richter! The only way to Brahms's heart was through his own compositions. Since Reményi's and Joachim's days, only great interpretive artists had had a chance with Brahms—the only exception being the more or less bourgeois nightingales of his time.

* * *

He assumed a singular posture in regard to the famous singers who performed his songs for Viennese audiences.

He was especially smitten with Hermine Spies, and it was said that two hearts had found each other. Strangely enough it was *me* in whom the hero of the piece, *Johannes Brahms*, confided this, without holding anything back.

On one of my daily strolls along the Ringstrasse, I passed the wing of the Court Opera where the music shop "Albert J. Gutmann" was located, the proprietor of which was my bosom friend. As soon as I was within earshot, the door of the music shop opened, and friend Gutmann called out jauntily: "Come on in! There's someone here who would really like to meet you!"

As soon as I entered, I recognized Hermine Spies and her elder sister, who greeted me warmly. Presently Hermine enthused over Brahms's newly published Cello Sonata no. 2 and raved about the audacity of the modulation from the first to the second movement (F to F-sharp). I told her that such chromatic rises and falls often occurred in Beethoven's second and third movements, as in the transition from the second to the third of his Fifth Piano Concerto, also in the *C-sharp movements to D Major in the Quartetto op. 131, and so on.*[13] Whereupon the ladies Spies quit the place in high dudgeon. Gutmann did not lose his good humor and even pressed me to accept a so-called *Cerclesitz* [i.e., a seat in the Dress Circle] for Fraulein Spies's recital the next week.

Several days later I made my way from Wollzeile to the Bösendorfersaal and installed myself in my *Cerclesitz*. The first part of the concert consisted of a set of short piano pieces for which Frau Barette Stepanov had originally been engaged.[14] Unfortunately, she had shut a door on her finger and had to cancel. There was considerable awkwardness, as our great prima donnas usually sang only a few short songs after their arias. Gutmann assails me: "You must take over for Stepanov! Please, do me the favor, out of friendship, of love!" What could I do? All eyes hang on me. I consent, go to the artist's room, and meet there—Johannes Brahms, who greets me cordially. I rush to the podium, am greeted with thunderous applause, play about thirty minutes' worth of Chopin, Liszt, and Schumann, but (inexplicably to me even today) no Brahms. I must play several encores. The morning papers seal the victory. An important journal writes: "We came to hear a concert featuring Spies with the participation of Barette Stepanov, but instead we heard a concert featuring Moriz Rosenthal with the participation of Hermine Spies." Eduard Hanslick begins [*sic*] his witty review in the *Neue Freie Presse* (a thoroughly anti-Liszt publication) with the words: "Herr Rosenthal was only present at the concert by coincidence, as a spectator, but his piano performance was in brilliant *Toilette*" [March 19, 1887].

[Hugo Wolf, who hated Brahms as fervently as Hanslick adored him, also reviewed this concert (March 20, 1887):[15]

I arrived at Fräulein Hermine Spies's concert just in time to hear Rosenthal. Stepanov had been announced, to be sure, but it was, in fact, Rosenthal who played. Unprepared as he was (he didn't even have time to don evening dress), this little pianistic devil stormed over the keys like a roaring flood. He played godlessly (godlike sounds too commonplace), and demonstrated beyond the shadow of a doubt that the devil is the supreme authority in art. I don't remember exactly what he played. I think it was the Hungarian Rhapsody No. 12, a Waltz in A-flat by Chopin, etc. When he finished I had the feeling of having escaped from a frightful deadly peril. As long as this exorcist cast his spell at the piano, I seemed to feel the glowing claws of Beelzebub at my neck, or I feared to be swept away in a heavy surf, or to be swallowed up in the fiery crater of a volcano. But I still live, thank God, to the delight of my fellow creatures and to the consolation of my unforgettable friend, Johannes Brahms.]

After returning to the artists' room, I approach Brahms first. He squeezes my hand affectionately and asks: "You must have another concert coming up, otherwise you wouldn't have been in such *tip-top*[16] shape!" I concurred, and he said: "I'll have to come to that one too, then." And as the flood of congratulations ebbed, he went on: "By the way, we still have a bone to pick with you! I heard that you oppugned my new cello sonata in a musico-aesthetic conversation with the ladies Spies." When I angrily rose from my seat, he replied reassuringly: "I didn't believe it anyway. You know what things like that are worth—women![17] I suppose you're invited for supper at Judge of the State Court Franz's house with Hermine Spies's friends. Maybe we'll see each other there. But I'll probably wind up my evening at the 'Roten Igel.'"

I must admit, I was stunned! I had rarely encountered negative stereotyping to such a degree, condemning the female sex *en bloc*; nor had I dreamt that it was possible. Evidently it was enough for Brahms to hear any fact told or confirmed by a female being in order not to believe it. I resisted only with great difficulty mentioning Clara Schumann and pointing her out as a highly organized individual, as a great artist,[18] but this would have embarrassed him after what he had said, and might therefore have cost me his trust and great good will. I mourned for his shattered ideals, but was very pleased that for my great friend at least no epithalamium would sound as a counterpoint to the leitmotif "Hermine Spies." Happily, his hatred of women diminished over the following years, and objective discussions became possible again.

* * *

This section begins with Brahms and Rosenthal breakfasting at Zauner's, the "pastry king of Bad Ischl," and Brahms telling the story on page 105.

We both laughed heartily. I couldn't very well imagine Brahms as an interpreter of his own Paganini Variations.[19] I did hear him play his most important piece, the Piano Concerto in B-flat. This was in Vienna, and the world premiere of this illustrious piece.[20] It was received with an admixture of applause and hisses, the opinion of the press also divided, and not, in a Brahmsian fashion, disciplined, as would be the case a decade later.[21] The two most important critics at that time were: Hanslick of the *Neue Freie Presse* and Ludwig Speidel of the *Wiener Fremdenblatt*. Shortly before this concert, Brahms had had the great honor of having bestowed upon him a certificate of the "Freedom of the City" from his city of birth, Hamburg. There was much to read in the papers about the certificate itself, the binding of which was a masterwork of leather craftsmanship. Here Speidel picked up his cue and wrote that the Piano Concerto was, like the certificate of honorary citizenship, *a masterwork of leather craftsmanship*.

This bad review outraged all musicians, and it created more than a little stir when Brahms spoke to the most famous musicians about this disgraceful assault, rallying them to write up a collective denunciation of Speidel. How very well I remember, even today, my astonishment at witnessing the great composer in formal combat mode against Speidel, on the warpath, and then at hearing of his wish that I become a member of the Vienna Tonkünstlerverein so that I might persuade its members to launch a counterattack! I would like to add that this counterattack was neither penned nor made public, presumably because Brahms lost interest, or maybe because in the end he realized just how unimportant Speidel was. Later, Speidel partly made up for his lapse in judgment of Brahms, while he continued to blast Richard Wagner with the same tiresome stubbornness.

In the first summer days of June, His Majesty, the Emperor Franz Josef I, customarily came to stay at his beautiful summer villa in Bad Ischl,[22] now and again going to the theater, now and again to concerts,[23] and—"last but not least"—now and again to his girlfriend, the once extremely interesting actress Katharina Schratt.[24] I visited her with Johann Strauss's brother-in-law, the good-natured Josef Simon, but found there was something a bit too majestic about the scene she set. But when she heard from Simon that I was court pianist to His Majesty, the Emperor, her initial iciness melted away in waves of friendly conversation, and I was allowed to recall to the illegitimate Empress of Austria many memories of her proud artistic career. For example, how Heinrich Laube's drama *Böse Zungen*[25] was saved from shipwreck by her talent, and how, later, her ingenious colleague Girardi was saved from ruin through an audience with the Emperor. She sighed: "Yes, those were wonderful times! Now I am old," to which I replied:

"Certainly not, Baroness! You've just been young for a long time!"

Everyone in attendance seconded my dictum. Hans, Count Wilczek—my talented piano pupil and dear friend—asked me: "Whatever happened to the comic opera, *da Graciosa*, by K. St.?"[26]

I answered with a sigh, my heart heavy: "At first it went admirably, and St. had gotten up to the third act, when suddenly his memory [of other writers' music] failed him, and his work started to stagnate."

"Not bad," observed Wilczek, "but through trying too hard to be original, one can go to the opposite extreme."

"The 'violet-blue Julika' can bear witness to that, as she flopped at her Vienna premiere because she didn't remind the audience of any singer they'd ever heard."

"Come on! Tell Brahms the two anecdotes the next time you eat with him at the Kaiserin Elisabeth restaurant.[27] He really likes to hear musical jokes!"

"Unfortunately," I said, "I improvised a somewhat similar anecdote a bit in his presence yesterday."

"So how did it go?" asked *La Schratt.*

"I was visiting an old friend, a composer of high rank, and found several scores by Tchaikovsky, Massenet, and Liadov scattered across the piano. Quite surprised at this, I pointed at the notes and asked, 'What's this, then? I thought you composed by memory,' to which my old, dear friend, Arthur [Friedheim], answered adroitly: 'You're not mistaken. These foreign scores are only here by accident!' 'Yes, I've heard that often happens,' Brahms said, 'to put foreign scores on the music stand, leave them there for a while, and eventually come to believe that they are one's own!' "[28]

Some time thereafter, on a rainy afternoon, I was sitting with Brahms and a harmony teacher named Wink in the Café de l'Opéra, enjoying our afternoon coffee. Suddenly Wink asked me: "Are you still playing so much Chopin? I'm willing to give it to you in writing that in ten years (it was the year 1890) no one will play even a single note by Chopin or Liszt."

"I know that," I replied calmly, "that's the real reason why I study both these masters with such perseverance, because I want to save them from impending oblivion."

After five minutes, Wink got up to take his leave of us. He hadn't spoken another word to me. But he'd had the effrontery to say to Brahms: "You sure have it good! I have to out in the rain to get to my lessons, while you sit here calmly reading your papers and enjoying yourself!"

That was too much even for Brahms, who had apparently been waiting calmly for just the right moment to intervene, and now broke loose: "Let me tell you something: first, study your theory and your counterpoint thoroughly. Impress your colleagues, then you'll be able to bring yourself to a point where you too can drink your afternoon coffee in peace! Good evening!"

Thus concluded the episode. Whether Wink ever changed his opinion about Chopin or Liszt, I don't know.

* * *

The scene just described had apparently rattled the master to such a degree that he began speaking about contemporary musicians and threw caution to the wind. We analyzed Joachim Raff, who got a very low mark in Brahms's book. We talked about Carl Tausig, any and all of whose creativity Brahms denied; about Franz Liszt, whom he tore to pieces and put on a level with Lachner;[29] finally about Anton Rubinstein, who was stripped of everything but his piano playing. After concluding this hussar ride, Brahms became noticeably calmer, but seemed to lose his usual vim and vigor, and became almost philistine, if a great man can be so described. For example, he said: "When a new musical dictionary or a music history book is published, I never look for my own name first,

I look for the names of other "shunned" people, such as Tausig, Rubinstein, Bülow, Raff, etc."

I was more than a little surprised to hear him list Tausig, Raff, and Rubinstein under the rubric "shunned people," and what was even more strange, to hear him list himself. I told him that Richard Heuberger had informed me that he was writing a piano concerto. After hearing this, Brahms's mood visibly lightened. He cried out: "Let him study the last few pages of Chopin's Ballade in f, and then he'll see if he's up to the job!"

* * *

It was the beginning of May 1889, when I returned to Vienna, "der alten Kaiserstadt," from my [first] American tour. Waiting for me at the train station were my dear mother, who broke out in tears of joy upon seeing me; my sisters, four younger and one older; and my old, faithful friends Max Breitenfeld, Professor Albert Seligmann, *Doctor medicinae* Eduard Schiff, and Doctor Harry Hirschl. The latter two have since passed on! *Requiescat in pace!* It was quite a bit past midnight when, after many hours of conversation, my family and I sought out our beds.

The next morning I celebrated my reunion with Vienna by driving through the most beautiful streets in a *Fiaker,* finally ending up at the Stadtpark. I ordered a light "Continental" breakfast, as well as coffee with cream and Viennese *Kipfeln* [crescent rolls], asked for the morning papers, and was reading with curiosity about international sensations and local events when a friendly pat on the shoulder roused me from my papers and my meditation. I looked up and saw in front of me no less a personage than Johannes Brahms himself, whom I had planned on visiting right after lunch.

As it happened, I had just given a two-piano concert in New York with my former teacher Rafael Joseffy in which we had played as encores, *unisono,* several Chopin etudes and the Schubert-Tausig *Military* March—a daring deed, but it worked out splendidly. I was more than a little surprised to learn that Brahms was familiar with the hussar piece. To wit, his first words were: "So you played 'à *quatre mains*' in New York!" while doing finger exercises in the air.

[The writer of an unidentified clipping from 1943 recalls this occasion:

> The finest bit of musical sportsmanship I can remember is when Rosenthal and Joseffy did a two-piano recital in New York and repeated it shortly after in Brooklyn. Joseffy lacked the physical strength of Rosenthal and the latter's 'orchestral' tone, but excelled in delicate colorings and runs of feathery lightness. Came the concerts, and *mirabile dictu,* Rosenthal the Thunderer was not in evidence; instead we heard Rosenthal the Charmer, curbing his might and co-coordinating to the point of exact imitation with Joseffy's gentler tone and touch. The pair devoted one section of their program to playing in unison, that is playing the same notes, merely doubling those of the compositions—Chopin's Etude on Black Keys [also op. 25, no. 2], Mendelssohn's Spring Song and Schubert's Marche Militaire. Not a hair's breadth of difference in tone, rhythm or dynamics. It was phenomenal, sheer incredible, and remains one of my most treasured pianistic memories.]

I told [Brahms] about my artistic relationship with my former teacher, explaining that Joseffy had become a complete Brahms convert and how gloriously he had played the master's Second Piano Concerto in New York, so ravishingly that he had to give the fourth movement again.

As was customary, Brahms tried not to seem surprised, and, affecting an indifferent mien, said breezily: "Yes, I know, but *it's always like that these days*, the final movement is always asked for *da capo!*" I didn't let his minimizing of my teacher's accomplishment annoy me, and later read through all the reviews of performances of the Concerto without once finding anything to corroborate Brahms's statement. I realized later that Brahms's behavior had already become "routine," that he received any surprising piece of news as if it were already known to him or unimportant. I recall that Kalbeck once remarked to him: "Did you know that D'Albert is going to America?" And he replied almost scornfully: "Fine, let him go then." (Meaning: That doesn't interest us in the least!) But anyway, to get back to the Stadtpark and its blossoming breakfast terrace: suddenly Brahms called out: "I'm swimming in melodies!" And when I looked at him in puzzlement, he said: "There are fifty-one, fifty-one finger exercises! And one of them friend Tausig stole from me and incorporated into *his* daily studies."

"But, master, his friend Ehrlich did that. *He* is the true editor of the Tausig-Ehrlich Studies!"[30]

"That doesn't matter," replied Brahms, "*melody stays melody*, you can't just steal one."

When I realized that the great master was determined to exalt his finger exercises into melodies, I played along and said: "This reminds me of Sicily, where tropical flowers grow out of and next to mighty stone colossi."

"Bravo!" Brahms exclaimed; and I had the lordly pleasure of giving him a ride home in my Fiaker.

* * *

The great soul of Brahms was not free of sunspots, and one of the most important and grievous of them was his envy of his colleagues, which caused him to speak sharply and out of turn. Thus he was once asked: "Master! Do you think Grädener (an excellent Viennese musician) actually has any talent as a composer?" Brahms's answer was as follows: "Oh yes, oh yes, *but very little!*" That he was not very tactful in his jokes is evidenced by a witticism often cited by Grädener himself: "Actually, Grädener's looking much better these days. Now he's *pale*; he used to be *green*."

Concerning the physiognomy of others, Brahms presided over a very strict court. He once invited me to have a sorbet with him on the Ischl Esplanade. Not far from us a married couple, by the name of Fleckmann, had just sat down; farther along, at another table, the famous concertmaster Grün was sitting with one of his female students.[31] Brahms began: "Look at how contorted Fleckmann's and Grün's faces are! It's always the same story: They try with might and main to say something witty, but they can't."

26 Brahms and Johann Strauss II

Unpublished

M. R.

During the Bad Ischl days a very popular story circulated in countless variations at tables in restaurants and coffee houses recounting the reciprocal appreciation, even admiration, which two masters of musical art held for each other: Johannes Brahms, the miracle worker from the north, and Johann Strauss, the "Second and Only," whose melodic flowers seemed to blossom out of the musical south.[1]

It was a well-known fact that Brahms had written the first few bars of "An der schönen blauen Donau" on the fan of Strauss's sparkly-eyed [third] wife, Adele, adding the epigram: "Unfortunately not by me." Strauss also made comments that revealed his profound understanding of and heartfelt admiration for the great North German composer of symphonies. Doubters naturally found this surprising. It was well known that Strauss was an early Wagnerian and that he included excerpts from Wagner's operas in his concerts. Those who were well informed also remembered that the heavenly "Danube" Waltz included a bacchanalian, indulgent, sinfully seductive chord which also reminded one of Chopin and Wagner, but by no means pointed at Brahms. Here the theory of "opposites attract" applies. Brahms's closeness had a morally uplifting and clarifying effect on others. When he stepped into the salon of Strauss's villa, his presence had a mellowing and balsamic effect on the Tarock waves rising in the salon.[2] Everybody put down their Daggers, Pagat, and Moon (sometimes even the Joker); in short, everyone felt the historic weight of the moment.

There also came the day when I spent some time alone and talked with His Majesty, the Waltz Monarch, in one of the comfortable rooms of his villa. Strauss spoke of his beginnings and his long-standing love of the piano. He told me that, in his youth, he had had ambitions to pursue the career of a concert pianist, and that he valued pianistic virtuosity highly. We spoke of Tausig and his poetic and whimsical Strauss paraphrases. We also discussed Chopin and Schumann, whose works Strauss highly admired. But suddenly a solemn austerity engulfed the room, the name Brahms rang out like a church bell. Strauss broke through the barrier, and both of us looked into far and foggy distances. "Monumentally important!" came from the lips of the Waltz King. This was the Cross of the Commander in the Straussian house order.[3]

Acknowledgment of the final conqueror, then a reverent pause. And then an iniquitous hand touched the Veil of Isis, and, half asphyxiated, my lips gave forth: "My dear master, do you believe that Brahms is as important to music and the piano as, for example, Chopin and Schumann?"

A pause of four three-quarter beats, and I still hear his words and tone of voice after thirty-five years, when Jean [Johann], as if in a trance, uttered: "Far from it! He doesn't have the imagination for it!"

27 Review of a Concert by M. R.

The Musical Times, March 1934

G. C.

This review of Rosenthal appeared in a round-up titled "Pianists of the Month," the others, in this case, being Solomon, Schnabel, Rudolf Firkusny, Kurt Appelbaum, and Lili Kraus.[1]

Moriz Rosenthal's second recital at Wigmore hall was unhappy. He began with Liszt's transcription of the Bach Organ Prelude and Fugue in A Minor, and it was a performance uncomfortable in its technique and musically incoherent. The Schumann "Fantasie" (op. 17), which followed, was played without fervour or imagination, and with an almost grotesque exaggeration of every vulgarity pianists are likely to commit. Were Rosenthal writing a book instead of playing the pianoforte the critics would say to him, "Begin again—and concentrate." For it is difficult to believe that Rosenthal understands the music he is playing. He had, many years ago, a wonderful technique; but he has his virtuosity no longer, and his lack of musicianship is therefore laid bare. "Disorder" in musical performance cannot be accidental: it is conceived in the mind—it must be, in fact, "organized disorder." For long stretches in the Schumann "Fantasie" Rosenthal indulged in whimsical disorder: not all the king's horses and all the king's men could have put the music together again. In the second movement, at the ninth bar, Rosenthal missed altogether the beauty and interest of the passage, which is that the first two bars are "marking time" while the next two move forwards, quite different in character. (There is a similar phrase in the first movement of the "Emperor" Concerto.) To play the inner part in the first two bars (which is an ugly "melody" and anticipates the next two bars in an undesired way), and to ignore the top B flats, is to destroy the sense and flow of the music. Schumann was certainly a pessimist in his indication of accents, but Rosenthal justified the greatest pessimism. At the *più animato* in this movement, Schumann is attempting, as so often in his pianoforte music (for instance, the end of the Sonata, op. 22), to obtain the effect of an orchestral *pizzicato;* Rosenthal played the semiquavers very nearly as quavers, and the *pizzicato* became a clattering of horses' hooves, incidentally along a very rocky path. The close of the "Fantasie" was most typically played; the music which in Schumann's intention rises to greater and greater movement, like ocean waves, was reduced by Rosenthal to the sentiment and proportions of a bathroom.

28 Letter to the Editor

The Musical Times, December 1934

M. R.

Rosenthal comes off very badly in this piece, for in attempting to decimate the one review (and critic) standing between him and unanimous praise for his recital in question, he shows himself to be not only mean-spirited, but unfocused—a cardinal sin for Rosenthal —in not representing the critic's words accurately. The critic did not write that Rosenthal played with "organized disorder," for instance: he wrote that "disorder" in musical performance cannot be accidental. This is true.

SIR,—When the criticism on my second London recital, initialed "G. C." and dated March, 1934, reached me some time after its publication, I was too busy to devote myself to the answer it deserved, having been engaged for a very strenuous tour through South America. Having returned again to old Europe, I request you kindly to publish the following answer:

The glory of Herostratos and other iconoclasts robs certain critics of their sleep.[1] Unable to shine by their (deficient) musical knowledge, or their more imaginary than real mastership of pen, they set works of art on fire in order to create a sensation which would otherwise be denied to their legitimate but feeble efforts. Their tombstones should bear the epitaph *Qualis aristicida pereo!*[2]

To the honor of musical and critical England be it said, there are very few critics of this mold in England, where, on the contrary, refined musical taste and gentlemanlike behavior are the unwritten and imperturbable law. A singular and very regrettable exception I found in your musical critic who writes under the initials of "G. C."

Let musicians and the musical public judge for themselves. At my second London recital, which won unanimous praise from all musicians, the greatest critics, and the whole musical public, I played the Schumann *Fantasie.* Mr. "G. C." asserts that I played it with "organized disorder," and that "not all the king's horses and all the king's men could have put the music together again." It is really astonishing that not a single critic felt this, and that the verdict was unanimously and completely in my favour. I must confess that I do not understand Mr. "G. C.'s" utterances on this point. In order to organize musical disorder one must follow a certain aim, and I wonder for what earthly or unearthly reason I should have organized a disorder. Everyone who has listened to my interpretations will agree that I avoid as much as possible all tempo rubato. If "G. C." states that not all the king's horses or men could put the music together, I may whisper to him the priceless information that Schumann's works have appeared in several hundred thousand of printed copies and that each single copy has the power to reconstruct the original text without the help of the king's horses or men, or even without the assistance of this wonderful master of style, "G. C."

Mr. "G. C." has one great idea—the idea he nurses about himself. He feels he has enough greatness in himself to administer a thrashing to a genius like Schumann. In speaking of the *Fantasie* by this composer he claims that in the second movement the inner part of the ninth and tenth bars forms an *ugly melody*. Here, as elsewhere, I am not in accord with Mr. "G. C." I think those bars beautiful; but think the assault on the great composer ugly beyond words, especially when committed by a novice against a demi-god. Mr. "G. C." continues: "At the *più animato* in this [second] movement, Schumann is attempting, as so often in his pianoforte music (for instance, the end of the Sonata, op. 22) to obtain the effect of an orchestral *pizzicato*"; and that the *pizzicato* became "a clattering of horses' hooves." In response to these fantastic statements I wish to say:

1. Neither in the *Fantasie* nor in the Sonata has Schumann attempted to obtain the effect of an orchestral *pizzicato*, for the simple reason that such a thing does not exist! (I would feel very surprised, and even upset, on suddenly hearing a *pizzicato* from a bass tuba together with a bassoon!)

2. Schumann has a definite picture in mind which does not correspond with this famous *pizzicato* but which goes very well with the clattering of horses' hooves. Perhaps if Mr. "G. C." were to read or study at least one of Schumann's biographies he would learn that the *Fantasie* was intended to be a Sonata "*ad gloriam* Beethoven" and dedicated to the glorious [*sic*] memory of this incomparable genius; that the second movement was intended to bear the inscription "Triumphbogen" (Arc de Triomphe), or later "Trophäen" (Trophies), which titles rather suggest battles and even the clatter of horses' hooves, but never a non-existing orchestral *pizzicato*.

Now, like a wise and artistic writer, Mr. "G. C." so arranged his fireworks that he may lead up to an astonishing climax. He finishes his article with the following *Salto mortale*: "The close of the *Fantasie* was most typically played; the music which in Schumann's intention (how do you know this, Mr. "G. C."?) rises to greater and greater movement, like ocean waves, was reduced by Rosenthal to the sentiment and proportions of a bathroom."

Wonderful! Now you see how infinitely greater "G. C." is than Rosenthal—"G. C." the tumultuous roaring ocean—Rosenthal reducing the mighty ocean to the proportions and sentiments of a bath tub. I have, of course, to bow to such greatness; but may I be permitted to ask in all modesty from whence "G. C." drew his notion that Schumann had in mind the rising ocean waves when he wrote the finishing pages of his *Fantasie?* It would appear that he possesses this knowledge exclusively, for curiously enough every biographer I know states that Schumann at different times named the last movement of the *Fantasie* "Palmen" and again "Sternenkranz" (Corona of Stars), which shows he imagined no roaring waves but an enchanting Southern landscape at night with quiet palms and glittering stars! Now "G. C." sees and hears the rolling ocean and not the magical Southern night with palms and stars which the great composer depicted. Why should I be ridiculed because I feel with the great composer instead of sharing in such ignorance? Let me give Mr. "G. C." one consolation: Lessing, the great German writer (born twenty years before Goethe, in 1729), wrote once, "There is one thing I almost prefer to truth, that is—striving after truth. In fact, nothing gives us such joy as to search after truth and to approach its throne." If Lessing is right, Mr. "G. C." must be considered as the happiest of all musical critics, because he is apparently the one who has most to learn.—Yours, &c.,

MORIZ ROSENTHAL.
Vienna.

29 Review of a Concert by M. R.

The Times (London), May 18, 1936

Mr. Moriz Rosenthal brought to a triumphant conclusion on Saturday the series of seven historical programmes of piano music which have been in progress at Wigmore Hall during the last three weeks. They have been the most consistent feature of an otherwise desultory concert season, and not the least part of the triumph was that after six opportunities of hearing him Mr. Rosenthal could make a large audience prefer Wigmore Hall to the open air on a summery Saturday and still want more when his official programme had been completed with a brilliant performance of Brahms's Variations on a Theme of Paganini.

The series has not been carried out quite as originally planned. It was entitled "From Bach to the Twentieth Century," but though, as has here been described, he began with Bach and Scarlatti, the "twentieth century" faded out from the final programme and nobody missed it. For what really brings us to listen to Mr. Rosenthal as often as possible is the pleasure and profit to be gained from hearing the music of the great masters of the piano played in the style inherited from Liszt and Tausig and enriched with his own lifelong experience. The historical character of this series allowed him to include in the penultimate programme last week specimens of those minor masters, John Field, Moscheles, Henselt, and Thalberg, rarely to be heard in the concert room to-day, but who contributed materially to the development of that great era of piano music and piano playing of which Mr. Rosenthal remains the foremost exponent.

In Saturday's programme, some of Rubinstein's more delicate works, Three Miniatures, the Barcarolle in G, and the "Valse allemande" on a theme from Weber [*Der Freischütz*], were added. We could wish that a small place had been found for Sterndale Bennett, who has some right to join such a company, at any rate when it visits London.[1] Mendelssohn was represented by a most lucid performance of the "Variations sérieuses" and two favourite "Songs without Words" ("The Spring Song" and "The Bees' Wedding"). Chopin was present, not for historical reasons since a whole programme had been given to him a week earlier, but because Mr. Rosenthal loves to play him and his audience loves to hear, and there is no better reason than that. Brahms was allowed the last word, indeed several last words, for the whole of the second part was given to the Hungarian Variations (op. 21, no. 2), some of the smaller pieces, among which the Capriccio in B Minor (op. 76, no. 2) was conspicuous for its delicate *staccato,* and an ample selection of the Paganini Variations. To this wide field of the last century's music Mr. Rosenthal's life has been devoted and he has made it his own. The twentieth century has developed other types owning different ideals. He can afford to leave them to other interpreters.

30 From Aphorisms

M. R.

In the realm of art and ideas, he who is without forebears is the highest aristocrat.

* * *

The keys are the scene where the musical plots are played out.

* * *

The favorite argument of the unimaginative against the indispensability of a melodically meaningful theme is: the beginning of Beethoven's Fifth Symphony. But these initial measures, however loaded with meaning they are, do not shape the theme at all but rather only the introduction to it. The theme itself only begins after the second pause and heralds Beethoven's melody.

* * *

Instrumentation heightens the sensory/sensuous enjoyment of the theme, its urgency, but never its inner spiritual value. If, say, a critic overlooks a work's shortcomings due to its brilliant instrumentation, then he resembles the listener who is compensated for the shortcomings of the poetry by the beautiful voice of the reciting poet.

* * *

Composers who are ambitious but lack in imagination prefer to express themselves with trumpets, trombones, and drum rolls. Platitudes are best delivered with a thundering voice.

* * *

For me, the greatest program artists are Beethoven and Chopin, although the former rarely drew up a program and the latter almost never did.

* * *

Schubert is the most burgeoning province in Beethoven's empire.

* * *

[John] Field: The sun never sets on his empire.

* * *

The melodies of Beethoven, Chopin, Schubert—in short, of our great composers —are the true musical events. Their performances function primarily as commentaries.

Grabbe wrote his ideas down on strips of paper that he then used as kindling. Their flame has not been extinguished to this day.

* * *

The scurrilous final scene following the death of Hannibal in Grabbe's epony-mous tragedy [1835] has an effect like the bone-chilling, hysterical laughter of Melpomene.[1] The hero is dead, long live human filth!

* * *

Heinrich Heine: Orient and Occident, the red glow of sunrise and the red glow of sunset, join together as one flame for him.

* * *

On the Dioscuri of the Romantic era: Schumann is broader-shouldered, but Chopin is taller.

* * *

How comforting it would be if there were a Last Judgment for ideas!

* * *

Stage fright (the only lucid interval in the artistic life).

* * *

The deep, almost pious seriousness with which so many pianists set to work on their choice of program and playing is very often derived from a weakness of the fourth finger.

* * *

This operetta was composed in an unusually diligent and businesslike man-ner, and is being launched by an imaginative, brilliant publisher.

* * *

It is not enough to be a true servant of the arts; its masters are what we long for and need.

31 On the Question of Applause

April 29, 1940
Unpublished

M. R.

Applause follows the performance of a work as surely as thunder follows lightning. There are many reasons why it is wrong to suppress it. If there is no applause, the artist infers unconsciously that the audience is cold and disinterested. He becomes uneasy, uncertain, and his initial nervousness grows. Moreover, he cannot know which of the movements were best or least liked.

But, say the opponents of applause, clapping disturbs the continuity of mood; the development of the work is disrupted. Yet has it never occurred to these super-clever people that intolerable monotony results from maintaining the same mood continuously throughout an entire symphonic work of several movements? Don't they know that often the composer himself prefers abrupt variations of mood?

Schumann's *Fantasie* illustrates the point. This work, which was originally dedicated to exalt Beethoven and bore the title "Beethoven," is divided into three movements. Schumann called the first part "Ruinen" and let it fade out in a most tender C Major *pianissimo*. The second movement, "Triumphbogen," comes in abruptly and almost forcibly with a strong E-flat Major *fortissimo*, destroying the mood of the first movement more radically than could any storm of applause. And without modulation it goes over into the C Major of the third and last movement, which the composer named "Sternenkranz" and later [changed to] "Palmen." Obviously, without the Dionysian applause that crowns the second movement ("Triumphbogen"), the work would seem to create no impression, because the closing movement of this powerful and noble song of a lofty and lonely soul is not directed to the brain centers that control the motor nerves of applause. The performance is rewarded with only mild approbation.

I raise the question, then, as to how our great composers such as Beethoven or Chopin would react to our problem.

In 1830 a young Polish pianist in Warsaw was giving a concert performance of Chopin's Concerto in E Minor. He opened the program with the first movement. Then Miss Constantia Gladkowska sang some arias and songs. These were

Translated from the German by E. K. Schwartz.

followed by a Rondo, "La sentinelle," by J. N. Hummel [and Mauro Giuliani], in which each of the five participating instruments [voice, piano, violin, guitar, and violoncello *ad lib.*] was provided with a *bravura* variation. Again, Miss Gladkowska appeared and sang her way into the hearts of all those present, and especially into the sensitive soul of the real concert-giver, who now closed this highly interesting evening with the playing of the second and third movements of his Concerto in E Minor. And what was the name of the man who arranged the entire program, the man who held all conservative program-bibles in contempt? His name has not remained unknown; it was Frédéric Chopin!

What would Beethoven have thought of a similar transgression? Would he have ranted and raved if the intense unity of his works had been broken by tactless applause? In answer, I quote from a letter of the Titan to his pupil and friend, Ferdinand Ries, occasioned by the sending of his greatest work for the piano, the so-called Sonata for Hammer-Klavier op. 106. Beethoven writes:

"If the sonata is not just right for London I can send another, or you can well omit the *largo* and begin immediately with the *fugue* in the last part, or the first part, *adagio* and, as a third, the *scherzo* and the *allegro risoluto*. I leave you to make the best of it."

Could there be a more effective death blow to concert hall snobbery than this letter of the master?[1]

And what is the moral of this discussion? Works and movements that close with Beethovenian triumphal fanfare, such as the first and last movements of the Sonata op. 106 or the four Scherzi and the First, Third, and Fourth Ballades of Chopin, rightly awaken stormy applause. Pieces like the *adagio* of op. 106 exclude applause just as does Chopin's "Funeral March." Therefore, heed your feelings, assuming, of course, that you have any!

Appendix A

Rosenthal as Humorist

Ambiguous truths

Once Rosenthal gave a concert in a city in the state of Ohio. Because his concert piano, which always followed him when he was on tour, had not arrived in time, he had to make do with a wretched piano for the night. But after the first few notes of Liszt's *Don Juan* Fantasie the badly screwed-in lyre, on which the pedals were hanging, fell down, and Rosenthal was forced to play the extraordinarily difficult piece without pedals. But when it rains it pours. In the middle of the piece a leg of the chair on which the artist was sitting broke off so that Rosenthal was forced to support the chair with his own leg and finish playing the piece in this condition. Rosenthal told me this story himself, and I commented jokingly: "Dear Rosenthal, I know that you are your own worst critic. How did you rate your play under such conditions?" Quick-witted as usual he answered: "I think I announced somewhat ambiguous truths to the audience like Pythia on her three-legged stool."[1] (Alfred Fischhof, *Neues Wiener Journal,* March 8, 1925)

On an audience member's snoring

On another occasion [Rosenthal] expostulated with a sleepy member of the audience at a concert he was attending, "For pity's sake, don't snore so loudly or you will waken up the whole audience." (*Musical America*)

On Teresa Carreño[2]

Recently [Rosenthal] was informed that Carreño almost refused to appear in a certain Western city because she had been advertised as the "Female Paderewski." The quick-witted Moriz replied: "They should have called her the 'Male Carreño.'" (Leonard Liebling)

On a colleague's besetting sin

[Rosenthal] attended a recital given by a colleague whose besetting sin was his abuse of the "loud pedal" by persistently holding it down. When a friend remonstrated with him for arriving somewhat late he replied: "Never mind, I can hear it all still."

On colleague W.'s performance of Rosenthal's arrangement of Chopin's "Minute" Waltz

Colleague W. [Alexander Winterberger?] put Chopin's so-called Minute Waltz in my difficult contrapuntal arrangement in thirds on his program. What I had foreseen came to pass: he played the piece in the safe slowest tempo. After the concert he asked me: "So, how did you like your Minute Waltz?" I replied: "Like is not the right word. It was the most beautiful quarter of an hour of my life."

On Ignaz Friedman not applauding him

Once, when the impresario George Kugel presented Rosenthal in the big hall of the Musikverein in Vienna, he invited Ignaz Friedman to share his box. During the intermission, Kügel went to the artists' room to see Rosenthal, and presently a pupil of Rosenthal's came in and said, "I saw Friedman sitting in Mr. Kügel's box, and he did not applaud at all." Rosenthal replied, "No wonder, he has a stiff wrist."

On his greatest pleasure

"In what do I take the greatest pleasure?" [Rosenthal] repeated after a reporter put that question to him. "Well, I sometimes think it is in reading critical praise of my piano playing. Then I decide that it is, after all, more from reading severe criticisms of other pianists." (*Musical America*)

On how to do a good business

"One of the managers I had was always trying to find something sensational by which to attract attention," [Rosenthal] said the other day, "and long after I had ceased to play under his direction he came to me for advice. He was a pianist himself, although a poor one, and had become an impresario after he had failed as a virtuoso.

"'What can I do,' he said to me, 'to make this concert attract the public? I want to do something to get the concert talked about.'

"'Take the largest hall in Vienna,' I told him, 'and charge no admission fee. The hall will be crowded.'

"'Yes, I know it will,' he answered, 'but I will not make any money by that.'

"'You just do as I tell you,' I urged him. 'You get the hall packed with people by letting them in free. Then you play the first number and the last on the program. Let the other artists come in between your selections.'

"'Yes, but then?'

"'Then put a notice on the program that everybody leaving the hall after your first number will have to pay a gulden. Everybody will get out rather than listen to you a second time and you will do a good business.'

"Whether or not he took my advice I never knew . . . "

On a low ceiling

The other night [Rosenthal] dined at the home of his manager, Henry Wolfsohn, on East Seventeenth Street. Mr. Wolfsohn lives in an old-fashioned house, and his dining room is in the basement.

"'I must apologize always for my very low ceiling," Mr. Wolfsohn said, "but we are accustomed to this dining room and never would be willing to give it up."

"The ceiling is low," said Mr. Rosenthal; "so low that you ought to serve only fried sole here." (*Musical America*)

On Ignace Jan Paderewski

In Syracuse [New York] Rosenthal submitted to the interviewer, and had some fraternal things to say of Paderewski: "He was made by the American matinée girl. He is a good pianist, but not the best. In Europe we have many we consider better than Paderewski. We have not the high opinion of his abilities that Americans have. But I am not an American, therefore I am not a good judge of Paderewski." (Leonard Liebling)

There is a story of Rosenthal's going, with another great pianist, Josef Hofmann, to hear Paderewski. In the middle of a slow movement by Beethoven, Rosenthal began to nod. Hofmann gave him a dig. "Are you going to sleep?" "No," answered Rosenthal, "Paderewski is." (Edward Sackville-West)

On a prodigy's repertoire

Once [Rosenthal] was forced to listen to a prodigy. The conversation is said to have run something like this:

"How old are you?"

"Seven, sir."

"And what would you like to play for me?"

"Please, sir, the Tchaikovsky concerto, sir."

"Too old!"

It may have been this prodigy whom Rosenthal met a few years later and asked, "Tell me, how old are you still?" (Harold Schonberg)

On Anton Rubinstein's eyesight[3]

Because of its wide leaps, the *Valse-Caprice* remained in the repertoire for several decades as a display piece. Walter Damrosch, ten years old at the time of Rubinstein's visit [to America], remembered an impromptu performance by the pianist in his family's home that included the work:

> I stood goggle-eyed behind him, watching his hands do incredible things on the piano despite the long black hair almost completely covering his face. I remember especially his last number, his famous waltz, which ends with a constant skipping in the right hand from the middle octave to an immediate reiteration on the piano's highest notes. I was beside myself with excitement as his hand made this terrific jump over the keys, again and again hitting the high notes with the precision of a marksman hitting the target in the center with every shot.

Other people remembered Rubinstein frequently missing those very same high notes. When the pianist Moriz Rosenthal heard him finally hit all the right ones, he supposedly remarked to a neighboring listener: "Poor Rubinstein! His eyesight is failing."

On X.'s octaves

At a dinner given to Rosenthal before his departure last week there was present a pianist, X., who is fond of playing Liszt's sixth rhapsody. He and Rosenthal are warm friends, and both being possessed of native Viennese wit they never fail to indulge in good natured badinage at each other's expense whenever they meet. Rosenthal takes a particular delight in aiming his satire at his friend X.'s playing of the famous octave episode in the sixth rhapsody. After Rosenthal's third New York recital, X. appeared in the artist room to greet him. "A nice friend you are," cried Rosenthal; "I have been in America a month and have given three recitals in New York, and yet this is the first moment you've had to come and see me." "You must excuse me," explained X.; "you see, I've been away on a tour and just got back, so I really had no time." "Nonsense," retorted Rosenthal; "if you have time to play the sixth rhapsody in the tempo which you take, then you certainly have time to come to see me."

The story which Rosenthal told at the dinner was this: "X. was giving a recital, and had reached the middle of the octave part in the sixth rhapsody when an usher approached the only auditor in the hall and asked to see his seat coupon. "I gave it to you when I came in," said the man addressed, a patriarch with snow white hair. "That is impossible," replied the usher, "for I remember distinctly that the only person who came through the gate was a little boy." "That was I," the patriarch made answer." (*Musical Courier*)

Appendix B

Annotated Concertography

By Mark Mitchell

The following list of works played in concert by Moriz Rosenthal does not pretend to be exhaustive since programs from each of his estimated 3,500 concerts are not extant.[1] Moreover, those that do exist often give imprecise information such as "five preludes" of Chopin or "sonata" of Scarlatti. This list is based upon the programs in the Archives of the Gesellschaft der Musikfreunde (incorporating the Bösendorfer Archives), Vienna, the Music Division of the New York Public Library, George Kehler's *The Piano in Concert,* and the collections of Steven Heliotes, Dr. Antonio Latanza (Director, Museum of Musical Instruments, Rome), and the authors, as well as more than one thousand concert reviews.

Louis Biancolli, who interviewed (and often reviewed) Rosenthal, set the number of works the pianist had in his repertoire at six hundred. Rosenthal himself calculated that Anton Rubinstein had only two hundred works in his repertoire; Sviatoslav Richter, on the other hand, brought more than two thousand works before the public. Privately Rosenthal played many other works, among them Godowsky's studies on the Chopin etudes.

Beethoven and Chopin were the composers of piano music to whom Rosenthal gave pride of place in his pantheon. "Of all the heroes of musical achievement," Rosenthal was quoted as saying in the *Neues Wiener Journal* of March 1, 1914, "Beethoven, Chopin, Schubert, Schumann, Weber, and Wagner are closest to my heart."

> Not by coincidence do I place Chopin next to Beethoven in the beginning of this list of noble monarchs. In accordance with a personal deep conviction, which, of course, I do not want to force on anyone, I feel that the great Pole is not lacking anything in musical genius in comparison with the master of the symphony. In spite of his diminutive forms, he has revolutionized music, enlarged the wealth of perception of the modern soul into infinitude, created new harmonies [Rosenthal called the Prelude op. 45 "the Bible of new harmonies"], and perfected all artistic means which relate to musical ideas. All this even though his artistic path was almost twenty years shorter than Beethoven's.

Nor did Rosenthal have any truck with received impressions of Chopin: "I have never had very much belief in the opinion that Chopin was a slave to his soul and his senses," he wrote ("The Genius of Chopin"). "I would far rather believe that he was more influenced by the inimitable chivalry and gallantry of his Polish race."

In the event Rosenthal was no less important an advocate of the music of Schumann and Liszt. However, he disdained Liszt's sonata! Steven Heliotes: "[Jorge Bolet, who studied with him circa 1935] said that Rosenthal once mentioned Liszt's sonata and said, sarcastically, as he hammered out the theme (when it makes its first 'lyrical' appearance), 'You call *that* a composer?' "[2] In an interview with the *Musical Courier* (September 15, 1940), Rosenthal admitted that he tired "of the 'bad weather' in Debussy's work, the 'stones of sound rather than the bread of melody' in Ravel," even as he respected their importance. On a less charitable occasion (*Neues Wiener Journal* of March 1, 1914) he said, "the works of Debussy and Ravel (not even to speak of cacophonicians à la Schönberg) seem to me like more or less successful flimflam." Rosenthal's attitude to Saint-Saëns, on the other hand, was humorously ambivalent: although publicly he called him the greatest living French composer—and, in fact, he had four works by Saint-Saëns in his repertoire—in private he seemed slightly antagonized by him. Surely one of the stranger items among Rosenthal's writings is the following Letter to the Editor of the New York *Evening Sun* (undated clipping; 1906?):

> Sir—I was quite astonished to read in your esteemed paper of my having audibly conversed during the recital of Mr. Saint-Saëns at Carnegie Hall and thereby having caused some persons to hiss. You would oblige me by most emphatically contradicting this. There was decidedly no hissing whatever and a few enthusiastic remarks uttered by me to my friend were whispered almost inaudibly.

In the event Rosenthal played less than a dozen works from the "répertoire hexagonal." (In 1906 he announced that he would program works by Fauré, but he seems not to have done so.) Rosenthal made a study of about thirty of Reger's piano works, and concluded that he did not admire any of them enough to play them, but lamented that Mahler, Richard Strauss, and Hugo Wolf gave so little to the piano. Nor did he play a number of works dedicated to him: Albeniz's Alhambra Suite; Godowsky's study on Chopin's Etude op. 10, no. 2 ("Ignis Fatuus," the fourth of his studies on the Chopin etudes) and the Toccata op. 13 ("Perpetual Motion"); and Stanford's Six Characteristic Pieces op. 132. (Stanford hoped that Rosenthal would play his Piano Concerto no. 2 in England and America in 1913; when Rosenthal did not, Leonard Borwick stepped in to give the premiere and was rewarded with the work's dedication.)

There are also programs of concerts which Rosenthal canceled listing works that he is not known to have programmed on other occasions. For instance, the conductor Georg Schneevoigt recalled that Rosenthal was scheduled to play three concertos in a single concert with him in Riga before World War I: an unspecified one by Beethoven, an unspecified one by Rubinstein, and Henselt's one and only. In the end, Rosenthal's program was played (and for Rosenthal's fee!) by Ignaz Friedman—who learned the Henselt Concerto in twenty-four hours. It is virtually inconceivable that Rosenthal would have programmed a work he could not actually play, so these works are listed but followed by a question mark.

Finally, it is just as well to list here those works that August Göllerich noted Rosenthal playing in Liszt's master classes at Weimar that he is not known to have played publicly: Schumann, Introduction and Allegro appassionato, op. 92 (June 5, 1884; with Caroline Montigny-Remaury); Meyerbeer-Liszt, Reminiscences de *Robert le Diable* (June 18); Anton Rubinstein, Variations on "Yankee Doodle" (July 4, 1885; Rosenthal was one of five pianists who took part in the performance, given to celebrate the Declaration of Independence of the United States); Beethoven-Liszt, Scherzo from the Symphony no. 9 (July 10); Joachim Raff, Sonata for Violin and Piano no. 1, op. 73: Scherzo (July 24; with Arma Senkrah); and C. F. Weitzmann, Canons—similar to "Chopsticks" (July 27; Rosenthal was one of three pianists who took part in the performance).

Albéniz

Cantos de España: Orientale (Rosenthal's piano roll has an extended cadenza.)
Ibéria: Triana

Auber-Liszt

La Muette de Portici (Tarantella)

C. P. E. Bach

Pièces de Caractère: La Complaisante and Les Langueurs tendres

J. S. Bach

Chromatic Fantasie and Fugue
French Suite no. 5 in G
Gavotte (unspecified)
Passepied en rondeau (from English Suite no. 5 in e?)
Sarabande (unspecified)
Well-Tempered Clavier (Prelude and Fugue in C-sharp, Book 1; Prelude and Fugue in d, but from which Book is not known; and unspecified)

In "The 'Grand Manner' in Piano Playing" (*Etude*, May 1937), Rosenthal spoke of Bach:

> He stands to all thinking musicians as one of the greatest composers of the world; but he has his limitations. The complete artist is fashioned from two elements: what he does and what he is. Now the Bach cult seems to lose sight of this fact. Its insistence upon Bach's magnificent craftsmanship (that is to say, what he *did*), tends to blot out the fact that what he *was*, as revealed in his powers of original thought and emotion, is not nearly so original, so revolutionary, though often quite as sublime as Beethoven. . . .
>
> Bach's characteristics are chiefly God-fearing piety, true depth of emotion, sincerity, contemplative thought, pride, and a sort of old-gentlemanly humor. But there is lacking the full wealth of upsoaring, even erotic, passion that stands revealed in Beethoven. Nor can it be said that this is due to the time in which Bach lived, for those qualities are evident in Shakespeare and even in Ovid, both of whom lived long before Bach.

J. S. Bach–Brahms

Chaconne from the Violin Partita no. 2 in d, BWV 1004

J. S. Bach–Liszt

Organ Prelude and Fugue in a

Balakirev

Unspecified work(s)

Beethoven

Three Bagatelles (E-flat and two unspecified)
Ecossaises
Piano Concerto (unspecified)
Piano Concerto no. 5 in E-flat, op. 73
Piano Sonatas no. 8 in c, op. 13 (*Pathétique*); no. 18 in E-flat, op. 31, no. 3; no. 19 in g, op. 49, no. 1; no. 23 in f, op. 57; no. 24 in F-sharp, op. 78; no. 26 in E-flat, op. 81a (*Les Adieux*); no. 28 in A, op. 101; no. 29 in B-flat, op. 106; no. 30 in E, op. 109; no. 31 in A-flat, op. 110; and no. 32 in c, op. 111
Piano Trios in c, op. 1, no. 3 (with Arnold Rosé and Friedrich Buxbaum) and B-flat, op. 97 (with Rosé and Buxbaum; with Johannes Woolf and Paul Ludwig)
Thirty-two Variations in c

Bortkiewicz

Etude op. 15, no. 8

Brahms

Capriccio op. 76, no. 2
Intermezzi op. 76, nos. 3 and 4; op. 118, no. 6; and op. 119, no. 3
Piano Concerto no. 2 in B-flat, op. 83
Piano Quintet in f, op. 34 (with Rosé Quartet)
Piano Sonata in f, op. 5
Rhapsody op. 119, no. 4
Variations on a Hungarian Song op. 21, no. 2
Variations on a Theme of Paganini op. 35

> Rosenthal played his own sequence (as, later, Arturo Benedetti Michelangeli would), omitting some variations.

Chopin

Allegro de Concert in A, op. 46
Ballades no. 1 in g, op. 23; no. 3 in A-flat, op. 47; and no. 4 in f, op. 52
Barcarolle in F-sharp, op. 60

> [From] Rosenthal's own program note to this work:

> All barcarolles composed before or after Chopin's time are quiet— reminiscent and descriptive of placid lakes. It was Chopin alone who made the barcarolle sing of the mysterious magic of the ocean—of its furious storms, of the sparkling brilliance of its sunny days, and the joy of happy lovers. Chopin's Barcarolle seems to sweep us always to the tropics of music. But in the op. 60, it is the imagination only which jour- neys, for the composer brings about an effective artistic relationship be-

tween the opening measure with its organ point on the dominant and the close of the work, where the same tremendous organ point is heard again on the tonic.

Berceuse in D-flat, op. 57

Etudes in C, op. 10, no. 1; a, op. 10, no. 2; E, op. 10, no. 3; G-flat, op. 10, no. 5; F, op. 10, no. 8; A-flat, op. 25, no. 1; f, op. 25, no. 2; F, op. 25, no. 3; g-sharp, op. 25, no. 6; G-flat, op. 25, no. 9; a, op. 25, no. 11; and c, op. 25, no. 12

Fantasie in f, op. 49

Impromptus no. 1 in A-flat, op. 29; no. 2 in F-sharp, op. 36; and no. 4 in c-sharp, op. 66 (Fantasie-Impromptu)

Mazurkas in A-flat, op. 24, no. 3; b-flat, op. 24, no. 4; g-sharp, op. 33, no. 1; D, op. 33, no. 2; C, op. 33, no. 3; b, op. 33, no. 4; c-sharp, op. 41, no. 1; e, op. 41, no. 2; B, op. 41, no. 3; G, op. 50, no. 1; A-flat, op. 50, no. 2; c-sharp, op. 50, no. 3; B, op. 56, no. 1; C, op. 56, no. 2; B, op. 63, no. 1; c-sharp, op. 63, no. 3; G, op. 67, no. 1; g, op. 67, no. 2; a, op. 67, no. 4; and op. posthumous

Nocturnes in E-flat, op. 9, no. 2; F-sharp, op. 15, no. 2; D-flat, op. 27, no. 2; G, op. 37, no. 2; f, op. 55, no. 1; E-flat, op. 55, no. 2; and E, op. 62, no. 2

Piano Concertos no. 1 in e, op. 11; and no. 2 in f, op. 21

Piano Sonatas no. 2 in b-flat, op. 35; and no. 3 in b, op. 58

Polonaise in A-flat, op. 53

Polonaise-Fantaisie in A-flat, op. 61

Prelude in c-sharp, op. 45

Preludes op. 28 (selection of at least fifteen, including no. 3 in G, no. 4 in e, no. 6 in b, no. 7 in A, no. 8 in f-sharp, no. 11 in B, no. 13 in F-sharp, no. 15 in D-flat, no. 19 in E-flat, no. 20 in c, no. 21 in B-flat, and no. 23 in F)

Scherzi no. 1 in b, op. 20; no. 2 in b-flat, op. 31; and no. 3 in c-sharp, op. 39

Tarentelle in A-flat, op. 43

Trois Nouvelles Etudes

Waltzes in a, op. 34, no. 2; F, op. 34, no. 3; A-flat, op. 42; D-flat, op. 64, no. 1; c-sharp, op. 64, no. 2; f, op. 70, no. 2; and e, op. posthumous

Chopin-Brahms

Etude op. 25, no. 2

Chopin-Liszt

Chants polonais nos. 1 (Maiden's Wish, arranged by Rosenthal—or, as a New York critic put it, "with five variations appended of Mr. Rosenthal's own contriving")[3] and 5 (My Joys, often played with a cadenza.)

Chopin-Rosenthal

Etude op. 25, no. 2

Studie über den Walzer op. 64, no. 1 (Leipzig, 1884; dedicated to Herrn Hans Grafen Wilczek Junior)

Göllerich wrote (June 18, 1885) that Liszt considered Rosenthal's study to be "handsomely and cleverly wrought, more charming than the Joseffy study [on the same waltz]." Göllerich added that Liszt "was of the opinion that the piece ended

too quickly and that Rosenthal ought to compose an ending for it; [Liszt] improvised three endings at the piano himself."

Rosenthal's performances inspired Elizabeth L. Bogle to compose verse in the
pianist's honor. Her poem "Rosenthal" was published in the *Tacoma New Herald*.
An excerpt:

'Tis done, and from five thousand eager hands
A clapping tears the breathless silence white,
Like toneless rip of cloth, zip of a lasso light,
Whose last flick blooms in tone, for he has tossed
The "Minute Waltz" in thirds ere it is known,
A trick, a bauble, worth a monarch's throne.

According to Carl Lachmund, Rosenthal played this study on the Minute Waltz in
less than 55 seconds.[4]

Clementi

Toccata

Couperin

La tendre Nanette

Cui

Feuillet d'album

Daquin

Le Coucou

Davidov-Friedheim

At the Fountain

Davidov-Rosenthal

Springbrunnen

Debussy

Images: Reflets dans l'eau
La plus que lente
Preludes: Les collines d'Anacapri and Minstrels

De Falla

Cubana

Field

Nocturnes in E (no. 18, "Le Midi") and E-flat (whether no. 1, 9, or 11 is unspecified)
Piano Sonata (unspecified)
Rondo (unspecified)

Gluck-Brahms

Gavotte

Goldmark

Bedrängnis (from ms.)
Traumgestalten (from ms.)

Gounod-Rosenthal

Faust Fantasie (dedicated to Josef Hofmann)

Grünfeld

Etude à la Tarantella (dedicated to Rosenthal)

Händel

Passacaglia (From Suite no. 7 in g, 1720?)
Suite no. 5 in E: Aria con variazioni ("Harmonious Blacksmith")

Haydn

Andante con variazioni

Heller

Two Preludes op. 81

Henselt

Berceuse
Nocturne
Piano Concerto in f?
Si oiseau j'étais

Hummel

Piano Sonata in f-sharp, op. 81: Finale
Rondo op. 11

Joseffy

Berceuse
Danse-Arabeske
Waltz in D-flat

Korngold

Three Pieces from *Much Ado about Nothing*

Lendvai, Erwin

Der Abenteurer op. 12: Allegro giusto

Leschetizky

Berceuse
Gavotte antique et Musette moderne
Valse-Caprice

Liadov

Berceuse
Preludes op. 46, nos. 1 and 3
Tabatiere à musique op. 32

Liszt

Années de Pélèrinage: Au bord d'une source and Au lac de Wallenstadt
Ballade no. 2 in b
Concert Etude in f (La Leggierezza)
Consolations (unspecified)
Don Juan Fantasie

In "If Franz Liszt Should Come Back Again" (*Etude*, April 1924), Rosenthal said:

> [Liszt] would be astonished at the tempo with which certain of his com-
> positions are ordinarily played in our concert halls.
> Take, for instance, Liszt's own *Don Juan Fantasie,* considered by some
> to be among the most difficult compositions ever written for the piano.
> In the *Champagne Song* it was the custom to play much slower than the
> air is sung upon the stage. When I was twenty-two years old I played
> this for Liszt and he marveled at my speed. If I should play it today at
> the same speed as I played it then, people would think me to be very cau-
> tious—perhaps losing my powers.

Fantasie on Hungarian Folk Melodies (based on Liszt's Hungarian Rhapsody no. 14)
Hexaméron

From Rosenthal's own note to this work:

When I played the Hexaméron before [Liszt] in Weimar he advised several changes and abbreviations. In this revised edition, which corresponds with the later one for two pianos, the piece opens with a very short introduction by Liszt, followed by his bold setting of the theme. Then Herz and Pixis appear, Chopin surprises us by metamorphosizing the March into an entrancing Nocturne, and this quite unique virtuoso work finished with the sparkling and buoyant, at the same time masterful "Finale" composed by Liszt.

Hungarian Rhapsodies nos. 2 (cadenza by Rosenthal), 11, and 12
Liebestraum no. 3
Mazurka brillante
Mephisto Waltz no. 1
Paganini Etudes: La Campanella
Piano Concertos no. 1 in E-flat and no. 2 in A

From "Rosenthal, Rex" (*Musical Courier*): "In the presence of such an epochal achievement as Rosenthal's [first] Liszt concerto, the average keyboard manipulator must have felt as Heine did when he first gazed on Goethe and Gibbon when he glimpsed the Rome of his dreams."

Rhapsodie Espagnole (arranged by Rosenthal)
Transcendental Etudes: Feux follets, no. 10, and Harmonies du soir
Valse-Caprice
Valse-Impromptu
Valse oubliée no. 1
Venezia e Napoli (more often than not, Rosenthal played just the Tarantella)
Waldesrauschen

Liszt-Rosenthal

Hungarian Rhapsody constructed from nos. 10 and 12

Padre Martini

Gavotte (Les Moutons) (with a coda by Rosenthal)

Mendelssohn

Rondo capriccioso op. 14
Songs without Words: op. 19, no. 1, op. 62, no. 6, and op. 67, no. 4
Variations sérieuses op. 54

Moscheles

Two etudes (Etude chromatique and unspecified)

Moszkowski

Unspecified work(s)

Mozart

Piano Sonata in A, K. 331

Poldini

Concert Etude op. 19, no. 1
Humoreske in 5/4 Time (from Petite Suite op. 97?)
Marche mignonne
Marionettes (excerpts)
Menuet
Rosen: Fünf Walzer für Klavier op. 55
Valse de ballet from Scènes de ballet op. 18 (from ms.)

Rachmaninoff

Unspecified work(s)

Rameau

Musette en rondeau
Tambourin

Reinecke

Impromptu on a Theme from Schumann's *Manfred* for two pianos (with Joseffy)

Rosenthal

Richard Specht ("Moriz Rosenthal," *Die Zeit* [Vienna], 1906):

> Rosenthal as composer: In his melodies noticeably a graduate of Chopin's school, talented and often astounding in his harmony. He has not published much, and his few compositions that have been printed have this great advantage: Nobody can play them but himself. That is particularly the case with his variations, which change a graceful theme brilliantly and, in details, captivatingly, but the difficulties of which, especially in the finale, hardly another pianist will be able to master. On the whole, he is one of the most interesting phenomena of modern art, if only for the reason that he does not pause, or allow anything to come in his way, because he possesses the rapid "tempo" of our race and the ability to find notes for the most delicate impressions and also always to find new possibilities of expression. He speaks of ourselves when he sits at the piano and speaks of himself and interprets a composition. Therefore not only the day belongs to him, but also the future.

Barcarolle (doubtful)
Mazurkas (doubtful)

Papillons (Fürstner, 1897; dedicated to Mademoiselle Régine Nicol)
Piano Concerto in g (doubtful)
Prélude (Fürstner, 1903; dedicated to Madame la Comtesse Robert de Fitz-James)
Romanza

> Robert Goldsand played this work, as well as the Papillons and Carneval de Vi-
> enne, at Rosenthal's 80th birthday "Gala Testimonial Concert" at Hunter College,
> December 18, 1942.

Tango-Habañera (doubtful; Rosenthal wrote about it often in his letters to Fred Gais-
berg)
Variationen über ein eigenes Thema (Fürstner, 1903—version for solo piano; ?—version
for piano and orchestra)
Theme
Arabeske
Scherzando ma deciso
Aria
Ballabile
Nocturne
À la Tarantella
Tempo di Mazurka
Petite Etude
Feuillet d'album
Finale con Intermezzi

> Rosenthal published a reworking of this composition under the title "Zehn Char-
> acterstücke" (Fürstner, 1928)

Rossini-Liszt

Overture to *William Tell*

Rubinstein

At the Brook
Bal Costumé: Andalouse and Toréador
Barcarolles (including nos. 4 and 5)
Miniatures: Sérénade, Valse, and Près du ruisseau
Piano Concerto (unspecified; probably no. 4 in d)?
Piano Trio in g, op. 15, no. 2
Valse allemande (containing a theme from Weber's *Der Freischütz*)
Valse-Caprice

Saint-Saëns

Etude en forme de valse
Piano Concerto no. 2 in g
Rhapsodie d'Auvergne
Variations on a Theme of Beethoven for two pianos (with Joseffy)

Sauer

Moto perpetuo en octaves [Octave Etude in E] (dedicated to Rosenthal)

Scarlatti

Sonatas (at least five, including ones in b, D, and e)

> Rosenthal is quoted on the first page of Hermann Keller's *Domenico Scarlatti, ein Meister des Klaviers* (Leipzig: Edition Peters, 1957); translated from the German by Justin Urcis):

> I am proud of my understanding of the music of Domenico Scarlatti, just as Nietzsche was in his way of understanding Epicurus. I hear his melodies light up in the darkness of time, I see them trickle down the volcanic soil of Naples. Let German scholars label him, in their scholastic delusion, merely as among the greatest old Italian virtuosos—the gentle boldness and ripe sweetness of his immortal melodies will earn him a higher place in art history than the technique of his keyboard writing, which, even though it is excellent, receives single-minded praise.

> He is also quoted in *Landowska on Music* (ed. Denise Restout; New York: Stein and Day, 1964):

> Once when Moritz Rosenthal was speaking to me of Scarlatti with enthusiasm, he said this significant thing, "It is too often believed that Scarlatti wrote only pieces of virtuosity. Yet what really reveals Scarlatti are his second themes, the slow ones, which prove that he was able to create feeling and profundity too." (381–382)

Scarlatti-Tausig

Capriccio (Sonata K. 20)

Scharwenka

Piano Concerto no. 1 in b-flat, op. 32

> [From] an interview with Harriette Brower, included in *Modern Masters of the Keyboard* (Freeport, N.Y.: Books for Libraries Press, 1926; reprint 1969), p. 20.

> [Scharwenka] has written several concertos which are excellent, but they are seldom heard, and are quite unknown in America. I consider them finer than the Saint-Saëns concertos. I have proposed the Fourth Concerto [in f] by Scharwenka to orchestral leaders here, but they refuse to put it on their programs. I suppose they don't want to take time to study a new work of that kind.

Schloezer

Etude de Concert in E-flat

Schubert

Impromptu in f, op. 142 (whether no. 1 or no. 4 is unspecified)
Moments Musicaux op. 94, nos. 1–4
Piano Sonata (Fantasie-Sonata) in G, op. 78

> Rosenthal also programmed just the menuet from this sonata (as did José Vianna
> da Motta, another Liszt pupil). Until the advent of Schnabel, this was just about
> the only Schubert piano sonata that anyone played, although both Conrad An-
> sorge and Vianna da Motta were playing the Sonata in B-flat, D. 960, as early as
> 1904, if not earlier.

Wanderer Fantasie op. 15

> From Rosenthal's own program note to this work:

> > [This] work was brought into vogue by Liszt, who arranged it for piano
> > alone and also with orchestra many years after his own virtuoso days
> > were over. His piano version greatly facilitates the execution, but it de-
> > tracts to some extent from the impressiveness of the work. It takes away,
> > too, from the brilliance which is characteristic of this composition and
> > which is hammered forth with a relentless and implacable mastery
> > worthy of Beethoven himself, who was Schubert's great and ever-present
> > ideal; for in the *Wanderer* Fantasie, the young eagle was trying, with his
> > already powerful wings, to reach the heights where his idol reigned.

Schubert-Liszt

Soirées de Vienne no. 6
Ständchen (Hark! Hark! The Lark!)
Winterreise: Der Lindenbaum

Schubert-Tausig

Marche Militaire (with Joseffy)

Schumann

Albumblätter op. 124: Ländler and Schlummerlied
Carnaval op. 9

> Rosenthal introduced counter-octaves in the March of the Davidsbündler after
> he heard Rubinstein play them—and after consulting with Liszt, who approved of
> the innovation.

Etudes symphoniques op. 13

> Because this work was a cornerstone of Rosenthal's repertoire, a review of one of
> his performances of it is in order. This one from *The Times,* London (April 18,
> 1898) is very significant insofar as it locates Rosenthal's interpretation in opposi-
> tion to the "official" tradition propagated by Clara Schumann:

It is true that Herr Rosenthal's reading of Schumann's masterpiece differs widely from that usually adopted by the pupils of the illustrious composer's widow, in that, to speak generally, he plays the first part more slowly and the finale more rapidly, and that preconceived ideals are apt to be rather upset. But the pianist is no iconoclast, no breaker of images for mere wanton pleasure. He builds up an image at least as effective as that he destroys, and his own remarkable individuality was intensely interesting as shown in his masterly performance.

Fantasie op. 17
Fantasiestücke op. 12: Des Abends, Warum?, In der Nacht, and Traumes-Wirren
Kreisleriana op. 16
Novellettes op. 21, nos. 2 and 4
Piano Concerto in a, op. 54
Piano Sonata no. 1 in f-sharp, op. 11: Aria

No performance of the entire sonata by Rosenthal has been found.

Six Studies for Pedal Piano op. 56
Waldszenen op. 82: Vogel als Prophet

Schytte

Etude (from ms.)
Pantomimen op. 30 for four hands: Pierrot, Harlequin, Columbine, and Finale (with the composer)
Piano Concerto in c-sharp, op. 28
Piano Sonata in B, op. 53
Schwedische Lieder und Tänze op. 52, nos. 2 and 3 for four hands (with the composer)
Über die Steppe
Valse noble
Vision

Scriabin

Etudes in D-flat, F-sharp, and f-sharp
Poème op. 32, no. 1

Sgambati

Nänie
Toccata op. 18, no. 4

Stanford

Unspecified work(s)

Johann Strauss II–Rosenthal

Rosenthal often played compositions of his own based on themes of Johann Strauss: In Vienna, between January 1891 and February 1902, he programmed the so-called *Wiener Carneval* at least five times; in January 1905, a *Humoreske über Themen von Johann Strauss,* while in November of that year, a *Fantasie über "An der schonen blauen Donau,"* etc. (to which this note was appended in the program: "Die Wiederkehr des dritten Walzerthemas nebst einigen Takten nach einer Version von Schulz-Evler"); in January 1909, a *Fantasie über Themen aus: "An der schonen blauen Donau" und "Die Fledermaus";* and in 1910, a *Fantasie über "An der schonen blauen Donau" u. andere Motive von Johann Strauss.* In other times and places, Rosenthal played a *Fantasia um Johann Strauss über die Walzer: "An der schönen blauen Donau," "Die Fledermaus" und "Freut euch des Lebens."* Essentially, these amount to two works: *Wiener Carneval* (published in 1925 by C. Fisher as *Carnaval de Vienne: Humoresque sur des thèmes de Johann Strauss,* but composed in May 1889) and *Blue Danube Fantasie* (circa 1906)—though Charles Rosen writes in his liner notes to his own recording of the work (on an Epic LP), "I doubt if Rosenthal ever played his *Carnaval de Vienne* without improvising something different each time." Among the manuscripts of the pianist Paul Wittgenstein auctioned by Sotheby's (London) in the spring of 2003 was an arrangement of the *Carneval de Vienne* for the left hand alone.

Ernest Newman compared the effect of Rosenthal's performance of one of these pieces to "that of a burning stick being made to revolve in the hands of a boy who knows all the rules of the burning-stick game. Mr. Rosenthal's fantastically difficult transcription does everything that can be done with the themes, except improve them." Of Rosenthal's H.M.V. recording of the Carneval de Vienne, Sorabji wrote (*New English Weekly,* June 18, 1936):

> This delicately flavoured and dazzling *entremet* already exists in a published form which, however, differs materially from the version under consideration. Rosenthal seems in these things a very incarnation of the spirit of Imperial Vienna, and over the incomparable elegance, grace, aristocratic *désinvolture* and distinction of his playing, not, of course, to mention its supreme brilliance, it were possible to dilate, but obviously the thing to do is to confine oneself to exhorting all lovers of fine playing and great style to get this record for themselves.

A film of Rosenthal playing his Blue Danube Fantasie was made by George Kossuth to go along with Rosenthal's Ampico roll of the work, but this has not been found.

Stravinsky

Etude in D, op. 7, no. 2

Szymanowski

Theme and variations in b-flat, op. 3

Tchaikovsky

Piano Concerto no. 1 in b-flat, op. 23
Romance in f, op. 5
Unspecified work(s)

Thalberg

Thème original et étude in a, op. 45 ("Repeated Notes")

Weber

Invitation to the Dance op. 65
Piano Sonatas no. 1 in C, op. 24: Rondo ("Perpetuum mobile") and no. 2 in A-flat, op. 39 (edited by Liszt)
Rondo brillante op. 62 ("La Gaîté")

Appendix C

Discography

By Allan Evans

Albéniz

Triana
1. May 29, 1929,* 2-21461; Parlophone (FR) 57063-ER, Odeon (G) 07641, Decca (US) 25875.

Chopin

Berceuse, op. 57
1. June 1, 1929, xxb 8350; Odeon (SP) 173.164.
2. c. 1930, 30475-1; Ultraphon (G) F 469, (F) FP 160, (CZ) E 11025, Royale (US) 105.

Concerto no. 1 in e, op. 11
1. March 1 & November 26, 1930, March 2, 1931, with Frieder Weissmann and the Berlin State Opera Orchestra; Parlophone (UK) R 902-3 E 11113-4, (G) B 12451-3, P 9558-9, Odeon (G) 0-25231-33, 0-6941-2, Columbia (J) set 206.

Concerto no. 1 in e, op. 11: Romanze
1. As above.
2. December 19, 1937, with Frank Black & the NBC Symphony; Biddulph CD LHW 040.

Etude in C, op. 10, nò. 1
1. April 4, 1929, (five takes), N838 (lateral) Edison 47004 (take A), 19145 (vertical) Edison 82353 (take B).
2. March 3, 1931, 2-21784; Parlophone (UK) E 11161, (AU) A4356, (G) P 9570, (FR) 59543-EC, Odeon (G) 0-6943, Decca (US) 25268.
3. June 23, 1939, Victor unissued.

Etude in G-flat, op. 10, no. 5
1. April 8, 1929, (five takes), Edison 19149 (vertical) & N842 (lateral) unpublished; Biddulph CD LHW 039.
2. May 2, 1930, 2-21703 unissued.
3. March 3, 1931, 2-21783; Parlophone (UK) E 11161, (AU) A4356.
4. March 3, 1931, 2-21783-2; Parlophone (G) P 9570, (FR) 59543-EC, Odeon (G) 0-6943, Decca (US) 25268.

---

*All recordings made on May 29 and June 1, 1929, used a Blüthner piano.

5. March 29, 1935, OEA 1369-1/3 HMV unissued; APR CD 7002 (take 1).

Etude in f, op. 25, no. 2
1. May 2, 1930, 2-21703 (possibly unissued); Parlophone (F) 2-21703?, Decca (US) 26875 (or 25875?)
2. March 29, 1935, 2EA 1365-1 HMV unissued; APR CD 7002.
3. June 22, 1939, Victor unissued.

Maiden's Wish (arr. Liszt)
1. March 2, 1929, (four takes), Edison N757 (lateral) & 19066 (vertical) unpublished, Biddulph CD LHW 039.
2. February 9, 1934, 2B 6004, 6006-1,2 HMV unissued; APR CD 7002 (take 1).
3. March 29, 1935, 2EA 1355-1,2 HMV unissued.
4. May 22, 1936, OEA 3646-1 HMV DB 2836, Victor 14300.

Mazurka in A-flat, op. 24, no. 3
1. March 2, 1929, (four takes), N755 (lateral) & 19064 (vertical) Edison unpublished; Biddulph CD LHW 039.
2. March 29, 1935, 2EA 1367-1,2 HMV unissued.
3. October 22, 1937, OEA 5506-1 HMV unissued; APR CD 7002.
4. October 23, 1937, OEA 5506-2,3 HMV unissued.

Mazurka in b-flat, op. 24, no. 4
1. May 29, 1929, xxb 8349; Odeon (F) 171.107, Columbia (J) 8233, Odeon (SP) 173.164.

Mazurka in g-sharp, op. 33, no. 1
1. May 3, 1930, 2-21703 (possibly unissued); Parlophone (F) 2-21703, Decca (US) 26875 (or 25875).

Mazurka in D, op. 33, no. 2
1. October 22, 1937, OEA 5505-1,2; (take 2) HMV DA 1660, Victor 1951 (take 2).

Mazurka in b, op. 33, no. 4
1. November 23, 1935, 2EA 2567-1; HMV DB 2773, Victor 14298, (J) 924.

Mazurka in A-flat, op. 50, no. 2
1. March 29, 1935, 2EA 1366-1 HMV unissued; APR CD 7002.
2. March 29, 1935, 2EA 1367-1,2 HMV unissued.
3. November 21, 1935, 2EA 2566-1; Victor 14304.
4. May 20, 1936, 2EA 2566-2 HMV unissued.
5. May 25, 1936, 2EA 2566-3; HMV DB 2773, Victor 14298, (J) 924.

Mazurka in B, op. 63, no. 1
1. October 22, 1937, OEA 5505-1,2; (take 2) HMV DA 1660, Victor 1951 (take 2).

Mazurka in c-sharp, op. 63, no. 3
1. March 2, 1929, (four takes) N755(lateral) & 19064 (vertical) Edison unpublished; Biddulph CD LHW 039.
2. May 3, 1930, 2-21704; Parlophone (F) 2-21703, Decca (US) 26875 (or 25875).
3. March 3, 1931, 2-21783; Parlophone (UK) E 11161, (AU) A4356.
4. March 3, 1931, 2-21783-2; Parlophone (G) P 9570, (FR) 59543-EC, Odeon (G) 0-6943, Decca (US) 25268.

5. October 23, 1937, OEA 5506-2,3 HMV unissued (uncertain if recorded).

Mazurka in G, op. 67, no. 1
1. 1928 (between March and June), 500006A Argentinean Odeon 132552 B (artist listed as "Morris Rosenthal, New York").
2. March 2, 1929, Edison 19064 unpublished; Biddulph CD LHW 039.
3. March 3, 1931, 2-21784; Parlophone (UK) E 11161, (AU) A4356, (G) P 9570, (FR) 59543-EC, Odeon (G) 0-6943, Decca (US) 25268.
4. November 21, 1935, 2EA 2566-1; Victor 14304.
5. May 25, 1936, 2EA 3649-1,2 HMV unissued.
6. October 22, 1937, OEA 5506-1 HMV unissued; APR CD 7002.
7. October 23, 1937, OEA 5506-2,3 HMV unissued.

Mazurka in a, op. 68, no. 2
1. May 25, 1936, 2EA 3649-1,2 HMV unissued.

My Joys (arr. Liszt)
1. May 29, 1929, xxb 8347; Odeon (F) 171.107, Columbia (J) 8233.
2. March 18, 1942, Victor unpublished CS 073452-1; Biddulph CD LHW 039.
3. March 18, 1942, Victor unpublished CS 073452-2; *Moriz Rosenthal in Word and Music* CD.

Nocturne in E-flat, op. 9, no. 2
1. April 8, 1929, (five takes), Edison 19150 (vertical) & M843 (lateral) unpublished; Biddulph CD LHW 039.
2. November 21, 1935, OEA 2564-1 HMV unissued.
3. May 20, 1936, OEA 3640-1,2 HMV unissued.
4. May 21, 1936, OEA 3640-3 HMV unissued.
5. May 22, 1936, OEA 3640-4; HMV DB 2926, Victor 14297, (J) 871.

Nocturne in D-flat, op. 27, no. 2
1. May 20, 1936, 2EA 3641-1 HMV unissued.
2. May 21, 1936, 2EA 3641-2,3 HMV unissued.
3. May 22, 1936, 2EA 3641-4, 5; HMV (take 5) DB 2926, Victor 14297, (J) 871.

Nouvelle Etude in A-flat
1. April 4, 1929, (five takes), N838 (lateral) Edison 47004 (take A), 19145 (vertical) Edison 82353 (take B).
2. March 29, 1935, 2EA 1365-1 HMV unissued; APR CD 7002.

Prelude in G, op. 28, no. 3
1. June 1, 1929, 2-21465 Parlophone E17021 (J).
2. November 21, 1935, 2EA 2562-2 HMV DB 2772, Victor 14299, (J) JD 836.

Prelude in e, op. 28, no. 4
1. June 1, 1929, 2-21465 Parlophone E17021 (J).

Prelude in b, op. 28, no. 6
1. March 1, 1929, N754 (two takes—lateral, B accepted); Edison 47004 & 19063 (two takes—vertical, B accepted) Edison 82353.
2. April 8, 1929, (five takes) Edison 19149 (vertical) & N842 (lateral) unpublished; Biddulph CD LHW 039.
3. November 21, 1935, 2EA 2562-2 HMV DB 2772, Victor 14299, (J) JD 836.

Prelude in A, op. 28, no. 7
1. March 1, 1929, N754 (two takes—lateral, B accepted); Edison 47004 & 19063 (two takes—vertical, B accepted) Edison 82353.
2. April 8, 1929, (five takes) Edison 19149 (vertical) & N842 (lateral) unpublished; Biddulph CD LHW 039.
3. November 21, 1935, 2EA 2562-2 HMV DB 2772, Victor 14299, (J) JD 836.

Prelude in B, op. 28, no. 11
1. March 1, 1929, N754 (two takes—lateral, B accepted); Edison 47004 & 19063 (two takes—vertical, B accepted) Edison 82353.

Prelude in F-sharp, op. 28, no. 13
1. October 23, 1937, OEA 5507-1 HMV unissued; APR CD 7002.

Prelude in E-flat, op. 28, no. 19
1. June 1, 1929, 2-21465 Parlophone E17021 (J).

Prelude in c, op. 28, no. 20
1. June 1, 1929, 2-21465 Parlophone E17021 (J) (possibly Prelude no. 1).

Prelude in B-flat, op. 28, no. 21
1. May 29, 1929, xxb 8348 Odeon unpublished.

Prelude in F, op. 28, no. 23
1 March 1, 1929, N754 (two takes—lateral, B accepted); Edison 47004 & 19063 (two takes—vertical, B accepted) Edison 82353.

Sonata in b, op. 58
I: Allegro Maestoso
1. June 27, 1939, Victor unpublished CS 040220/1; Biddulph CD LHW 039.
II: Scherzo
1. June 22, 1939, Victor unpublished CS 040206; Biddulph CD LHW 039.
III: Largo
1. March 23, 1935, BBC broadcast (almost complete); *Moriz Rosenthal in Word and Music* CD.
2. June 23, 1939 Victor unpublished CS 040211/12; Biddulph CD LHW 039.
IV: Finale
1. June 26, 1939, Victor unissued CS 040214 (one side); Biddulph CD LHW 039.
2. June 26, 1939, Victor unpublished (two sides); *Moriz Rosenthal in Word and Music* CD.

Tarantella
1. March 18, 1942, Victor unpublished CS 073453; Biddulph CD LHW 039.

Waltz in a, op. 34, no. 2
1. March 29, 1935, 2EA 1368-1 HMV unissued.

Valse in F, op. 34, no. 3
1. June 22, 1939, Victor unissued.

Valse in A-flat, op. 42
1. March 2, 1929, (four takes) Edison N756 (lateral) & 19065 (vertical) unpublished; Biddulph CD LHW 039.
2. April 28, 1930, 2-21691 unissued.

3. February 9, 1934, 2B 6004, 6006-1,2 HMV unissued; APR CD 7002 (take 2).
4. November 21, 1935, 2EA 2561-1 HMV DB 2772, Victor 14299, (J) JD 836.

Valse in D-flat, op. 64, no. 1
1. November 14, 1927, 7843 Parlophone unissued.

Valse in c-sharp, op. 64, no. 2
1. November 14, 1927, 7844 Parlophone unissued.
2. 1928 (between March and June), 500005B Argentinean Odeon 132552 B (artist listed as "Morris Rosenthal, New York").
3. May 29, 1929, 2-21457; Columbia (J) 8325. Parlophone E17021 (J).
4. June 1, 1929, 2-21457-2 unissued?
5. April 28, 1930, 2-21692; Parlophone (G) P 9520, (UK) E 11043, Odeon (G) 0-6940, (AU) A 4258, (SP) P 55044, Decca (US) 25121.
6. March 29, 1935, 2EA 1364-1,2 HMV unissued.
7. November 21, 1935, OEA 2565-1 HMV unissued.
8. May 20, 1936, 2EA 2565-2 HMV unissued.
9. May 21, 1936, 2EA 2565-3 HMV unissued.
10. May 22, 1936, 2EA 2565-4 HMV DB 2772, Victor 14299, (J) JD 836.

Valse in e, op. posthumous
1. 1928 (between March and June) 500006A Argentinean Odeon 132552 B (artist listed as "Morris Rosenthal, New York").
2. May 29, 1929, 2-21458 (two takes) unissued.
3. April 28, 1930, 2-21693; Parlophone (G) P 9520, (UK) E 11043, (F) 59523-EC, Columbia (J) 8325, Odeon (G) 0-6940, (AU) A 4258, (SP) P 55044, Decca (US) 25121.

Debussy

Reflets dans l'eau
1, May 29, 1929, 2-21460-1; Parlophone (FR) 57063-ER.
2. May 29, 1929, 2-21460-2; Parlophone (FR) 57063-ER, Parlophone (UK) E 11145, Odeon (G) 07641, Decca (US) 25317.

Handel

Air and Variations (Suite no. 5 in E)
1. June 21, 1939, Victor unissued.
2. June 22, 1939, Victor unissued.
3. June 23, 1939, Victor CS 040200 unissued; Biddulph CD LHW 039.

Liadov

Prelude in B-flat, op. 46, no. 1
1. May 29, 1929, 8348 unissued.
2. May 3, 1930, 2-21705; Parlophone (UK) E 11145, (FR) 59523-EC, Decca (US) 25317.

Tabatière à musique
1. November 14, 1927, BW 1345-1, 2 unissued.

2. February 11, 1929, Edison experiment #185A (30 rpm disc: may survive on metal part in Edison archive or elsewhere).
3. May 29, 1929, 8348 unissued.
4. May 3, 1930, 2-21705; Parlophone (UK) E 11145, (FR) 59523-EC, Decca (US) 25317.
5. December 16, 1931, 2831 (Berlin) German Radio disc (lost).

Liszt

Au lac du Wallenstadt
1. March 23, 1935, BBC broadcast (not extant: only part of Chopin's Sonata Op. 58 survives from this broadcast).

Hungarian Rhapsody no. 2 (cadenza by Rosenthal)
1. February 11, 1929, Edison experiment #185A (30 rpm disc: may survive on metal part in Edison archive or elsewhere).
2. 1930, 30473-1/74; Ultraphon (F) FP 107, (G) F 468, Royale (US) 104.

La Leggierezza
1. No date (Gramophone Co., Paris, November 15, 1927?): According to the National Sound Archives of London, "an official of Pathé-Marconi once told the Institute that a test pressing of Liszt's Etude in F Minor existed, but no details are available." Surviving evidence of recordings made a day earlier leads one to doubt whether this is true, although one hopes to be proven wrong.

Liebestraum no. 3
1. 1930, 30476; Ultraphon (F) FP 107, FP 160, (G) F 468, Royale (US) 104.

Mendelssohn

Song without Words, op. 62, no. 6
1. May 21, 1936, OEA 3641-1 HMV unissued.

Rosenthal

Blue Danube Waltz (after Strauss)
1. May 8, 1928, A 45018/9; Electrola (G) EJ 329, HMV ES 560 (Cz).
2. March 6, 1931, 2-21785-1,2/86-1,2 Parlophone (G) P 9562 & 59.544.

New Carnaval de Vienne
1. February 9, 1934, 2B 6004, 6005-1,2 HMV unissued; APR CD 7002 (take 2 of 6005).
2. March 29, 1935, 2EA 1356-1,2 (part 1) HMV unissued.
3. November 23, 1935, 2EA 2568,69-1; HMV DB 2836, Victor 11-8175.

Papillons
1. November 14, 1927, BW 1344-1,2 (20456-57) unissued.
2. May 3, 1930, 2-21704; Parlophone (F) 2-21703, Decca (US) 26875 (or 25875).
3. February 9, 1934, 2B 6008-1 HMV unissued.
4. March 29, 1935, 2EA 1357-1 HMV unissued.
5. November 21, 1935, OEA 2563-1,2 HMV unissued.
6. November 23, 1935, OEA 2563-3,4 HMV unissued.
7. May 22, 1936, OEA 3644-1 HMV unissued.

8. October 23, 1937, OEA 644-2,3 HMV unissued; APR CD 7002 (take 3).
9. June 22, 1939, Victor unissued.

Wiener Carnaval (after Strauss)
1. June 1, 1929, 2-21462-1,2/63 unissued.
2. May 3, 1930, 2-21706, 2-21707-2; Parlophone (G) P 9542, (UK) E 11079, (FR) 59522-EC, (I) P 56086, Decca (US) 25839.
3. December 19, 1937, unissued NBC radio broadcast (at IPAM).

Schubert

Moment Musical no. 3
1. May 22, 1936, OEA 3645-1 HMV unissued.
2. October 22, 1937, OEA 3645-2,3 HMV unissued; APR CD 7002 (take 2).

Soirée de Vienne no. 6 (arr. Liszt)
1. May 25, 1936, OEA 3647/8-1,2; HMV (take 1) DA 1510, Victor 1951.

Notes

1. Editors' note: Although a length of four-and-a-half minutes was the industry standard, the 78 could actually accommodate more than five-and-a-half minutes of music. For example, Beethoven's Duo for Violin and Cello, played by Paul and Rudolf Hindemith, lasts about 5′40″ on one side of a Brunswick 78; additionally, several 78s on the Japanese Nitto label of traditional music made before 1910 are more than five minutes per side (and they are ten-inch discs!).

2. Editors' note: Vladimir de Pachmann invented the standard fingering for this piece.

3. Editors' note: This was not really typical of Liszt, whose master classes began punctually and were always announced in advance.

4. Editor's note: Rosenthal also played pianos by, among others, Bechstein, Blüthner, Bösendorfer, Knabe, Steinway, and Weber.

Chronology

1. An important history of Liszt's teaching is August Göllerich's *The Piano Master Classes of Franz Liszt 1884–1886,* edited by Wilhelm Jerger, translated, edited, and enlarged by Richard Louis Zimdars (Bloomington: Indiana University Press, 1996). Rosenthal played in these classes a handful of times, yet Liszt made no significant remarks about his performances. For example, after Rosenthal played the Chopin Barcarolle (June 20, 1885), Göllerich wrote, "The master said [Rosenthal] takes a fairly fast tempo"; Göllerich wrote nothing after Rosenthal played Liszt's "Au bord d'une source." In general, the playing of his pupils provided an occasion for Liszt to make important pronouncements about the art of the piano—an art that he ultimately felt could not be taught.

2. Xaver Scharwenka was also in Leipzig for the premiere. In his autobiography (*Klänge aus meinem Leben: Erinnerungen eines Musikers* [Leipzig, 1922]), he recounted: "On the day after the performance, while I was having afternoon coffee in my hotel room, there was a knock at the door. Four young men, responding to my 'Come in,' trooped into the room. There in a row stood Moriz Rosenthal, Emil Sauer, Arthur Friedheim, and Bernhard Stavenhagen. I learned that they were pupils of Liszt and had accompanied him from Weimar. They found my name on the hotel's guest list and wanted to meet me. I thanked them for the honor they paid, ordered coffee, cognac, and cigars, and invited the merry quartet for a splendid dinner at Ackerlein's Keller. During the course of the evening we visited another tavern where 'Fidelitas' reached its highest point. In the midst of the liveliest talk we were suddenly aware that a staunch companion was missing; Rosenthal had slipped away unnoticed. After a lengthy search we found him in a quiet, out-of-the-way room where he was practicing passages in sixths with solemn dedication on a broken-down piano." (Translated from the German by Charles Suttoni.)

3. Hedwig Loewy Kanner (1882–1959), Austrian pianist, pedagogue, and music critic. Sources that give the date of Rosenthal's marriage to Kanner as 1922 are in error: Rosenthal identified Kanner as his wife in a letter dated October 14, 1921.

Introduction

1. That Brahms's presence is more vivid than Liszt's in Rosenthal's writings is not to be wondered at. Liszt was half a century older than Rosenthal, and their relationship, though cordial, was essentially that of teacher and pupil. Liszt died when Rosenthal was twenty-three years old. Brahms, on the other hand, was a generation closer to Rosenthal, and though he was already an eminence when Rosenthal met him, their relationship was collegial. It lasted until Brahms's death in 1897, when Rosenthal was thirty-five.

2. Rosenthal also spoke Polish and some Italian.

3. Arthur Friedheim (1859–1932), German pianist, conductor, and composer. He was also the author of some memoirs, *Life and Liszt: Recollections of a Concert Pianist*, edited by Theodore L. Bullock (New York: Taplinger, 1961). The quotation is from p. 26.

4. Oddly enough, Rosenthal did not play the *Davidsbündlertänze* or the *Humoreske* in concert—at least not according to programs and reviews from more than one thousand of his concerts.

5. Mark Hambourg (1879–1960), Russian-born British pianist and composer. He wrote two volumes of memoir, *From Piano to Forte: A Thousand and One Notes* (London: Cassell, 1931) and *The Eighth Octave: Tones and Semi-tones concerning Piano-playing, the Savage Club and Myself* (London: Williams and Norgate, 1951).

6. Ignaz Friedman (1882–1948), Polish-born pianist. His playing of the Chopin mazurkas alludes to the rhythmic practice of the composer himself. Allan Evans has completed a biography of this remarkable Leschetizky pupil. Aleksander Michałowski (1851–1938), Polish pianist, composer, and teacher (Wanda Landowska was one of his pupils). He made some recordings for the Gramophone and Typewriter Company (London).

7. Lina Ramann (1833–1912), German writer and music teacher.

8. In his article "Franz Liszt, Memories and Reflections" (*Die Zeit* [Berlin], October 1911), Rosenthal pointed out that this was not the only time Liszt's work showed the influence of Chopin: "one needs only to compare Liszt's great *Transcendental* Etude in F Minor and the arpeggiated chords of his magnificent "Harmonies du soir" with Chopin's Etudes in F Minor and E-flat Major, op. 10 (published earlier) to see the many stimuli Liszt had received from the genius of Chopin, in spite of the former's originality. Liszt, however, appears as an innovator and pioneer in the orchestral effects of his transcriptions for the piano, a progeny which was not to find any epigone." (Elsie Braun Barnett's translation from the German of the complete article was published in *Current Musicology* 13 [1972].)

9. On this occasion it was the one in the Scherzo in b-flat that Rosenthal was shown. Richard Specht wrote of a similar occasion ("Moriz Rosenthal," *Die Zeit* [Vienna], 1906): "I, myself, was present at the decision of a bet when Rosenthal pledged himself to recognize every composition of Chopin by any single measure shown to him, the rest of the page being covered. One may easily understand that they did not make it very easy for him. The strangest measures, very often composed of only one chord, and in one case consisting of only a single note, were submitted to him, and almost without hesitation he named the composition to which the measure belonged, and played it from memory."

10. It is worth remarking that while Rosenthal was intimately aware of Chopin's music, he did not always play it as the composer wrote it. In the Etude op. 10, no. 5, he often substituted a pianissimo double-octave glissando—as on his March 1931 recording of the piece—for Chopin's original ending. (Ignaz Friedman also took this liberty.) In the Scherzo in b, he often played the final passage in interlocking octaves instead of single notes.

11. This essay was published in an (unsigned) English translation from the German in *The Independent*, November 15, 1906; *The Musical Courier; The Musical Observer: A Journal for Musical People*, March 1907; etc.

12. Liszt himself was thoroughly unimpressed by exploits. According to August Göllerich (*The Piano Master Classes of Franz Liszt, 1884–1886*), Liszt refused to allow Rosenthal to play the *Don Juan* Fantasie for him on at least two occasions.

13. Edward Sackville-West, "Rosenthal," *Recorded Sound* 7 (summer 1962), pp. 214–215.

14. Harold C. Schonberg, *Horowitz: His Life and Music* (New York: Simon & Schuster, 1992), p. 73. Horowitz's judgment must be taken *cum grano salis*, since he had been the object of one of Rosenthal's more biting witticisms. After hearing Horowitz play the Tchaikovsky Concerto in b-flat at his Vienna debut, Rosenthal had remarked: "He is an Octavian, but not a Caesar."

15. Joseph Bennett (1831–1911), English music critic and writer. Rosenthal's letter was published in Bennett's *Forty Years of Music, 1865–1905* (London, 1908).

16. Arthur Shattuck (1881–1951), American pianist. He studied with Leschetizky.

17. *The Memoirs of Arthur Shattuck,* edited by S. F. Shattuck (Neenah, Wis.: Privately published, 1961).

18. Ignacy Jan Paderewski (1860–1941), Polish pianist, composer, and statesman.

19. In America, where early on Rosenthal had had to play the week after Paderewski in city after city, he had enormous posters put up announcing that whereas Paderewski had played such and such a piece in so many minutes and seconds, he (Rosenthal) would play it faster.

20. Conte Enrico di San Martino Valperga. *Regia Accademia di Santa Cecilia: I concerti dal 1895 al 1933. Parte I. Ricordi del Presidente* (Rome, 1933), pp. 66–67.

21. Frédéric Kalkbrenner (1785–1849), French pianist, teacher, and composer of German extraction.

22. Julian Fontana (1810–1869?), Polish musician and writer. He had been a schoolmate and close friend of Chopin's and later copied out his manuscripts and mediated between him and his publishers. Rosenthal is correct that Fontana "ended his life with a pistol shot," but incorrect that he did so after going deaf as a result of taking some bad advice from his landlady. (She had supposedly told him to put cotton wool dipped in ether in his ears to cure a "slight pain.") In any case, Fontana's life was crowded with pursuits that had nothing to do with Chopin.

23. Erica Morini (1904–1995), Austrian violinist.

24. Eileen Wood (1908–1982). Five of Rosenthal's letters to her are in the Music Division of the New York Public Library.

25. Ludvig Schytte (1848–1909), Danish pianist, composer, and pedagogue. This "school" comprised sixteen sequences of exercises: with the still hand; with the moving hand; putting the thumb under, etc.; scales; broken chords and arpeggios; finger change on any given key; thirds, sixths, fourths, and fifths; trills; broken octaves; staccato octaves; legato octaves; alternating the hands; glissandos; extension, and for developing the independence and strength of the fingers; chords; jumps and chance movements.

26. Quoted in Edward Herbst, *Voices in Bali* (Hanover: University Press of New England, 1997), pp. 23–24.

27. Specht obviously did not know Rosenthal's "program" for the section in A-flat from Brahms's Rhapsody op. 119, no. 4 (see the Preface, p. xi).

28. Richard Specht, "Moriz Rosenthal," *Die Zeit* (Vienna), 1906.

29. Soma Morgenstern, *Kritiken, Berichte, Tagebücher* (Lüneberg: Dietrich zu Klampen Verlag, 2001), p. 258. Wilhelm Furtwängler (1886–1954), German conductor, composer, and writer.

30. Sigmund Herzog, pianist, composer, and pedagogue. Marcella Sembrich (1858–1935), Polish-born naturalized-American soprano.

31. It is not difficult to turn up a copy of Julius Eker's English translation of *Lucrezia Floriani* (Chicago: Academy Chicago Publishers, 1985).

32. Adolf Weismann, *Chopin* (Berlin & Leipzig: Schuster & Loeffler, 1912).

1. Autobiography

1. Rosenthal's mother was the former Augusta Kanner, whose family originally came from Odessa. Leo Rosenthal, Moriz's father, was her second husband. By her first husband, she had a daughter, Laura, a pianist of whose gifts Moriz was believed by the rest of the family to be jealous. Laura was mentally disturbed, however, and was eventually committed to an asylum. Upon her release, she sat at the piano and played very well, as if time had not intervened.

2. According to a Kanner family history, Rosenthal had at least four full sisters: Rosa, Marie, Clara, and Fanny. Marie's husband, Berthold Hatschek (1854–1941), was a professor of zoology at the German University in Prague, then chairman of the zoology department at the University of Vienna. She herself was a painter of some repute whose subjects included members of the Hapsburg family; today her portrait of the zoologist Ernest Haeckel hangs in the Lilly Library at Indiana University. Fanny Rosenthal married a Yugoslavian army doctor named Schraga; after his death, she lived with the Hatscheks in Vienna, and during World War II she went to Yugoslavia, where the sisters were murdered. Fanny was said to be almost as lively a wit as her brother.

3. Albert Jungmann (1823 or 1824–1892), Austrian composer and music publisher. Tekla Bądarzewska-Baranowska (1834–1861), Polish composer. "The Maiden's Prayer" had been published in Warsaw in 1856.

4. The American critic James Gibbons Huneker called Rosenthal "the Napoleon of the Pianoforte," and not only because of his height.

5. Jósef Antoni Poniatowski (1763–1813), Polish prince and French marshal who aided Napoleon in his ill-starred campaign against Russia. He drowned in the Elster on October 19, 1813. When Chopin visited Leipzig in 1836, he laid on a wreath on a monument to Poniatowski.

6. On a narrative level, it is worth noting that Rosenthal pretends to learn things about his father from the swim coach that he certainly already knew.

7. Sir Hudson Lowe (1769–1844) was the governor of St. Helena and custodian of Napoleon I.

8. Friedrich August Noesselt was the author of world histories for both boys and girls: respectively, *Lehrbuch der Weltgeschichte für Bürgerschulen* and *Lehrbuch der Weltgeschichte für Töchterschulen*.

9. Friedrich von Schiller (1759–1805), German poet, dramatist, and historian.

10. "Pedallosigkeit" in the original German is also a neologism.

11. "CL" is the Roman numeral for 150; "Esel" is the German word for donkey.

12. Marie Edmé Patrice Maurice de MacMahon (1808–1893), French marshal and second president of the Third Republic.

13. Karol Mikuli (1819–1897), Romanian pianist, composer, conductor, and teacher. He settled in Lemberg in 1858 and became artistic director of the Galician Music Society, also director and professor of the Lemberg Conservatory. Robert Freund confirms that Marek studied with Liszt in *Musical Memories and Letters, 1860–1960,* translated from the German by Nicholas Milroy and Allan Evans (unpublished): "Towards Easter 1871, Liszt left Pest, but returned the same year in November and moved into a third floor apartment on the corner of Nador and Szechenyi streets—now Freedom Square. It was in the winter in which I served the six months of my one-year's military service (from which I was discharged in the spring of 1872). Even though I had little time for playing the piano, I visited him regularly twice a week, often for two or three hours. Other than myself, Louis Marek, a thirty-year-old musician from Lemberg, studied with him at that time."

14. A remarkable insight into how Rosenthal's elders perceived Chopin at the time.

15. Hans Guido von Bülow (1830–1894), German pianist, conductor, and composer.

16. Probably Princess Anna Czartoryska (*née* Sapieha), wife of Prince Adam Jerzy Czartoryski and a patron of Chopin. "Sapiegyna" is the feminine form of the surname "Sapieha." Chopin dedicated his *Rondo à la krakowiak* (op. 14) to her.

17. In the lesson he wrote on Chopin's A-flat Waltz, op. 42, Rosenthal observed that Kalkbrenner was the father not only of *legatissimo* playing, but of using a loose wrist for octaves and *staccato* playing.

18. Rosenthal is conflating the opening lines of two poems by Rainer Maria Rilke: "In diesem Dorfe steht das letzte Haus" from *The Book of Hours (II: The Book of Pilgrimage)* and "Das ist dort, wo die letzten Hütten sind."

19. Carl Czerny (1791–1857), Austrian pianist, composer, and pedagogue. He was a pupil of Beethoven and a teacher of Liszt.

20. The letter, written from Schloss Wilhelmsthal, is dated July 27, 1875.

21. Karl Holz (1798–1858), a minor government official and amateur violinist (he played in the second chair in Ignaz Schuppanzigh's quartet). He acted as Beethoven's secretary and factotum from 1825 to 1826.

22. Beethoven's quote continues: "In the future I shall write in the manner of my grand-master Handel annually only an oratorio or a concerto for some string or wind instrument, provided I have completed my tenth symphony (C minor) and my Requiem." Quoted in *Thayer's Life of Beethoven,* revised and edited by Elliot Forbes (Princeton: Princeton University Press, 1967), p. 984.

23. The joke, presumably, is that Mikuli ate so many of the Count's *swiecone* that he had no room left for his own.

24. August Wilhelmj (1845–1908), German violinist.

25. Rudolph Niemann (1838–1898), German pianist and composer. Walter Niemann (1876–1953), German composer and writer on music.

26. Adam Mickiewicz (1798–1855), Polish poet and patriot. E. L. Voynich: "According to [Alfred] Cortot, [Chopin's] G minor Ballade is based on [Mickiewicz's] epic poem: 'Konrad Wallenrod'; and the other three on ballads, written by Mickiewicz on the legends which he had learned in Lithuania from the local peasantry; the F major on that called 'Switez'; the A-flat major on 'Switezianka'; and the F minor on 'Trzech Budrysow'"

(*Chopin's Letters*, collected by Henryk Opienski, translated and with a preface and editorial notes by E. L. Voynich [New York: Alfred Knopf, 1931], p. viii).

27. David Popper (1843–1913), Austrian cellist and composer, and Sophie Menter (1846–1918), German pianist and composer whom Liszt called "my only legitimate piano daughter." They married in 1872 and divorced in 1886. In 1896 Aubrey Beardsley wrote to his sister Mabel: "I saw the advertisement of the concert you went to in *The Times*. I was so interested to see that Sophie Menter (the heroine of [Beardsley's poem] the 'Three Musicians') was playing again in London. I should so much have liked to have heard her. The C minor [concerto of Saint-Saëns, the fourth] is a sweet and beautiful thing."

28. In English in the original.

29. Perhaps the origin of an arrangement Rosenthal offered early in his career. He had scant success with this work. After he played it at Carnegie Hall in 1898, one critic wrote: "It is really a pity that these compositions in their original form are neither bad enough nor hard enough for Mr. Rosenthal."

30. Crossed out in the original.

31. Jozéf Wieniawski (1837–1912), Polish pianist and composer. Henryk Wieniawski (1835–1880), Polish violinist and composer.

32. Rafael Joseffy (1852–1915), Hungarian pianist, composer, and teacher. He himself was a pupil of both Liszt and Tausig.

33. Anton Grigor'evich Rubinstein (1829–1894), Russian pianist, composer, conductor, teacher, and founder of the St. Petersburg Conservatory.

34. There were many touches (half-staccato, *jeu perlé, portato*) which are now lost to most pianists. *Jeu perlé* is an almost legato, with more accented notes (like a string of pearls); half-staccato is a lighter legato, with more space between the notes. The difference between these touches is subtle, but these were subtle musicians.

35. Carl Tausig (1841–1871), Polish-born pianist and composer of Czech ancestry. His father was a pupil of Sigismond Thalberg (1812–1871), the Austrian pianist and composer.

36. In "The Training of a Virtuoso," an interview with Harriette Brower (*Etude,* March 1928), Rosenthal said: "Soon after beginning to study with Joseffy I found my new master had ideas of touch quite different from the former one. Whereas Mikuli had always insisted on the closest legato, the most exact connection of tones, Joseffy taught a half-staccato touch, which was quite the opposite. The former was more smooth and flowing, the latter more scintillating and brilliant; the former more in the Chopin manner, the latter in the manner of the great virtuoso. Naturally this new manner of touch added a new aspect to my style of playing. Not that I entirely gave up my legato manner of playing, but I endeavored to cultivate also the detached, brilliant, delicate style of which my new teacher was such a master."

37. A characteristic of Rosenthal's recording of the work.

38. "Today" refers to the time of Rosenthal's writing.

39. Joseph Dachs (1825–1896), a pupil of Czerny, came to the Conservatory in 1850, at the age of twenty-five, and maintained a fine pianistic career of his own. He was regarded as a pioneer for his performances of Schumann's music. His many illustrious pupils included Annette Essipov, Vladimir de Pachmann, Benno Schönberger, Anthony Stankowitch, and Hugo Wolf. Anton Door (1833–1919) taught at the Conservatory from 1869 until 1901. Julius Epstein (1832–1926), the pianistic idol of both Anton Rubinstein and Leschetizky, taught there from 1867 until 1901.

40. Louis Plaidy (1810–1874), pianist, violinist, and teacher. John Francis Barnett studied with both Plaidy and Moscheles in Leipzig and wrote in his autobiography (*Musical Reminiscences and Impressions* [London: Hodder and Stoughton, 1906], pp. 41–42): "The student soon finds that musicians, like doctors, often disagree. Thus Plaidy initiated us into the mysteries of staccato from the loose wrist, while Moscheles advocated octaves from the arm. The student, therefore, had to exercise his discretion as to which theory to accept in this, as in some other matters. On the whole, in regard to technique one learnt the most from Plaidy, in respect to style, the most from Moscheles."

41. Charles Camille Saint-Saëns (1835–1921), French composer, pianist, and organist.

42. Heinrich Heine (1797–1856), German writer.

43. The *Memoirs* were Heine's second attempt at a novel and contain the story of the Flying Dutchman which Wagner took as the basis for his opera of the same title.

44. Friedrich Nietzsche (1844–1900), German philosopher and composer. This sentence comes from Nietzsche's *Ecce Homo*, translated from the German by Walter Kaufmann (New York: Random House/Vintage, 1989), p. 245.

45. George Gordon Lord Byron (1788–1824), English poet.

46. According to Adele Kanner, one of Rosenthal's sisters was a highly gifted pianist whom her family speculated could have equaled or even surpassed her brother had she pursued advanced studies. See n. 1 above.

47. In English in the original.

48. Eduard Suess (1831–1914) invented the term "biosphere," in 1875.

49. Pierre Simon Laplace (1749–1827), French mathematician and astronomer known for his writings on gravitation. His theory involved probability. See Charles Coulston Gillispie, *Pierre-Simon Laplace, 1749–1827: A Life in Exact Science* (Princeton, N.J.: Princeton University Press, 2000).

50. The most virtuosic of the piano sonatas of Johann Nepomuk Hummel (1778–1837), Austrian pianist, composer, and teacher.

51. Antonia Raab (1846–1902), Austrian pianist.

52. The Bösendorfersaal was located in the former riding school of Prince Liechtenstein, at 6 Herrengasse. It closed with four concerts in the spring of 1913. The last of them, given by the Rosé Quartet, ended with the second movement of Haydn's *Kaiser* Quartet (op. 76, no. 3).

53. Ludwig Bösendorfer (1835–1919), head of the Vienna piano firm after his father's death in 1859, and a much-esteemed gentleman. Rosenthal signed a note to him dated June 26, 1892, "Hofpianish von Ludwig Bösendorfer." "Hofpianish" is Viennese dialect; "Hofpianist," standard German.

54. A *bluette* is a piece of brilliant character.

55. Paul von Schloezer (c. 1840–1898), pianist, composer, and professor at the Moscow Conservatory.

56. Liszt, in a letter to Wilhelm von Lenz (no. 117 in volume 2 of the Liszt letters collected and edited by La Mara) in Constance Bache's English translation (New York: Greenwood Press, 1969), pp. 217–220), asked if he knew Wagner's epigraph "Für Carl Tausig's Grab": "Ripe for Death's harvest, / The fruits of life long tarrying, / Full early to pluck them / In the fleeting bloom of spring— / Was it thy lot, was it thy bourn? / Thy lot and thy destiny both must we mourn."

57. Wilhelm von Lenz (1809–1883), Russian official and writer on music. Vladimir de Pachmann (1848–1933), Russian-born naturalized-Italian pianist. Mark Mitchell is the author of the pianist's biography: *Vladimir de Pachmann: A Piano Virtuoso's Life*

and Art (Bloomington: Indiana University Press, 2002). Johann Strauss II (1825–1899), Austrian composer, conductor, and violinist. "Nachtfalter," "Man lebt nur einmal," and "Wahlstimmen" are published by Musica Obscura as *Three Valses-Caprices d'après J. Strauss.*

58. Alfred Grünfeld (1852–1924), Prague-born Viennese pianist, composer, and teacher. He was the first major pianist to record extensively.

59. Karl Goldmark (1830–1915), Austro-Hungarian composer. He also wrote a memoir, *Erinnerungen aus meinem Leben* (Vienna, 1922). This was published in English as *Notes from the Life of a Viennese Composer* (1927).

60. Joachim Raff (1822–1882), German-Swiss composer, critic, and teacher.

61. Eduard Hanslick (1825–1904) was a champion of Brahms's music and was rewarded by the composer with the dedication of the Waltzes op. 39. Rosenthal, who had studied with Hanslick at the university, spoke of his teacher in "If Franz Liszt Should Come Back Again" (*Etude*, April 1924): "Like many music critics, he studied music itself for a time, with a master, in his youth (Tomaschek); but never was a professional, practicing musician, in the larger sense. He surrounded himself with iron-clad theories of beauty, so thick that he could not see out to view the beauties of Wagner. I was repelled by his theories and left him very soon. Therefore I do not find myself in accord with Hanslick in any way. His theory—that music is '*ein Reihe bewegte Tone*' (a range of moving tones), like the little bits of colored glass in the kaleidoscope, and nothing more, is hopeless to me. He tried to make the world believe that beauty in any musical masterpiece had nothing to do with any emotions, but lay in the musical tones themselves. This takes away the whole significance of music."

62. Pablo de Sarasate (1844–1908), Spanish violinist and composer. He was considered to be superior to Joachim as a virtuoso, but inferior to him as an interpreter.

2. Review of a Concert by M. R. in Vienna

1. Rosenthal's decision to play works of Liszt and Brahms in Vienna was audacious; the bad blood between these two composers being common knowledge. In "Last of the Pianistic Titans" (*Hi Fi/Stereo Review*, February 1965), an interview with Louis Biancolli, Rosenthal said: "[Liszt] told me once he missed a certain excitement in the music of Brahms. He used the Latin word *saluber*—healthy, *gesund*—to describe it." [Biancolli asked] "Do you remember exactly how he put it?" "[Liszt] said, 'It does not make you ill, it does not make you excited, it does not give you a fever.' To Liszt it was music of bourgeois contentment." (For the record, Liszt thought Brahms's Paganini Variations superior to his own Paganini Etudes, though he pointed out that Brahms's were written after knowing his.)

5. Rosenthaliana

1. Josef Hofmann (1876–1957), Polish-born American pianist, composer, teacher, and inventor. Fritz Kreisler (1875–1962), Austrian-born American violinist and composer. For Hambourg, see the Introduction, n. 5.

2. E. T. A. Hoffmann (1776–1822), German writer (notably, the stories upon which Tchaikovsky's *The Nutcracker*, Offenbach's *Les Contes d'Hoffmann*, and Delibes's *Coppelia* are based), composer, and painter.

3. Eugène D'Albert (1864–1932), Scottish-German pianist and composer. He was one of Liszt's favored pupils.

4. Ferruccio Busoni (1866–1924), German-Italian composer and pianist. Important works on Busoni include Edward J. Dent's *Ferruccio Busoni* (London: Oxford University Press, 1933), Antony Beaumont's *Busoni the Composer* (Bloomington: Indiana University Press, 1985), *Ferruccio Busoni: Selected Letters* (New York: Columbia University Press, 1987), and Gottfried Galston's *Kalendernotizen über Ferruccio Busoni* (Wilhelmshaven: Verlag der Heinrichshofen-Bücher, 2000). Galston's diary has been translated into Italian as *Busoni: gli ultimi mesi di vita* (Rome: Ismez Editore, 2002).

5. This novel was the basis for an opera by Marziano Perosi (1875–1959), *Gli ultimi giorni di Pompei*. Marziano was the brother of a more famous composer, Lorenzo Perosi (1872–1956).

6. Max Breitenfeld (1860–1942, deported, at age eighty, first to the Terezin "model" camp where many musicians were sent and then to the Treblinka death camp), pianist and composer.

6. The Diémer Competition, Paris [1903]

1. Louis Diémer (1843–1918), noted French pianist and pedagogue whose pupils included Alfredo Casella (1883–1947), Alfred Cortot (1877–1962), Vincent d'Indy (1851–1931), Yves Nat (1890–1956), and Edouard Risler (1873–1929). The first Diémer competition was held in 1903.

2. Jules Massenet (1842–1912), French composer. Gabriel Fauré (1845–1924), French composer, teacher, pianist, and organist. Francis Planté (1839–1934), French pianist. Arthur de Greef (1862–1940), Belgian pianist and composer: he was a pupil of Liszt and a protégé of Albéniz, Grieg, and Saint-Saëns. Emile Paladilhe (1844–1926), French composer. André Alphonse Wormser (1851–1926), prolific French composer. Raoul Pugno (1852–1914), French pianist, composer, and teacher. Isidore Philipp (1863–1958), French pianist and teacher of Hungarian birth among whose many exceptional pupils were Youra Guller (1895–1980), Nikita Magaloff (1912–1992), Guiomar Novaës (1895–1979), and Madeleine de Valmalete (1899–1999). Philipp himself performed well into his nineties. Camille Chevillard (1859–1923), French conductor, composer, and pianist.

3. Joaquín Malats (1872–1912), Catalan pianist. Lazare Lévy (1882–1964), French pianist and teacher. He succeeded Cortot at the Paris Conservatory.

4. Rosenthal errs here either in his age or in the work that inspired him. *Hérodiade* was premiered in 1881 (Brussels), when he was nineteen.

5. Isaac Albéniz (1860–1909), Spanish composer and pianist. He composed the work for which he is most famous, and to which Rosenthal here refers, between 1905 and 1908—the second two books under the stimulus of Malats's playing. Rosenthal's wording of events therefore gives rise to some confusion: since *Iberia* was not completed until 1908, Malats certainly could not have played it in 1903!

8. From *Music, The Mystery and the Reality*

1. Alexander Siloti (1863–1945), Russian pianist and conductor. Charles Barber is the author of a biography of this musician, *Lost in the Stars: The Forgotten Musical Life of Alexander Siloti* (Lanham, Md.: Scarecrow, 2002). Emil von Sauer (1862–1942), German pianist, teacher, and composer. He also wrote a memoir of his early life, *Meine Welt*

(1901). His recordings of Liszt's "La Ricordanza" and the E-flat concerto (with Felix Weingartner, who studied composition with Liszt) are still among the most exalted interpretations of this composer's music. Frederic Lamond (1868–1948), Scottish pianist and composer and the author of both an autobiography—*The Memoirs of Frederic Lamond* (Glasgow: William Maclellan, 1949)—and a reminiscence of Anton Rubinstein ("Memories of Rubinstein," *Recorded Sound,* January 1977).

9. On Liszt's *Don Juan* Fantasie

1. Tirso de Molina (pseudonym of Fray Gabriel Téllez, 1584?–1648), Spanish dramatist. It is in Tirso de Molina's *El Burlador de Sevilla y el Convidado de Piedra* (1630) that the character of Don Juan makes his first appearance on the stage.

2. Pierre Corneille (1606–1684), French dramatist. Jean Baptiste Poquelin Molière (1622–1673), French actor and dramatist. Christian Dietrich Grabbe (1801–1836), German dramatist. His *Don Juan und Faust* (1829) was the only one of his works he lived to see staged. Nikolaus Lenau (1802–1850), Austrian poet. *Don Juan* (1844), his last work, remained a fragment at the time of his death.

3. Translator's note: pun in the German "Un-Sinnlichkeit": "Un-Sinnlichkeit" is a neologism for the opposite of sensuality, while "Unsinn" means nonsense.

10. A Stroll with Ferruccio Busoni

1. Ferruccio Busoni, *Sketch of a New Aesthetic of Music,* in *Three Classics in the Aesthetic of Music* (New York: Dover, 1962), p. 97.

11. Mahleriana

1. Richard Epstein (1869–1919), Austrian pianist.

2. A chief specialist in a hospital. Mahler would die of bacterial endocarditis.

3. Breitenfeld seems always to have been on the scene.

4. Riemann's theory was based on regularity in phrasing—an arbitrary way of analyzing music, as exceptions to any rule often matter more.

5. Richard Heuberger (1850–1914), Austrian composer, conductor, teacher, and music critic. He wrote a biography of Schubert, as well as "Recollections of Brahms" (published in 1971).

6. Hans Richter (1843–1916), Austro-Hungarian conductor who worked closely with Wagner and conducted the premiere of the *Ring* (Bayreuth, 1876). Although a Wagnerite, he was also a dedicated interpreter of Brahms and Bruckner. He took over the Hallé Orchestra in 1899.

7. Ludwig Karpath (1866–1936), writer on music. In addition to music criticism (most notably for the *Neue Wiener Tageblatt*), he wrote *Siegfried Wagner als Mensch und Künstler* (1902), *Zu den Briefen Richard Wagners an eine Putzmacherin* (1906), and *Richard Wagner, der Schuldenmacher* (1914). See the Introduction (p. xi) on Brahms's role in getting some of these letters published.

8. Rosenthal probably means that Walter was conducting for Mahler. Bruno Walter (1876–1962), German-born conductor. Gempler may be Karl Gemperle (1853–1934), Austrian actor and librettist.

9. Mahler conducted in New York part of each year from 1908 until 1911.

12. Czar Alexander II

1. Ivan Turgenev (1818–1883), Russian writer.
2. Fritz Schrödter (1855–1924), tenor. Antonie Schläger (1859 or 1860–1910), dramatic soprano. Her debut in London, in Meyerbeer's *Les Huguenots* (Paris, 1836), received the following notice in *The Musical Visitor* (August 1889): "the Valentina was Frau Schlager, the distinguished *prima donna* of the Vienna Opera, who now made her first appearance in this country. Frau Schlager, who, it is assumed, is a relative of the distinguished director of the Mozarteum at Salzburg, is not the slender Valentina such as we might expect would impel the emotion of Raoul to deeds of 'derring-do,' nor is her voice in the first freshness of youth. But she proved herself a great actress, and in the grand duet in the last act she was a worthy partner of the Polish tenor [Jean de Reszke]."

14. Letter to the Editor

1. Theodor Helm (1843–1920), Austrian writer on music. *Fünfzig Jahre Wiener Musikleben (1866–1916): Erinnerungen eines Musikkritikers,* edited by M. Schönherr, was reprinted in 1977.
2. Anton Felix Schindler (1795–1864), Moravian musician and writer and biographer of Beethoven. For the most part he was an unreliable source.
3. Jan Matejko (1838–1893), Polish nationalist painter. His most promising student was Maurycy (Moriz) Gottlieb (1856–1879); Gottlieb's family later claimed that he was poisoned by Matejko out of jealousy over his abilities. Gottlieb's second cousin was the Polish pianist Ignace Tiegerman (1893–1968), a remarkable musician who studied under Leschetizky and Friedman.
4. This anecdote reminds one of Gertrude Stein's response to a portrait of her by Pablo Picasso. When she told the artist that it did not look like her, he agreed that it didn't, but promised that it would.

15. As Others See Us

1. From Gilbert and Sullivan's operetta *The Mikado.*

16. The Korngold Scandal

1. Julius Korngold (1860–1945), prominent Viennese critic. Erich Wolfgang Korngold (1897–1957), Austrian composer.
2. "He has no choice, God help him . . . " is an allusion to a famous passage from a sermon by Martin Luther.
3. Piano Sonata in E, op. 2. Korngold wrote three piano sonatas.
4. Artur Schnabel (1882–1951), Austrian-born naturalized-American pianist and composer. He was the first to record all of Beethoven's piano sonatas.
5. As Jacques Mayer told it: "Rosenthal was asked by another virtuoso if he would not place on his programs a composition by a boy wonder (Erich Korngold), whose father, critic of the Vienna *Freie Presse,* was making, publicly and privately, ardent propaganda for his child's compositions. 'As you say, my dear friend,' replied Rosenthal, 'the compositions are not grateful, but the father will surely be.' "

6. Eduard Gärtner (1862–1918), singer at the Vienna Opera. Ignaz Friedman set some of his melodies as *Six Viennese Dances*. Heinrich Schenker (1868–1935), Austrian theorist. Like Rosenthal, he studied with Mikuli in Lemberg.

17. From *Franz Liszt*

1. Or, as Richard Specht wrote of Rosenthal: "Nietzsche has played."

18. The Old and the New School of Piano Playing

1. Quoted in *Thayer's Life of Beethoven,* revised and edited by Elliot Forbes (Princeton, N.J.: Princeton University Press, 1967). Ferdinand Hiller (1811–1885), German conductor, composer, pianist, and teacher.

2. *Chopin's Letters,* collected by Henryk Opienski, translated and with a preface and editorial notes by E. L. Voynich (New York: Alfred Knopf, 1931), Letter no. 58 (pp. 126–129).

3. Elias Parish Alvars (1808–1849), English harpist and composer, much admired by Berlioz, Liszt, and Mendelssohn.

4. See Suetonius, *The Twelve Caesars.* Rosenthal was not the first to compare musicians to various Caesars. Goldmark (*Notes from the Life of a Viennese Composer*): "On one occasion a considerable number of prominent musicians had been invited to meet in the restaurant of the Musikverein for the purpose of founding a musical art society. Liszt, Rubinstein and Brahms were present, and sat near each other at supper. Seeing this, someone called out, 'The triumvirate.' At that Rubinstein, indicating Liszt, said: 'Caesar'; pointing at himself: 'Brutus' and then at Brahms: 'Lepidus'!"

5. We give the part of the letter quoted by Rosenthal (no. 169 in volume 2 of the Liszt letters collected and edited by La Mara) in Constance Bache's English translation (New York: Greenwood Press, 1969), pp. 278–279, Rosenthal's italics.

6. And yet just a page earlier Rosenthal has credited Rubinstein with introducing this innovation.

7. Ludwig Deppe (1828–1890), German pianist, teacher, conductor, and composer based in Hamburg. Amy Fay, the author of the minor classic *Music Study in Germany,* and Emil von Sauer were among his pupils. He himself studied with Eduard Marxsen (Brahms's teacher).

20. Letter to Herbert Hughes

1. Adolph Gutmann (1819–1882), German pianist and composer. Marcelina Princess Czartoryska, *née* Radziwill (1817–1894), Polish pianist.

2. The exact dedication reads: "dédié à Monsieur Adolpho Gutmann."

3. Thomas Tellefsen (1823–1874), Norwegian pianist and composer.

4. Mikuli was from Czernowitz, now in the Ukraine. Bukovina ("Land of Beech Trees") was, from the 1775–1918, the easternmost crown land of the Austro-Hungarian empire.

5. Jane Wilhelmina Stirling (1804–1859), pianist, cellist, and pupil of Chopin. He dedicated his Nocturnes op. 55 to her. She is the subject of a 1960 biography by Audrey Evelyn Bone. Countess Delfina Potocka (1807–1885), Polish pianist and singer. She was the dedicatee of Chopin's Concerto in f and "Minute" Waltz. Julius Schulhoff (1825–

1899), pianist and composer of Czech origin. An account of Schulhoff's introduction to Chopin is given in Moritz Karasowski's *Frederic Chopin: His Life and Letters,* translated by Emily Hill (London: William Reeves, 1938). Henry Brinley Richards (1817–1885), Welsh pianist. Camille Stamaty (1811–1870), Greco-French pianist, composer, and teacher. (Saint-Saëns was one of his pupils.) Edward Wolff (1816–1880), Polish pianist and composer. Jeanne de Caraman was the dedicatee of the Scherzo op. 54; Catherine Maberly of the Mazurkas op. 56. Sir Charles Hallé (1819–1895), German-born English pianist and conductor. He was the first pianist to play all of Beethoven's piano sonatas in Paris.

6. George Sand (1804–1876), pseudonym of Amandine Aurore Lucile baroness Dudevant (*née* Dupin). French novelist and femme fatale. She is the subject of an excellent biography by Curtis Cate (*George Sand: A Biography* [New York: Houghton Mifflin, 1975]).

7. Alfred de Musset (1810–1857), French poet.

8. Auguste Jean-Baptiste Clésinger (1814–1883), French sculptor.

9. *Chopin's Letters,* collected by Henryk Opienski, translated and with a preface and editorial notes by E. L. Voynich (New York: Alfred Knopf, 1931), Letter no. 245 (pp. 346–347

10. Rosenthal may be alluding here to his own witticism about the poor composer who writes from memory, recalling the works of others.

21. Moriz Rosenthal—Emil Sauer

1. Carl August Peter Cornelius (1824–1874), German composer most famous for his comic opera *Der Barbier von Bagdad* (Weimar, 1858).

2. Cf. the book of Job in the Bible.

3. Hardly! When Rosenthal played the Sonata in A, K. 331, in Aeolian Hall in 1927, W. J. Henderson wrote in the *New York Sun* (January 28): "Few who present this composition remember that the Turks bombarded the Parthenon, but Mr. Rosenthal did not forget it and we heard the heavy guns in the bass. There were some minor explosions in the variations, but there was also some of the old time Rosenthal swiftness of finger and incomparable smoothness in scales."

22. Schumann's *Carnaval*

1. Karl Grädener (1812–1883), distinguished composer and pedagogue. His son, Hermann Grädener (1844–1929), studied at the Conservatory and thereafter remained in Vienna, active as organist, violinist, conductor, composer, and teacher.

2. *Flegeljahre: eine Biographie* (1804–1805).

3. Schumann wrote of this concert: "To certain doubts that I expressed as to whether such rhapsodic carnival life would make an impression upon so large an audience Liszt said only that he hoped so. I fear that he was too sanguine. . . . There are things in [*Carnaval*] which may delight this person or that, but the musical moods change too quickly for a large audience to follow without being wakened every minute or two. My amiable friend had not, as I have said, taken this into consideration. Sympathetically and wonderfully as he played, he may have reached a few individual listeners, but not the whole audience" (*The Musical World of Robert Schumann,* translated, edited, and annotated by Henry Pleasants [New York: St. Martin's Press, 1965], p. 161).

4. Rosenthal ("Is Culture Progressing in Musical Art?" *Etude,* November 1931): "[The *Fantasie*] always produced a curious reaction upon him [Liszt]. Liszt would never divulge what the actual associations were, but he could never bear to hear it. Four separate times I was present when that glorious, sweeping first movement was played to him; and each time he turned quite pale and stopped the playing before the movement was done." However, after [Max] Van de Sandt played the *Fantasie* in one of Liszt's master classes (June 20, 1884), August Göllerich (*The Piano Master Classes of Franz Liszt, 1884–1886*) wrote: "At the end of the first movement, the master, totally transported by the last sixteen bars, said, 'I can never hear that without emotion, that is exquisite, not music manufacturing! That belongs to a higher region!'"

5. W. von Wasielewski, author of *Robert Schumann* (Dresden, 1858; 2nd ed., 1906) and *Schumanniana* (Bonn, 1883).

6. Rosenthal introduced counter-octaves in this March after he heard Anton Rubinstein play them—and after consulting with Liszt, who approved of the innovation.

7. These qualities were certainly combined in Rosenthal's playing. Richard Specht ("Moriz Rosenthal," *Die Zeit,* 1906): "[Rosenthal] is certainly the master of the climax. . . . The modifications of the touch which give to the piano the most varying plenitude of different colorings, seem to increase in the *fortissimo* instead of growing monotonously hard, as we should expect or as is generally the case. The most peculiar rhythmic complications, instead of persistently hindering him as is the case with others, serve only to increase the climax. It is one of his own peculiar gifts thus to overcome every difficulty in such a way that it is quite unnoticed."

8. Friedrich Wieck (1785–1873), German music teacher and writer on music.

9. Rosenthal told Biancolli (in "Last of the Pianistic Titans"): "I asked [Liszt] one day if Schumann made the same impression on him that Chopin did. Do you know what his reply was? 'Schumann has broader shoulders, but Chopin is taller.'"

23. Anton Rubinstein's Concert in Pressburg

1. Bratislava is now the capital of Slovakia. Both Bartók and Dohnányi studied in the city, then known as Pozsony, when it belonged to Hungary.

2. Pauline Viardot-Garcia (1821–1910), French mezzo-soprano, composer, and teacher. Turgenev was her lover.

3. Ludwig Rellstab (1799–1860), German music critic, poet, librettist, and novelist. His father was the music publisher and composer Johann Carl Friedrich Rellstab (1759–1813).

4. "Es war ein alter König," *Neuer Frühling,* no. 29, here translated from the German by Kate F. Kroeker (in *The Poetry and Prose of Heinrich Heine,* selected and edited with an introduction by Frederic Ewen [New York: Citadel Press, 1948]), p. 107.

5. In spite of his argument against Rubinstein's interpretation of this movement, one notes—with some amusement—that Rosenthal himself was known to perform it in much the same way. Indeed, after Rosenthal played it in London, in May 1910, the critic for *The Times* (May 19, 1910) wrote: "It was rather a pity that . . . some concession should have been made by the player to Rubinstein's foolish 'band-at-a-distance' effect, a falsification of the text which is now happily quite unusual." Rachmaninov's recording of the sonata gives an idea of this practice.

6. A paraphrase from the *Agamemnon* of Aeschylus (here translated by Edith Ham-

ilton): "Drop, drop—in our sleep, upon the heart / sorrow falls, memory's pain, / and to us, though against our very will, / even in our own despite, / comes wisdom / by the awful grace of God."

7. An allusion to Siegfried's tasting the dragon Fafner's blood in Wagner's *Siegfried,* which allows him to understand the forest bird. Elsie Braun Barnett's translation from the German of the complete article was published in *Current Musicology* 13 (1972).

8. One wonders why Rosenthal did not simply ride in the boat with his friend.

24. My Memories of Johannes Brahms

1. Max Kalbeck (1850–1921), poet, music critic, librettist, translator, and, most significantly, biographer of Brahms.

2. Rosenthal is calling up a passage from Goethe's *Faust* (here translated from the German by George Madison Priest). Mephistopheles [to Faust]: "Don't give way, Doctor! Quick! Don't tarry! / Keep close by as I lead the way. / Out with your duster, out, I say! / Thrust hard at him and I will parry."

3. Actually, this is not true (cf. Charles Rosen's preface). The Italian pianist Arturo Benedetti Michelangeli (1920–1995) also performed and recorded his own selection and arrangement of these variations.

4. The Hörselberg was the locale of Venus's court in Wagner's *Tannhaüser.* Wagner was the only composer Brahms hated more than Liszt.

5. Franz Grillparzer (1791–1872), Austrian dramatist, poet, and short story writer. John Irving (*The World According to Garp*): "[Grillparzer] is one of those nineteenth-century writers who did not survive the nineteenth century with any enduring popularity, and Garp would later argue that Grillparzer did not deserve to survive the nineteenth century." Grillparzer delivered Beethoven's funeral oration and wrote the epitaph for Schubert's tombstone.

6. "The mountains are in labor; a ridiculous mouse will be brought forth."

7. *Letters of Hans von Bülow to Richard Wagner and Others,* translated by Hannah Walter, edited and with a preface and notes by Scott Goddard (New York: Da Capo, 1979).

25. Brahmsiana

1. See the opening note to the previous chapter for an explanation of the bracketed passages.

2. Referring to the factitious tales of the fictitious Baron of Münchhausen.

3. Ludwig Rottenberg (1864–1930), conductor, composer, and teacher. His daughter Gertrud married Paul Hindemith.

4. Alexander Winterberger (1834–1914), German pianist and organist. He was a pupil of—and rumored to be an illegitimate son of—Liszt.

5. The cure at Bad Ischl consisted of brine vapor baths and the drinking of "cocktails" of salty and sulphuric waters.

6. The Kniesel Quartet, formed in 1885 by Franz Kneisel (1865–1926), then the concertmaster of the Boston Symphony Orchestra.

7. Ilona Eibenschütz (1873–1967), Hungarian pianist. Clara Schumann arranged for her to play Beethoven's Sonata op. 111 for Brahms, so sufficiently impressing him that he later played for her, in private, his then unpublished Klavierstücke op. 119. She

recorded op. 119, nos. 2 and 3—no. 2 published on a Pearl CD titled "Pupils of Clara Schumann" —as well as the Intermezzo op. 76, no. 4.

8. Ede Reményi (1828–1898), Hungarian-born violinist who often performed with Brahms, as did Joseph Joachim (1831–1907), Austro-Hungarian violinist, composer, conductor, and teacher.

9. Bernhard Stavenhagen (1862–1914), German pianist, conductor, and composer.

10. Siegmund Bachrich (1841–1913), violist, composer, and teacher.

11. In his lesson on this work (*Etude*, April 1934), Rosenthal wrote that the secondary theme "is almost always interpreted wrongly, that is, in the sense of the German waltz, with the accent on the first quarter note. But here Chopin was apparently possessed by his Polish temperament, and introduced an episode which should rather be played in mazurka style. The writer now always takes (at all events, in the repetition) the first eight measures of the mazurka-rhythm with the accent on the third quarter note."

12. H. G. Bonavia Hunt? [Sir] Charles Villiers Stanford (1852–1924), English composer.

13. The italicized section appears in English in the original.

14. Barette Stepanov, Russian (?) pianist. On July 1, 1889, she played a novelty at one of the Richter concerts in London: "a movement from the recently discovered pianoforte concerto in D, alleged to be by Beethoven" (*The Musical Visitor*, August 1889). The work in question was the piano version of Beethoven's violin concerto in D, op. 61.

15. *The Music Criticism of Hugo Wolf*, translated, edited, and annotated by Henry Pleasants (New York: Holmes and Meier, 1978).

16. In English in the original.

17. "Frauenzimmer" comes from the Late Middle High German "Fruwenzimmer," literally "a women's room." Though probably once neutral in sense, in the seventeenth century the word acquired a mildly derogatory one, as in "gelehrtes Frauenzimmer" (educated woman), before taking a definite downward plunge during the last two hundred years. Today the word has a slightly impatient, sometimes affectionate, sometimes frankly contemptuous sense. Brahms intended the last of these. An English equivalent might be "women," said with a certain intonation.

A letter from Eugène D'Albert to a English friend dated March 15, 1882, and quoted in Christopher Fifield's *True Artist and True Friend: A Biography of Hans Richter* (Oxford: Clarendon Press, 1993), offers additional evidence of Brahms's misogyny: "Brahms is glad I was not with Leschetitsky [sic] as he cannot bear the lady-pianists. These females, he said, have no artistic feeling and practise away with the window wide open like machines. Most of Leschetitsky's pupils are young ladies" (184). As counterweight, however, one must note the regard in which he held Eibenschütz (see n. 7 above), Etelka Freund, and Clara Schumann, among other women musicians, as interpreters (and even dedicatees) of his piano music. It would seem that Brahms's "problem" was not with individual women, but with "women" generally.

18. Liszt, on the other hand, did not have a high opinion of Clara Schumann, whose tendency to sway about on the piano stool he caricatured in his master classes; when told by pupils that his thoughts on Schumann interpretation were at odds with Clara's, his habitual reply was: "Madame Clara is the Pope, of course!!"

19. Hanslick on Brahms's playing (1862): "It may appear praiseworthy to Brahms that he plays more like a composer than a virtuoso, but such praise is not altogether unqualified. Prompted by the desire to let the composer speak for himself, he neglects— especially in the playing of his own pieces—much that the player should rightly do

for the composer. His playing resembles the austere Cordelia, who concealed her finest feelings rather than betray them to the people." Philip Hale expressed his opinion of Brahms's playing more succinctly: "Brahms—what a pianist! One of ten thumbs!"

20. The premiere took place in Budapest, November 9, 1881.

21. Liszt, to whom Brahms was and had been anything but kind, nonetheless made public his admiration for the concerto, even allowing it to be performed (with the orchestral part reduced for a second piano) in his master classes in Weimar (July 1, 1885).

22. Maria Jeritza, in *Sunlight and Song: A Singer's Life,* translated by Frederick H. Martens (New York: Arno Press, 1977), recalled that, though the villa was beautiful, it had neither hot running water nor bathtubs (64).

23. Mostly the emperor liked to hunt. The Imperial Archives record that he killed 50,556 animals during the many summers he spent at Bad Ischl. The emperor always returned to Vienna on August 18th.

24. Katharina Schratt (1853–1940), Austrian actress. Maria Jeritza: "[Franz Josef] firmly believed in those old traditions of kingship which hark back to the founders of his dynasty. To him the official 'placing' of Frau Schratt at court was a matter of self-evident necessity. Any more direct personal contact with a Hapsburg emperor and empress had to be grounded in a recognized court position. So Frau Schratt was officially appointed *Vorleserin* ('Reader') to the imperial pair some time during the eighties, a post for which she was especially qualified by reason of her natural gifts. And Frau Schratt did, in fact, read aloud to the Emperor: her official title was no misnomer" (*Sunlight and Song,* p. 120).

25. Heinrich Laube (1806–1884), German dramatist and member of the radical Young German Movement.

26. Here and elsewhere, "K." is shorthand for "Kollege" (i.e., "colleague").

27. The restaurant of the Kaiserin Elisabeth Hotel.

28. Versions of this story were told by, among many others, Bennett Cerf (*The Saturday Review of Literature,* January 22, 1944, p. 14), Henry T. Finck (*Musical Laughs* [New York: Funk & Wagnalls, 1924], p. 66), and Robin Legge.

29. Franz Paul Lachner (1803–1890), German composer and conductor.

30. Tausig's *Tägliche Studien* were posthumously revised and edited by Heinrich Ehrlich.

31. Jakob Grün (1837–1916), Hungarian violinist and professor at the Conservatory from 1877 until 1909. He taught Erica Morini and showed many kindnesses to Goldmark.

26. Brahms and Johann Strauss II

1. Jules Massenet defined the difference between Brahms and Strauss thus: "Brahms est l'âme de Vienne, Strauss en est le parfum" (Brahms is the soul of Vienna, Strauss is its perfume).

2. Tarock is a card game.

3. A "Cross of the Commander" is a medal or other decoration bestowed by royalty upon a person of exceptional attainment.

27. Review of a Concert by M. R.

1. Solomon Cutner (1902–1988), English pianist. Rudolf Firkusny (1912–1994), American pianist of Czech birth. Kurt Appelbaum (1914–1990), Austrian-American pianist. Lili Kraus (1905–1986), British pianist of Hungarian birth.

28. Letter to the Editor

1. Ancient Greek terrorist who burned down the Ephesian temple (and possibly library) of Artemis in 356 B.C. in order to become famous.

2. Rosenthal is paraphrasing the last words of the Emperor Nero, quoted by Suetonius: "Qualis artifex pereo" ("what an artist dies in me," or "what an artist the world is losing in me"). After a particularly incomparable bit of playing of his own, Pachmann often uttered the same remark.

29. Review of a Concert by M. R.

1. [Sir] William Sterndale Bennett (1816–1875), the most distinguished English composer of the Romantic era.

30. From Aphorisms

1. Melpomene was the Muse of Tragedy.

31. On the Question of Applause

1. Charles Rosen, letter to Mark Mitchell (February 20, 2002): "[Beethoven] didn't care about the English edition for which only the money interested him, and he thought that eliminating the fugue and maybe the adagio would make it sell better to the barbarians. It was about to be published correctly in Vienna, which is what counted and he was pushing Ries to get it out fast in England where it mattered less except financially."

Appendix A

1. Pythia was the name given to the woman who, sitting on a three-legged stool, was the medium of the Apollo Oracle at Delphi and who gave answers that were ambiguous in their meaning.

2. Teresa Carreño (1853–1917), Venezuelan-born pianist, composer, conductor, and singer.

3. In R. Allen Lott, *From Paris to Peoria: How European Piano Virtuosos Brought Classical Music to the American Heartland* (New York: Oxford University Press, 2003), pp. 203–204.

Appendix B

1. This figure was given in *Musical America* (October 10, 1938), *Newsweek* (November 14, 1938), and *Musical Courier* (January 1, 1941). One obituary of the pianist stated that he gave 4,500 concerts.

2. According to Kevin Bazzana, pianist Ervin Nyiregyhazi recalled hearing Rosenthal play seven or eight times in Berlin during World War I and said that not a single work by Liszt appeared on any of his programs.

3. Liszt used the same Polish folk melody that had captivated Chopin here in his

own Glanes de Woronince (no. 2). Marcella Sembrich used to sing "The Maiden's Wish" in the lesson scene in Rossini's *Il barbiere de Siviglia.*

4. *Living with Liszt: From The Diary of Carl Lachmund, an American Pupil of Liszt, 1882–1884,* edited, annotated, and introduced by Alan Walker (Stuyvesant, N.Y.: Pendragon Press, n.d.), p. 305.

Index

Page numbers in italics refer to illustrations.

"Brahmsiana" (Rosenthal), 104, 107–16
Breitenfeld, Max
  and Brahms, 107, 109
  in "Rosenthaliana" (Liebling), 47
  trips with Rosenthal, 103, 108
  upon Rosenthal's return to Vienna, 115
Breithaupt, Rudolf, 77
Breuer, Robert, 17
The Brothers Karamazov (Dostoyevsky), 59
Bullock, Theodore, 1
Bülow, Hans von
  on Bösendorfer, 97
  and Brahms, 104, 105, 106, 115
  influence and success, 37–38
  and Liszt, 105
  performances, 24, 25
  and Rosenthal, xii, 4
  Rubinstein compared to, 102
Busoni, Ferruccio
  Don Juan Fantasie, x, 54, 55
  in "Rosenthaliana" (Liebling), 47
  at Rosenthal's performance, xviii
  Rosenthal's relationship with, 12, 56–57
Byron, George Gordon, 33, 54

Caland, 77
cantabile touch, xiii
Caraman, Jeanne de, 87
Caramiello, Francesco, 10
Carreño, Teresa, 129
Chevillard, Camille, 49–50
Chopin, Frédéric
  and applause, 127–28
  and Beethoven, 133
  and George Sand, 87–88
  and Hummel, 75
  influence and success, xix, 1, 35, 47, 75, 76,
    77, 85, 114, 133
  as instructor, 85
  and Kalkbrenner, 8
  and Liszt, 3–4, 158n 8
  Mahler on, 59
  Mazurka-Intermezzo, 3
  mazurkas, xiii
  on meaning of Unisono-Finale, 13
  and Mikuli, 24–25, 26
  pedal technique, 77
  piano preferences, 20
  programs, 125
  pupils, 85–87
  and Rellstab, 99
  Rosenthal's performance of (general), xiii,
    2, 3, 28, 159n 10
  and Schumann, 93, 96
  stature, 126

Strauss on, 117
style, 2
use of scales, 32
works performed
  Allegro de Concert, ix
  Berceuse, 44
  Concerto in f, 35
  Etude in F Minor, 40
  Etude on Black Keys, 115
  mazurkas, 29
  Minute Waltz (Rosenthal's arrangement),
    129–30
  nocturnes, 72
  in Rosenthal's repertoire, 136–38
  Sonata in B-flat Minor, 99–100, 101
  Sonata op. 58, 110
  unspecified, 56, 59, 62, 102, 104, 124
  Waltz in c-sharp, 29
  Waltz in D-flat Major, 91
  works recorded, 149–53
Christina of Spain, 61
chronology, xvii–xx
citizenship in United States, xx
Clementi, Muzio, 35, 138
Clésinger, Auguste Jean-Baptiste, 88
Clésinger-Sand, Solange, 87–88
composers. See also specific composers
  intentions of, 63–68
  Rosenthal as, 142–43
concertography (Mitchell), 133–48
concerts. See performances
conferences, 13
contract negotiations, 9
Corneille, Pierre, 54
Cornelius, Peter, 91
Couperin, François, 138
Crimp, Bryan, 14
critics, music, 113, 121–23, 130. See also
  reviews of concerts
Cui, César Antonovich, 138
Curtis Institute of Music, xix, 10
Cutner, Solomon, 119
"Czar Alexander II" (Rosenthal), 61–62
Czartoryska, Marcelina, 85, 86

Dachs, Josef, 30, 31, 32, 38, 162n 39
Da Ponte, Lorenzo, 54, 55
Daquin, Louis-Claude, 138
Davidov, Karl, 138
Davidsbündler, 95, 96
death, xx
Debussy, Claude, 138, 153
debuts. See performances
demeanor of Rosenthal, 91
Deppe, Ludwig, 77

MARK MITCHELL is author of *Virtuosi: A Defense and a (Sometimes Erotic) Celebration of Great Pianists* and *Vladimir de Pachmann: A Piano Virtuoso's Life and Art,* both published by Indiana University Press. He is writing a history of performances of Western classical music in Bombay.

ALLAN EVANS is the founder of Arbiter Cultural Traditions, and has published more than 150 recordings by historic interpreters. He has also completed a biography of the pianist Ignaz Friedman. He teaches at the Mannes College of Music, New York.